Josh and Hazel's Guide to Not Dating

CHRISTINA LAUREN

Gallery Books

NEW YORK   LONDON   TORONTO   SYDNEY   NEW DELHI

G

Gallery Books
An Imprint of Simon & Schuster, Inc.
1230 Avenue of the Americas
New York, NY 10020

First Gallery Books trade paperback edition September 2018

GALLERY BOOKS and colophon are registered
trademarks of Simon & Schuster, Inc.

For information about special discounts for bulk purchases,
please contact Simon & Schuster Special Sales at
1-866-506-1949 or business@simonandschuster.com.

The Simon & Schuster Speakers Bureau can bring authors to your live event.
For more information or to book an event, contact the Simon & Schuster Speakers
Bureau at 1-866-248-3049 or visit our website at www.simonspeakers.com.

Interior design by Jaime Putorti

Manufactured in the United States of America

10 9 8 7 6 5 4

Library of Congress Cataloging-in-Publication Data

Names: Lauren, Christina, author.
Title: Josh and Hazel's guide to not dating / Christina Lauren.
Description: First Gallery Books trade paperback edition. | New York, NY :
    Gallery Books, an imprint of Simon & Schuster, Inc., 2018.
Identifiers: LCCN 2018021709 (print) | LCCN 2018024190 (ebook) | ISBN
    9781501165863 (eBook) | ISBN 9781501165856 (paperback)
Subjects: | BISAC: FICTION / Romance / Contemporary. | FICTION / Romance /
    General. | GSAFD: Love stories.
Classification: LCC PS3612.A9442273 (ebook) | LCC PS3612.A9442273 J67 2018
    (print) | DDC 813/.6—dc23
LC record available at https://lccn.loc.gov/2018021709

ISBN 978-1-5011-6585-6
ISBN 978-1-5011-6586-3 (ebook)

For Jen Lum, and Katie and David Lee.

PROLOGUE

HAZEL CAMILLE BRADFORD

*B*efore we get started, there are a few things you should know about me:

1. I am both broke and lazy—a terrible combination.
2. I am perpetually awkward at parties and in an effort to relax will probably end up drinking until I'm topless.
3. I tend to like animals more than people.
4. I can always be counted on to do or say the worst possible thing in a delicate moment.

In summary, I am *superb* at making an ass out of myself.

At the outset, this should explain how I have successfully never dated Josh Im: I have made myself entirely undatable in his presence.

For instance, the first time we met, I was eighteen and he was twenty and I vomited on his shoes.

Surprising no one who was there (and consistent with point number two, above), I don't remember this night, but trust me—Josh does. Apparently I'd toppled an entire folding table of drinks mere minutes after arriving at my first real college party, and retreated to the shame corner with my fellow freshmen, where I could drown my embarrassment in the remaining cheap alcohol.

When Josh tells this story he makes sure to mention that before I threw up on his shoes, I charmed him with a dazed "You are the hottest guy I've ever seen, and I would be honored to give you sex tonight."

I chased down the bitter taste of his horrified silence with a badly advised body shot of triple sec off Tony Bialy's abs.

Five minutes later, I was vomiting all over everything, including Josh.

It didn't end there. A year later, I was a sophomore, and Josh was a senior. By then I'd learned you don't do shots of triple sec, and when a sock is slid over the doorknob, it means your roommate is getting laid, so don't come in.

Unfortunately, Josh didn't speak sock, and I didn't know he was rooming with Mike Stedermeier, star quarterback *and* the guy I was currently banging. *Currently banging*, as in that very moment. Which is why the second time I met Josh Im, he walked into his dorm room to find me naked, bent over his couch, going for it on fourth and long.

But I would say the best example comes from a little story we like to call The Email Incident.

Spring semester of my sophomore year, Josh was my anatomy TA. Up until that point, I'd known he was good-looking, but I'd had no idea that he was actually *amazing*. He held extra office hours to help people who fell behind. He shared his old notes with us and held study sessions at coffee shops before exams. He was smart, and funny, and laid-back in a way I already knew I would never master.

We were all infatuated with him, but for me it went deeper: Josh Im became my blueprint for Perfect. I wanted to be his friend.

So, I'd just had my wisdom teeth out. I was convinced beforehand that it would be simple: pull a few teeth, take a few ibuprofen, call it a day. But as it happens, my teeth were impacted and I had to be knocked out for their removal. I woke up later at home, in a painkiller-induced sweat, with hollow aching caves in my mouth, cheeks full of cotton tubes, and the frantic recollection that I had a paper due in two days.

Ignoring my mom's suggestion that she soberly send one for me, I composed and sent the following email, which Josh currently has printed out and framed in his bathroom:

Dera Josh.,

In class you sed that if we email you our paper you would look over them. I wanted to send you my paper and

I put it in my calendar so as not forget. But the thing that happened is that I had a witsdom tooth out actually all of them. I have tried very hard in this clas and have a solid B (!!!). You are very smart and I nknw that I will do better if you help me. Can I have a few extra days???? I'm not feeling very well with this pills and please I know that you can't make exceptions for all the pope but if you do it for me this one thing I will give all my wishes in a fountain for youfrom now on

    i love you,

    Hazel Bradford (it's Hazel not Haley like you said it's ok don't be embearassed emberessed sad)

Incidentally, he also has his reply printed out, and framed just below it:

Hazel-not-Haley,

    I can make this exception. And don't worry, I'm not embarrassed. It's not like I puked in your shoes or rolled around naked on your couch.

    Josh

It was at this moment precisely that I knew Josh and I were destined to be best friends and I could never, ever mess it up by trying to sleep with him.

Unfortunately, he graduated, and sleeping with him

wouldn't be a problem because it would be nearly a decade before I saw him again. You'd think in that time I would have become less of a hot mess, or he would have forgotten all about Hazel-not-Haley Bradford.

You'd be wrong.

ONE

HAZEL

*A*nyone who knew me in college might be horrified to hear that I ended up employed as an elementary school teacher, responsible for educating our wide-eyed, sponge-brained youth, but in truth, I suspect I'm pretty great at it. For one, I'm not afraid of making a fool of myself. And two, I think there's something about the eight-year-old brain that just resonates with me on a spiritual level.

Third grade is my sweet spot; eight-year-olds are a *trip*.

After two years spent student-teaching fifth grade, I felt constantly sticky and harried. Another year in transitional kindergarten and I knew I didn't have the endurance for so much potty training. But third felt like the perfect balance of fart jokes without the sometimes-disastrous intentional farting, hugs from kids who think I'm the smartest person alive, and having enough authority to get everyone's attention simply by clapping my hands once.

Unfortunately, today is the last day of school, and as I take down the many, many inspirational pages, calendars, sticker charts, and art masterpieces from my classroom walls, I register that this is also the last day I'm going to see *this* particular third grade classroom. A tiny ball of grief materializes in my throat.

"You have Sad Hazel posture."

I turn, surprised to find Emily Goldrich behind me. She's not only my best gal, she's also a teacher—though not here at Merion—and she looks tidy and recently showered because she's a week ahead of me into summer break. Em is also holding what I pray is a bag full of Thai takeout. I am hungry enough to eat the little jeweled apple clip in her hair. I look like a filthy mop head covered in the fading glitter eight-year-old Lucy Nguyen decided would be a fun last-day surprise.

"I am, a little." I point around the room, at three out of four empty walls. "Though there's something cathartic about it, too."

Emily and I met about nine months ago in an online political forum, where it was clear we were both childless because of all the time we spent there ranting into the void. We met up in person for venting over coffee and became immediate fast friends. Or, maybe more accurately, I decided she was amazing and invited her to coffee again and again until she agreed. The way Emily describes it: when I meet someone I love, I become an octopus and wind my tentacles around their heart, tighter and tighter until they can't deny they love me just the same.

Emily works at Riverview teaching fifth (a true warrior among us), and when a position opened for a third grade teacher there, I sprinted down to the district with my application in hand. So desperate was I for the coveted spot in a top-ten school that only once I got out of my car and started the march up the steps to HR did I register that I was (1) braless and (2) still wearing my Homer Simpson slippers.

No matter. I was properly attired for the interview two weeks later. And guess who got the job?

I think it's me!

(As in, it isn't confirmed but Emily is married to the principal so I'm pretty sure I'm in.)

"Are you coming tonight?"

Em's question pulls me out of the mental and physical war I'm waging with a particularly stubborn staple in the wall. "Tonight?"

"Tonight."

I glance at her patiently over my shoulder. "More clues."

"My house."

"More specific clues?" I've spent many a Friday night at Em's, playing Mexican Train dominoes with her and Dave and eating whatever meat Dave has grilled that night.

She sighs and walks to my desk, retrieving a hammer from my dalmatian-print box of tools so I can more easily pry the metal from the plaster. "The *barbecue*."

"Right!" I brandish the hammer in victory. That little ass-hole staple is mine to destroy! (Or recycle responsibly.) "The work party."

"It's not officially work. But a few of the cool teachers will be there, and you might want to meet them."

I eye her with faint trepidation; we all remember Hazel Point Number Two. "You promise you'll monitor my booze intake?"

For some reason, this makes her laugh, and it causes a silver pulse of anticipation to flash through my blood when she tells me, "You'll be just fine with the Riverview crowd."

....

I get the sense Emily wasn't yanking my chain. I hear music all the way to the curb when I climb out of Giuseppe, my trusty 2009 Saturn. The music is by one of the Spanish sing-ers that Dave loves, layered with the irregular sound of glass clinking, voices, and Dave's awesome braying laugh. My nose tells me he's grilling carne asada, which means that he's also making margaritas, which means I'll need to stay focused to keep my shirt on tonight.

Wish me luck.

With a deep, bracing breath, I do one more check of my outfit. I swear it's not a vanity thing; more often than not, something is unbuttoned, a hem is tucked into underwear, or I've got an important garment on inside out. This characteristic might explain, in part, why third graders feel so at home in my classroom.

Emily and Dave's house is a late Victorian with a shock of independently minded ivy invading the side that leads to the backyard. A winding flower bed points the way to the gate; I follow it around to where the sound of music floats up and over the fence.

Emily really went all out for this "Welcome, Summer!" barbecue. A garland of paper lanterns is strung over the walkway. Her sign even has the correct comma placement. Dinner parties at my apartment consist of paper plates, boxed wine, and the last three minutes before serving featuring me running around like a maniac because I burned the lasagna, insisting I DON'T NEED ANY HELP JUST SIT DOWN AND RELAX.

I shouldn't really get into the comparison game with Emily, of all people. I love the woman but she makes the rest of us look like limp vegetation. She gardens, knits, reads at least a book a week, and has the enviable ability to eat like a frat boy without ever gaining weight. She also has Dave, who, aside from being my new boss (fingers crossed!), is progressive in an effortless way that makes me feel like he's a better feminist than I am. He's also almost seven feet tall (I measured him with uncooked spaghetti one night) and good-looking in an *Are you sure he isn't a fireman?* kind of way. I bet they have amazing sex.

Emily shrieks my name, and a backyard full of my future friends turns to see why she's just shouted, "Get your rack over here!" But I'm immediately distracted by the sight of the yard tonight. The grass is the kind of green you'll only find in the Pacific Northwest. It rolls away from the stone path like an emerald carpet. The beds are full of hostas just starting to unfurl their leaves, and a massive oak stands in the center of it all, its branches heavy with tiny paper lanterns and stretched in a canopy of leaves protecting the guests from the last bit of fading sun.

Emily waves me over and I smile at Dave—nodding like, *Duh, Dave,* when he holds up the margarita pitcher in question—and cross through a small group of people (maybe my new colleagues!) to the far end of the yard.

"Hazel," Em calls, "come over here. Seriously," she says to the two women at her side, "you're going to love her so much."

So, hey guess what? My first conversation with the third grade teachers at Riverview is about breasts, and this time I wasn't even the one to bring them up. I know! I wouldn't have expected that, either! Apparently Trin Beckman is the most senior teacher in our grade, and when Emily points to her breasts, I readily agree she's got a great rack. She seems to think they need to be in a better bra and then mentions something about three pencils I don't entirely catch. Allison Patel, my other third grade peer, is lamenting her A cups.

Emily points to her own A's and frowns at my perky C's. "You win."

"What does my trophy look like?" I ask. "A giant bronze cock?"

The words are out before I can stop them. I swear my mouth and my brain are siblings who hate each other and give each other wedgies in the form of mortifying moments like this. Now it seems my brain has deserted me.

Emily looks like a giant bird has just flown into her mouth. Allison looks like she's contemplating this all very seriously. We all startle when Trin bursts out laughing. "You were right, she *is* going to be fun."

I exhale, and feel a tiny bolt of pride at this—especially when I realize she's drinking water. Trin isn't tickled by my lack of filter because she's already tipsy on one of Dave's killer margaritas; she's just cool with weirdos. My octopus tentacles twitch at my side.

A shadow materializes at Emily's right but I'm distracted by the perfectly timed margarita Dave presses into my hand with a whispered, "Take it slow, H-Train," before disappearing again.

My new boss is the best!

"What's going on over here?"

It's an unfamiliar male voice, and Emily answers, "We were just discussing how Hazel's boobs are better than all of ours."

I look up from my drink to see whether I actually know the person currently studying my chest and . . . oh.

Ohhhh.

Dark eyes widen and quickly flicker away. A carved jaw twitches. My stomach turns over.

It's him. *Josh*.

Josh fucking *Im*. The blueprint for Perfect.

He coughs out a husky breath. "I think I'll skip the boob talk."

Somehow Josh is even better-looking than he was in college, all tanned and fit and with his flawlessly crafted features. He's ducking away in horror already but my brain takes this opportunity to give my mouth a revenge wedgie.

"It's cool." I wave an extremely casual hand. "Josh has already seen my boobs."

The party stops.

Air stills.

"I mean, not because he *wanted* to see them." My brain desperately tries to fix this. "They were forced on him."

A wind chime rings mournfully in the distance.

Birds stop flying midair and fall to their deaths.

"Not forced, like, by *me*," I say, and Emily groans in pain. "But like his roommate had me—"

Josh puts a hand on my arm. "Hazel. Just . . . stop."

Emily looks on, completely confused. "Wait. How do you guys know each other?"

He answers without taking his eyes off me. "College."

"Glory days, am I right?" I give him my best grin.

With an expectant look tossed to each of us Trin asks, "Did you guys *date*?"

Josh pales. "Oh my God. *Never*."

Holy crap, I forgot how much I like this guy.

....

That little shyster Dave Goldrich, principal, waits until I've had three margaritas before telling me I officially have the job as Riverview's newest third grade teacher. I'm pretty sure he does this to see what astounding response comes out of my mouth, so I hope he isn't disappointed with "Holy shit! Are you fucking with me?"

He laughs. "I am not."

"Do I already have a thick HR file?"

"Not officially." Bending from somewhere up near the International Space Station, Dave drifts down to plant a kiss on the top of my head. "But you're not getting the favorite treatment, either. I separate work life from personal. You'll need to do the same."

I pick up on the only thing that matters here. "I'm your favorite?" I bare my teeth, flashing my charming dimple. "I won't tell Emily if you won't." Dave laughs and makes a dramatic reach for my glass, but I evade him, leaning in to add, "About Josh. Is he a tea—?"

"My sister didn't tell me you're joining the staff at Riverview." Josh must be part vampire because I swear he just materializes in empty spaces near warm bodies.

I straighten, flapping at the air in front of my face and trying to clear the confusion. "Your *sister*?"

"My sister," he repeats slowly, "known to you as Emily Goldrich, known to our parents as Im Yujin."

All of a sudden, it clicks. I've only ever known Em's married name. It never occurred to me that the beloved big brother—or *oppa*—I'm always hearing about is the very same Josh I barfed on all those years ago. Wow. Apparently this is the grown-up version of the metal-mouthed tween brother I've seen in the row of photos in Emily's living room. Well done, puberty.

Turning, I yell over my shoulder, "Emily, your Korean name is Yujin?"

She nods. "He's Jimin."

I look at him like I'm seeing a new person in front of me. The two syllables of his name are like a sensual exhale, something I might say immediately preorgasm when words fail me. "That might be the hottest name I've ever heard."

He blanches, like he's afraid I'm about to offer to have sex with him again, and I burst out laughing.

I realize I should be mortified that Past Hazel was so dramatically inappropriate, but it's not like I'm that much better now, and regret isn't really my speed anyway. For the count of three quick breaths, Josh and I grin at each other in intense shared amusement. Our eyes are cartoon-spiral wild.

But then his smile straightens as he seems to remember that I am ridiculous.

"I promise to not proposition you at your sister's party," I tell him, pseudo–sotto voce.

Josh mumbles an awkward "Thanks."

Dave asks, "Hazel *propositioned* you?"

Josh nods, holding eye contact with me for a couple more seconds before looking over to his brother-in-law—my new boss. "She did."

"I did," I agree. "In college. Just before vomiting on his shoes. It was one of my more undatable moments."

"She's had a few." Josh blinks down when his phone buzzes, pulling it out of his pocket. He reads a text with absolutely no reaction and then puts the phone away.

There must be some male pheromone thing happening, because Dave has extracted something from this moment that I have not. "Bad news?" he asks, brows drawn, voice all low, like Josh is a sheet of fragile glass.

Josh shrugs, expression even. A muscle ticks in his jaw and I resist reaching out and pressing it like I'm playing *Simon*. "Tabitha isn't going to make it up for the weekend."

I feel my own jaw creak open. "There are real people named Tabitha?"

Both men turn to look at me like they don't know what I mean.

But come on.

"I just—" I continue, haltingly. "Tabitha seems like what you'd name someone if you expect them to be really, *really* . . . evil. Like, living in a lair and hoarding spotted puppies."

Dave clears his throat and lifts his glass to his mouth, drinking deeply. Josh stares at me. "Tabby is my girlfriend."

"Tabby?"

Swallowing back a strangled laugh, Dave puts a gentle hand on my shoulder. "Hazel. Shut up."

"HR file?" I look up at his familiar face, all bearded and calm. It's dark out now, and he's backlit by a few strings of outdoor lights.

"The party doesn't count," he assures me, "but you're a maniac. Ease Josh in a little."

"I think the fact that I'm a maniac is partly why I'm your favorite."

Dave nearly breaks, but he manages to turn and walk away before I can tell. I am now alone with Josh Im. He studies me like he's looking at something infectious through a microscope.

"I always thought I caught you in . . . a phase." His left eyebrow makes a fancy arch. "Apparently you're just like this."

"I feel like I have a lot to apologize for," I admit, "but I can't be sure I won't be constantly exasperating you, so maybe I'll just wait until we're elderly."

Half of his mouth turns up. "I can say without question I've honestly never known anyone else like you."

"So completely undatable?"

"Something like that."

TWO

JOSH

*H*azel Bradford. Wow.

Pretty much everyone we went to college with has a Hazel Bradford story. Of course, my old roommate Mike has many—mostly of the wild sexual variety—but others have ones more similar to mine: Hazel Bradford doing a mud run half marathon and coming to her night lab before showering because she didn't want to be late. Hazel Bradford getting more than a thousand signatures of support to enter a local hot dog eating contest/fund-raiser before remembering, on-stage and while televised, that she was trying to be a vegetarian. Hazel Bradford holding a yard sale of her ex-boyfriend's clothes while he was still asleep at the party where she found him naked with someone else (incidentally, another guy from his terrible garage band). And—my personal favorite—Hazel Bradford giving an oral presentation on the anatomy and function of the penis in Human Anatomy.

I could never quite tell whether she was oblivious or just
didn't care what people thought, but no matter how chaotic
she was, she always managed to give off an innocent, unin-
tentionally wild vibe. And here she is in the flesh—all five
foot four of her, a hundred and ten pounds soaking wet, huge
brown eyes, with her hair in an enormous brown bun—and I
don't think anything has changed.

"Can I call you Jimin?" she asks.

"No."

Confusion flickers across her face. "You should be proud
of your heritage, Josh."

"I am," I say, fighting a smile. "But you just said it 'Jee-
Min.'"

I'm given a blank stare.

"It's not the same," I explain, and say it again: "*Jimin.*"

She takes on a dramatic, seductive expression. "Jeee-
minnnn?"

"No."

Giving up, Hazel straightens and sips her margarita, looking around. "Do you live in Portland?"

"I do." Just behind her, in the distance, I see my sister
walk up to Dave, pull him down to her level, ask him something, and then they both look at me. I'm positive she's just
asked where Tabby is.

I knew, when Tabitha took the job in L.A.—her dream job
to write for a fashion magazine—that there would be weekends when one or the other of us would be stuck and unable to

fly south (me) or north (her), but it sucks that on three out of four of her weekends to come up here, she's flaked last minute.

Or maybe not flaked so much as had a last-minute work emergency.

But what kind of emergencies do they have at a style magazine?

Honestly, I have no clue. Whatever.

Hazel is still talking.

I turn my attention back down to her just as she seems to wrap up whatever it was she was asking. She stares at me expectantly, grinning in her wide-open way.

"What's that?" I ask.

She clears her throat, speaking slowly, "I asked whether you were okay."

I nod, tilting my bottled water to my lips and trying to wipe away the irritation she must see slashed across my mouth. "I'm good. Just mellow. Long week." I do a mental tally: I averaged eleven hours and thirty-five clients a day this week alone so I could be free all weekend. Knee replacements, hip replacements, bursitis, sprains, torn ligaments, and one dislocated pelvis that made my hands feel weak before I even attempted to work on it.

"It's just that you're sort of monosyllabic," Hazel says, and I look down at her. "You're drinking water when there are Dave's margaritas to be had."

"I'm not very good at . . ." I trail off, gesturing with my bottle to the growing melee around us.

"Drinking?"

"No, just . . ."

"Putting words together into sentences, and then sentences together into conversation?"

Pursing my lips at her, I say primly, "Socializing in large crowds."

This earns me a laugh, and I watch as her shoulders lift toward her ears and she snickers like a cartoon character. Her bun wobbles back and forth on the top of her head. A guilty pulse flashes through me when I realize that despite being goofy, she's sexy as hell, too.

I can feel the reaction work its way from my heart to my groin, and cover with "You are so weird."

"It's true. I'm around kids all day—what do you expect?" I'm about to remind her that it seems like she's always been this way when she continues, "What do you do for a living?"

"I'm a physical therapist." I look around the yard to see whether my business partner, Zach, has shown up yet, but I don't see a flash of orange hair anywhere. "My partner and I opened our practice about a year ago, downtown."

Hazel groans in jealousy. "You get to talk about cores all day, and working things nice and deep. I would never get any actual work done."

"I mean, I occasionally get to tell people to take their pants off, but it's rarely the people you want to see naked from the waist down."

She gives me a thoughtful frown. "I sometimes wonder what the world would be like if clothes were never invented."

"I literally never wonder that."

Hazel rolls on without pause. "Like if we were just naked all the time, what things would have been developed differently?"

I take a sip of my water. "We probably wouldn't ride horses."

"Or we'd just have calluses in weird places." She taps her lips with her index finger. "Bike seats would be different."

"Very likely."

"Women probably wouldn't shave their labia."

A jarring physical reaction cracks through me. "Hazel, that is a terrible word."

"What? We actually don't have hair inside our *vaginas*." I stifle another shudder and she levels me with the fiery stare of a woman scorned. "Besides, no one winces at the word 'scrotum.'"

"I absolutely wince at 'scrotum.' And 'glans.'"

"Glaaaans," she says, elongating the word. "*Terrible*."

I stare at her for a few quiet seconds. Her shoulders are bare, and there's a single freckle on her left one. Her collarbones are defined, arms sculpted like she exercises. I get a flash of a mental image of Hazel using watermelons as weights. "I feel like you're making me drunk just by speaking." I peer into her glass. "Like some kind of osmosis is happening."

"I think we're going to be best friends." At my bewildered silence, she reaches up and ruffles my hair. "I live in Portland, you live in Portland. You have a girlfriend and I have a huge assortment of Netflix series backlogged. We both hate the word 'glans.' I know and love your sister. She loves me. This is the perfect setup for boy-girl bestship: I've already been unbearable near you, which makes it impossible to scare you away."

Quickly swallowing a sip of water, I protest, "I'm afraid you're going to try."

She seems to ignore this. "I think *you* think I'm fun."

"Fun in the way that clowns are fun."

Hazel looks up at me, eyes on fire with excitement. "I seriously thought I was the only person alive who loves clowns!"

I can't hold in my laugh. "I'm kidding. Clowns are terrifying. I won't even walk too close to the storm drain in front of my house."

"Well." She threads her arm through mine, leading me closer to the heart of the party. When she leans in to whisper, my stomach drops somewhere around my navel, the way it does at the first lurch of a roller coaster. "We have nowhere to go but up."

....

Hazel sidles us up to a pair of guys standing near the built-in grill—John and Yuri, two of my sister's (and now Hazel's) colleagues. Their conversation halts as we approach, and Hazel holds out a firm hand.

"I'm Hazel. This is Josh."

The three of us regard her with faint amusement. I've known them both for years.

"We go way back," John says, tilting his head to me, but he shakes her hand, and I watch her methodically take in his shoulder-length dreads, mustache, beret, and T-shirt that reads SCIENCE DOESN'T CARE WHAT YOU BELIEVE. I hold my breath, wondering what Hazel is going to do with him because, as a white dude with dreadlocks, John has made it pretty easy for her, but she just turns to Yuri, smiling and shaking his hand.

"John and Yuri work with Em," I tell her. I use my bottle to point to John. "As you may have guessed, he teaches science to the upper grades. Yuri is music and theater. Hazel is the new third grade teacher."

They offer congratulations and Hazel curtsies. "Do third graders get music?" she asks Yuri.

He nods. "Kindergarten through second is vocal only. In third they begin a string instrument. Violin, viola, or cello."

"Can I learn, too?" Her eyebrows slowly rise. "Like, sit in on the class?"

John and Yuri smile at Hazel in the bemused way that says, *Is she fucking serious?* I imagine most elementary school teachers nap, eat, or cry when they have a free period.

Hazel does a little dance and mimes playing a cello. "I've always wanted to be the next Yo-Yo Ma."

"I . . . guess so?" Yuri says, disarmed by the power of Hazel Bradford's cartoon giggle and bewitching honesty. I turn and look at her, worrying about what Yuri has just gotten himself into. But when he checks out her chest, he doesn't seem worried at all.

"Yo-Yo Ma began *performing* when he was four and a half," I tell her.

"I'd better get cracking, then. Don't let me down, Yuri."

He laughs and asks her where she's from. Half listening to her answer—only child, born in Eugene, raised by an artist mother and engineer father, Lewis & Clark for college—I pull out my phone and check the latest texts from Tabby, each of them sent about five minutes apart. I hate that I get a tiny bit of pleasure knowing that she kept checking her phone.

> Don't be mad at me.

> I told Trish this was the last Friday
> I could work so late.

> Do you want me to try to come up tomorrow,
> or would it be a waste?

> Josh, Josh, don't be mad at me,
> I'm so sorry.

I blow out a controlled breath, and type,

> At Em's party, so only seeing these now. I'm not mad.
> Come home tomorrow if you want, but it's totally up
> to you. You know I always want to see you.

....

"She said you were going to be best friends?" My sister frowns at a shirt and drops it back on the pile at Nordstrom Rack. "*I'm* her best friend."

"It's what she said." A laugh rises in my chest but doesn't make its way out when I remember Hazel accepting her fourth margarita from Dave and asking me to staple her shirt to her waistband. "She's a trip."

"She's made me weird," Em says. "It'll happen to you, too."

I think I know exactly what Em means, but seeing the effect Hazel has had on my sister—making her more fun-loving, giving her social confidence that only now, in hindsight, can I really attribute to Hazel—I don't consider this oddness a bad thing. And Hazel is so unlike Tabby and Zach—so unlike everyone, really, but maybe the polar opposite of my girlfriend

and best friend, who both tend to be quiet and observant—
that I think it might be fun to have her around. Like keeping
interesting beer in the fridge that you're always surprised and
pleased to find there.

Is that a terrible metaphor? I glance at my sister and
mentally calculate the amount of physical damage she could
inflict with the hanger she's holding.

"She's half 'hot exasperating mess' and half 'color in a
monotone landscape.'" Em pulls the shirt from the hanger
and hands it to me. I fold it over my arm, letting her—as
usual—pick my clothes. "I can't believe Tabby isn't here,
again."

I don't bite. It's the third time she's tried to bait me into a
conversation about my girlfriend.

"Doesn't she know that relationships take work?"

Sliding my gaze over to her, I remind her, "She has a
deadline, Em."

"Does she really, though?" Her voice is high and tight and
she takes out her frustration on a pair of shorts she throws
back down on the stack in front of her. "Doesn't this evasion
of hers feel like . . . like . . ."

I prepare for this with a deep breath, hoping my sister
doesn't go there.

"Like she's cheating?" she asks.

And she went there.

"Emily," I begin calmly, "when Dave is working crazy

hours at the school, and you come over and eat dinner at my place and vent about how you haven't seen him in *days*, do I tell you, 'Well, maybe he's got someone on the side'?"

"No, but Dave is also not a flaky asshole."

This trips my fuse. "What is your deal with Tabby? She's only ever been nice to you."

She flinches at my volume, because it's pretty high, which I know is rare. "It's not even that you're too good for her, or she's too good for you," she says, "it's like you guys are in different circles. You have different *values*."

It's true that our parents—who moved here from Seoul when they were newly married and nineteen—aren't huge fans of Tabitha, but I also think they might not be huge fans of any non-Korean girl I date. Unfortunately, I don't think that's what Emily means. I give her a bewildered look.

She turns to face me fully, ticking reasons off on her fingers. "Tabby is the only person I know who has *silk sheets*. She spends hours getting ready to end up looking like she's just rolled out of bed. You, on the other hand, love camping and still occasionally wear the sweatpants I got you for Christmas nine years ago."

I shake my head, still not following.

"She thinks of *Heathers* as a pretty good guide to social etiquette." Emily stares at me. "She laughs at *Romy and Michele's High School Reunion* completely without irony but has sat through *four* Christopher Guest films with us without cracking a single smile. Even when she does come home to visit you, she spends half her time battling out *Who Wore It Better* debates in the comments on Instagram."

I blink, trying to connect the dots. "So your issue with her is . . . you think she's shallow?"

"No, I'm not saying that. If those things make her happy, then *fine*. What I'm saying is I think you don't have a lot in common. I watch you guys interact and it's, like, silence, or 'Can you hand me the carrots over there on the counter?' She is very, *very* enmeshed in the world of fashion, and Hollywood, and appearances." Emily stares up at me, and I get the silent communication as I shuffle the load of clothes she's selected for me from one arm to the other.

"Well, then it's convenient for both her and me that I don't care what I wear. *Obviously*, I let the women in my life choose."

My sister's eyes narrow and I watch as she shrewdly takes a different tack. "What do you guys do when she's here?"

I file through the images of Tabby's last few visits. Sex. Walking to the corner for groceries. Tabby didn't want to go canoeing or hiking and I didn't feel like hitting the bars, so we stayed in for more sex. Dinner out nearby, followed by sex.

I'm pretty sure my sister doesn't want that level of specificity, but she doesn't need me to answer, apparently, because she rolls on. "And what do you do when you visit her?"

Sex, clubs, crowded restaurants, everyone on their phones texting people across the room, more clubs, me complaining about the clubs, me hiking Runyon Canyon alone, coming back to her place and having more sex.

Emily looks away. "Anyway, I'm meddling."

"You are." I guide her toward the cashier; I'm getting bored looking at clothes.

I pay for our items, thank the woman at the register, and we leave, walking along the paved path of the outdoor mall, ducking past kiosk workers aggressively waving skin cream samples at us. Emily looks up at me with reconciliation in her smile. "Let's get back to what we were talking about before."

We are in agreement here. "I think we were talking about the barbecue."

She slides her eyes to me. "You mean we were talking about *Hazel*."

Ah. Clarity slaps me. Turning, I stop her with a hand on her shoulder. "I already *have* a girlfriend."

My sister gives me a pruney face. "I'm aware."

"In case you're trying to start something between me and Hazel Bradford, I can tell you without any question that we are not compatible."

"I'm not trying anything," she protests. "She's just fun, and you need more fun."

I give her a wary glance. "I'm not sure I'm man enough to handle Hazel's brand of fun."

Emily swings a shopping bag over her shoulder and flashes me a toothy grin. "I guess there's only one way to find out."

THREE

HAZEL

I'm sure the man in front of me understands my dilemma—*nay*, I'm sure he sees this several times a day. "Indecision personified," I say, pointing to my chest. "The problem here is you have so many good choices."

"Um." The PetSmart cashier stares at me, maneuvering his gum from one side of his mouth to the other. "I can try to help?"

"I'm deciding between a betta fish and a guinea pig."

"I mean, that's kind of a big difference?" His glasses slowly slide down his nose, and I'm transfixed because their path is halted by an enormous, angry whitehead perched there like a doorstop.

"But if it were you," I say, waggling my eyebrows, "what direction would you go? Fish or furry? I already have a dog"—I gesture to the leashed Winnie at my side—"and a rabbit, and a parrot. They just need one more friend."

The teenager looks at me like I'm completely lacking any marbles. "I mean—"

"*Lick it good.*"

He stares at me and it takes me a beat to realize it's my phone that's just blasted these three words from Khia's "My Neck, My Back (Lick It)."

I burst into motion, scrambling for my purse. "Oh, God!"

"*Suck this pussy just like you should, right now.*"

"Oh my God, oh my God." I fumble inside my bag, pulling the phone out.

"*Lick it good.*"

"Oh—I'm so sorry—"

"*Suck this pussy just like you should, my neck, my back . . .*"

I drop my phone and have to push Winnie's excited, exploring nose away from it before I can grab it—"*Lick my pussy and my crack*"—and silence it with the swipe of a finger.

"*Emily!*" I sing-yell to cover my abject horror, and apologize to the elderly pug owner looking at leashes. I may have just given her a stroke. Her dog is now barking maniacally, setting off Winnie, who sets off three other dogs in line to check out at the registers. One squats to poop from all the stress.

"Good God, Hazel, where *are* you?"

"PetSmart." I wince. "Getting . . . something?"

The line falls dead for several seconds and I look at the screen to see if I've lost the call. "Hello?"

"You think what your apartment needs is another animal?" she asks.

"I'm not getting a Great Dane, we're talking rodent or fish." I look up at the PetSmart employee—Brian, he's apparently named—and excuse myself with a tiny humiliated wave. "By the by, old friend," I say to Emily, "did you perchance change my ringtone again?"

"I couldn't stand that *Tommy Boy* line one more time— I'm not even kidding."

I imagine sending a flock of dragons to her house to feast on her. At the very least a hungry swarm of mosquitoes. "So Khia is better? Sweet Jesus, you could have just made it *ring*."

She laughs. "I was sending a message. Stop using all these weird ringtones, or turn your phone on silent."

"You are so bossy."

As anticipated, she ignores this. "Look, is it cool if I give Josh your number?"

"Not if he's going to call me before I have a chance to change the ringtone."

"We're out shopping," she tells me. "He's such a sad sack now that Tabitha is in L.A., and I know you guys had fun at the party. I just want him to get out more."

I hear Josh's sullen growl in the background: "I'm not a sad sack."

The idea of hanging out with Josh Im makes me oddly giddy. The idea of hanging out with a sad sack Josh Im sounds like a challenge. "Ask him if he wants to come over for lunch tomorrow!"

Emily turns, repeating the request presumably to Josh, and then there's silence.

A lot of silence.

Awkward.

I imagine a host of sibling glares being fired back and forth like bullets:

Way to put me on the spot, jerk!

You'd better say yes or you're going to make her feel bad!

I hate you so much right now, Emily!

She's not as crazy as she seems, Josh!

Finally, she comes back. "He says he'd love to."

"Great." I bend down, making fish kisses at the beautiful teal betta I think I'm going to adopt. "Tell him to bring take-out from Poco India when he comes."

"Hazel!"

I burst out laughing. "I'm *kidding*, oh my God. I'll make lunch. Tell him to come over anytime after eleven." I end the call and pick up the fish in the tiny plastic cup. "You are going to love your new family."

....

Winnie and I head out with fish in hand to meet Mom for lunch. My mom moved to Portland from Eugene a few years ago, when I finished college and it became apparent that I was unlikely to move back home anytime soon. I'm far more my mother's daughter than my father's, personality-wise, but I look exactly like my dad: dark hair, dark eyes, dimple in the left cheek, wiry and not as tall as I'd like to be. Mom, on the other hand, is tall, blond, and curvy in all the best snuggly-mom ways.

My dad was a decent parent, I suppose, but the predominant emotion I got from him throughout my life was disappointment that I wasn't sporty. A son would have been ideal, but a tomboy would have sufficed. He wanted someone to jog in the park with, and throw around a football with for a couple of hours. He wanted weekend-long sportsball tournaments, with shouting and maybe some unfriendly opposing-team fatherly shoving. Instead, he got a goofy chatterbox daughter who wanted to raise chickens, sang Captain and Tennille in the shower, and worked at the pumpkin patch every fall since she was ten because she liked dressing up as a scarecrow. If I wasn't entirely bewildering to him, then I was surely more work than he'd signed up for.

My parents divorced when I was twenty and happily established with a life and friends in Portland. I'll be honest: I wasn't the least bit surprised. My response reveals me to be the monster I am because primarily I was irritated that I would have to make two separate stops when I went home, and when I visited Dad, Mom wouldn't be the buffer of joy anymore.

But even though I knew I was technically an adult at twenty, I kept telling myself that Dad and I would bond when I was older . . . when I was out of college . . . that he'd be so proud at my wedding someday . . . that he'd make a great grandpa because he could play and then hand back the kid and return to the game without a wife glaring at him from across the room.

Unfortunately, it wasn't in the cards. Dad died a few weeks before Christmas the year I turned twenty-five. He was at work, and, according to his longtime coworker Herb, Dad basically sat down at his desk and said, "I'm feeling tired," fell unconscious, and never woke up.

A weird honesty developed between my mom and I after Dad died. I always knew that my parents didn't have the tightest romantic bond, but I didn't realize how flat they had been, either, to the point that they were essentially two strangers moving around the same house. The ways I'm like Mom—a little wacky, I admit—were totally exasperating to Dad. Mom and I are both huggers, maybe overly enthusiastic about the things we love, and terrible joke tellers. But where I love animals and costumes and seeing faces in clouds and singing in the shower, Mom favors making wild skirts out of bold fabrics, creating artwork out of colored glass, wearing flowers in her hair, quoting musicals, and dancing while mowing the front lawn in her red cowboy boots.

Dad couldn't stand her eccentricities, even though they're what attracted him in the first place. I remember clearly one fight they had in front of me where he told her, "I hate it when you act like a weirdo out in public. You're so fucking embarrassing."

I don't know how to explain it. I was fourteen when he said that to her, and those last four words broke something in me. I saw myself and Mom from the outside in a way I hadn't before, like Dad represented this mainstream ideal and she and I were these loud, bouncing yellow dots outside of the standard curve.

When I looked up at her, I'd expected her to be shattered by what he'd said. But instead, she looked at him pityingly, like she wanted to console him but knew it would be a wasted effort. Dad missed out on so much by not enjoying every second he had with her, and in the end, she was terribly disappointed that he was so dull. I learned a very important thing that day: my mom would never try to change for a man, and I wouldn't, either.

....

She's waiting for me at Barista when we walk up, but it's apparent that she's really been awaiting Winnie, because it's a full two minutes of puppy voice and ear ruffling before I even get a glance. At least it gives me time to decide what I'm going to order.

Mom looks up just as the waitress delivers a muffin and latte to her. "Hey, Hazie."

"You already ordered?"

"I was hungry." With a hand bearing rings on every finger, Mom peels the paper wrapping away from the muffin, staring down at Winnie. "I bet I could drop this entire thing and she wouldn't notice."

I order a curry chicken salad and black coffee and look over at my dog. Mom's right, she's obsessed with the trio of speckled finches under the table next to us, casually pecking at sandwich crumbs. I can see Winnie's insanity ratcheting higher with every peck.

A car honks, a couple passes by with Winnie's favorite thing ever—a baby in a stroller—and nothing.

But then Mom drops a huge chunk of muffin and Winnie pounces on it in a flash as if she sensed some change in the atmospheric pressure. Her movement is so fast and predatory that the birds burst away, escaping into a tree.

Mom drops another piece of muffin.

"Knock it off, you're ruining her."

"She's named Winnie the Poodle," Mom reminds me. "Already ruined."

"Because of you I can't eat a single meal without her watching me like I'm dismantling a bomb. You're making her fat."

Mom leans down and kisses Winnie on the nose. "I'm making her happy. She loves me." This time, Winnie catches the bite of muffin before it even lands on the sidewalk.

"You're the worst."

Mom sings to my dog, "Best, best, best."

"Best," I agree, thanking the waitress when she delivers my coffee. "By the way, Sassypants, I like your haircut."

Mom reaches up, touching it like she forgot she had hair, without any self-consciousness whatsoever. She's always worn it long, mostly because she *does* forget it's there, and luckily it's low maintenance: thick and straight. Now it's trimmed so it lands just below her shoulders, and for the first time ever, there are some layers at the front.

I reach over, touching the ends. "Call me crazy but it looks like you actually had someone else cut it this time."

"I couldn't do layers like this," she agrees. "Wendy has a girl who does her hair." Wendy is Mom's best friend, who moved up to Portland about ten years ago, and was another draw for Mom to relocate here. Wendy is a Republican first, a real estate agent second, and any time left over she devotes to hassling her husband, Tom, about being lazy. I love her because she's basically family, but honestly I have no idea what she and Mom ever find to talk about. "I went to see her yesterday. I think her name was Bendy. Something like that."

Delight fills me like sunshine. "Please let it be Bendy. That is fantastic."

Mom frowns. "Wait. Brandy. I think I combined Brandy and Wendy."

I laugh into a hot sip. "I think you did."

"Anyway, I hadn't cut it in forever, and Glenn seems to like it."

I pause and then take another long, deliberate sip as Mom looks directly at me, her green eyes shining with mischief.

"*Glenn*, eh?" I pretend to twirl my mustache.

JOSH AND HAZEL'S GUIDE TO NOT DATING   41

She hums and spins her rings.

"You've been seeing a lot of him lately." Glenn Ngo is a podiatrist from Sedona, Arizona, and about four inches shorter than Mom. They met when she went in because her feet were killing her, and instead of telling her to stop wearing her cowboy boots, he just gave her some orthopedic inserts for them and then asked her out to dinner.

Who says romance is dead?

I knew they were dating but I didn't know they were *I'll cut my hair the way you like it since I have zero vanity* dating.

"Mom," I whisper, "have you and Glenn . . . ?" I dunk my spoon in and out of my coffee cup a few times.

Her eyes widen and she grins.

I gasp. "You *floozy*."

"He's a podiatrist!"

"That's exactly my point!" I drop my voice to a hush, joking, "They're known fetishists."

"You shut up," she says, laughing as she leans back in her chair. "He's good to me, and he likes to garden. I'm not saying anything for certain, but there's a chance he might be visiting on a more . . . permanent basis."

"Shacking up! I am scandalized!"

She gives me a cheeky smile and takes a sip of her drink.

"Does he mind the singing?" I ask.

Her look of victory is everything. "He does not."

Our eyes hold, and our smiles turn from playful to something softer. Mom found a good one, someone I can tell really gets her. An ache pokes at my chest. Without having to say it, I know we both question whether those guys really exist. The world seems full of men who are initially infatuated by our eccentricities, but who ultimately expect them to be temporary. These men eventually grow bewildered that we don't settle down into calm, potential-wifey girlfriends.

"What about you?" she asks. "Anyone . . . *around*?"

"What's with the emphasis? You mean, around inside my pants?" I take a bite of the salad deposited in front of me and Mom gives a little *Yeah, that's not exactly what I meant but go ahead* shrug.

"No." I straighten and push away the mild concern that her question immediately triggered this next thought: "But guess who I did run into? No, never mind, you'll never guess. Remember my anatomy TA?"

She shakes her head, thinking. "The one with the prosthetic leg on your roller derby team?"

"No, the one I wrote the email to while high on painkillers."

Mom's laugh is this breathy little twinkle. "Now, *that* I remember. The one you liked so much. Josh something."

"Josh Im. I also threw up on his shoes." I decide to leave out the roommate sex for now. "So, weirdest thing: he's Emily's *brother*!"

This seems to take a few seconds for Mom to process. "Emily *your* Emily?"

"Yes!"

"I thought Emily's last name was Goldrich?"

I love that it would never occur to my mother that a woman would take her husband's name. "She's married, Mom. That's her married name."

She feeds Winnie a handful of muffin crumbs. "So, you and her brother . . . ?"

"No. *God* no. I'm an established idiot with him, and he's most likely a Normal Dude." Our shared code for the kind of man who wouldn't appreciate our particular brand of nuts. "Besides, he has a girlfriend. Tabitha," I can't help but add meaningfully, and Mom makes a *yeeesh* face. "He calls her Tabby."

Mom's *yeeesh* face deepens.

"I know, right?" I poke at my salad. "But he's actually pretty cool? Like, you wouldn't look at him and automatically think he's a banker."

"Well, what is he?"

"A physical therapist. He's all muscley." I maneuver an enormous piece of lettuce into my mouth to beat down the image of Josh Im working his strong hands over my sore thighs.

Mom doesn't say anything to this; she seems to be waiting for more, so I swallow with effort and venture onward into Babble County.

"We hung out together at Emily's barbecue last night, and it's weird because I feel like since he's already seen me at my most insane, and he has a girlfriend, I don't have to try to pull up the crazy plane around him. I always wanted to be friends with him and here he is! My new friend! And he looks at me like I'm this fascinating bug. Like a beetle, not a butterfly, and it's fine because he already has a butterfly and when you think about it, beetles are pretty great. It's nice." For some inexplicable reason, I repeat it again. "It's nice."

"That *is* nice." The way Mom studies me is making me feel like I forgot to dress myself this morning; it's with this *Does my adult daughter know her own mind?* kind of maternal focus.

I shake my head at her and she laughs, absently petting Winnie.

"You" is all she says.

I growl. "No, *you*."

She looks back at me with such adoration. "You, you, you."

FOUR

JOSH

I pull in front of Hazel's apartment complex and stare up at the flat gray buildings. From the outside, they look like perfect cubes. Structures like these make me wonder whether an architect actually took time to *design* this. Who would create a concrete block with bland windows and look back at the blueprint and go, "Ah. My masterpiece is complete!"

But the tiny garden out front is pretty, full of bright flowers and neatly spaced ground cover. And there's underground parking, which can't be beat in a town like . . .

Clearly, I'm stalling.

I reach for the bag on the passenger seat and carry it with me up the walkway to the buzzer at the front door.

Pressing the button for 6B, I hear a shriek from several floors up and step back to see Hazel leaning out the window, waving a pink scarf.

"Josh! Up here!" she yells. "I'm so sorry, the stairs are broken so you're going to have to scale the outer walls. I'll throw down some ropes!"

I stare at her until she laughs and shrugs, disappearing. A few moments later, the front door buzzes loudly.

The elevator is small and slow, giving me a mental image of a bored teenager riding a stationary bicycle in the basement, sweatily coaxing a pulley to raise and lower tenants and guests. Down a yellow hallway I go, stopping at 6B, where the welcome mat bears three colorful tacos and reads COME BACK WITH TACOS.

Hazel opens the door, greeting me with an enormous grin. "Welcome, Jeee-Meeeeeen!"

"You're a maniac."

"It's a gift."

"Speaking of gifts." I hand her the bag of fruit. "I got you apples. Not tacos."

In the Korean community, it's customary to bring fruit or a gift when visiting someone's home, but Hazel—the *teacher*—inspects the bag with amusement.

"I usually only earn one of these at a time," she says. "I'll have to be very impressive today."

"It was either apples or a bag of cherries, and apples just seemed more appropriate."

She guffaws at this before motioning for me to come inside. "Want a beer?"

Given the awkwardness of this semiblind friend-date, I absolutely want a beer. "Sure."

I toe off my shoes near a group of hers, and Hazel looks at me like I'm stripping. "You don't have to do that. I mean, you can if you want, but know that pile of shoes has a lot more to do with me being too lazy to pick them all up than it does with wanting to save the carpet."

"Family habit," I explain.

But one look around and . . . I believe her. Her apartment is tiny, with a small living room and galley kitchen, a tiny nook for a table, and a hall that leads to what I assume is the only bedroom and bathroom. But it's airy and bright, with a couple of windows in the living room and a balcony on the far wall.

It's also full of stuff, everywhere. When Emily and I were young, our mother would read us a book about mischievous *gwisin* who would slip out at night and play with children's toys, pull food from cabinets and pots from shelves. When the family awoke, the *gwisin* would disappear, leaving whatever they'd been playing with out for someone else to clean up.

I'm reminded of this as I take in Hazel's space. Still, it's not messy so much as it is *full*. Books are stacked on the coffee table. Pages of brightly colored construction paper sit in piles on the floor. Folded clothes are draped over the arms of chairs, and a basket of laundry pushes rebelliously against a closet door. I know most people would call this *lived in*, but it presses like an itch against the part of my brain that thrives on order.

I watch her turn and walk into the kitchen, taking in her cutoffs and pale yellow sweatshirt that falls off one shoulder, revealing a red bra strap. Her hair is in that same huge bun right on top of her head, and her feet are bare, each toenail painted a different color.

She catches me staring at her feet.

"My mom's boyfriend is a podiatrist," she says with a teasing smile. "I can totally introduce you."

"I was just admiring your fine art."

"I'm an indecisive type." She wiggles her toes. "Winnie picked out the colors."

I look around for a roommate, or any sign of someone else living here. Emily implied that Hazel lives alone. "Winnie?"

"My labradoodle." Hazel turns to the fridge, bending and digging, presumably, for beer. I shoot my gaze to the ceiling when I realize I've let my eyes go blurry on the view of her ass. "My parrot is Vodka." Her voice reverberates slightly from inside as she reaches to the far back. "My rabbit is Janis Hoplin." She looks over her shoulder at me. "Janis gets really crazy around men. Like, *humping* crazy."

Humping? I glance around the apartment. "That's . . . hmm."

She has a dog, a rabbit, and a parrot.

"Oh, and my new fish is Daniel Craig." She straightens with two bottles of Lagunitas in one hand, cracks open our

JOSH AND HAZEL'S GUIDE TO NOT DATING   49

beers on a brass mustache mounted to her kitchen wall, and hands me one. "I thought it best to ease you in, so they're all at my mom's."

"Thanks." We clink the necks together, both take a sip, and she's looking at me like it's my turn to speak. Generally I have no problem making conversation, but rather than feeling uncomfortable around Hazel, I actually feel like the most entertaining thing for both of us would be if she would just keep babbling. I swallow, wiping the liquid from my upper lip. "You like animals, huh?"

"I like babying things. I swear I want, like, seventeen kids."

I freeze, unsure whether she's being serious.

Her mouth curves up in a thrilled arc. "See?" Her index finger aims at her chest. "Undatable. I like to drop that one on the first date. Not that this is a date. I don't really want seventeen kids. Maybe three. If I can support them." She bites her lip and begins to look self-conscious just when I'm starting to dig the way she's throwing the kitchen sink at me. "This is where Dave and Emily usually tell me I'm babbling and to shut up. I'm really glad you came for lunch." A pause. "Say something."

"You named your fish Daniel Craig."

She seems delighted that I'm actually listening. "Yes!"

She pauses again, reaching up to brush away a wayward strand. Is it weird that I like that her hair seems to be as resistant to being tamed as she does?

I dig around in my brain for something not related to my current train of thought. Apparently I fail, because what comes out is "Summer vacation looks good on you."

She relaxes a little, looking down at her cutoffs. "You'd be amazed what a few days without an alarm clock can do."

The words *alarm clock* are enough to make the shrill blast of mine echo in my thoughts. "Must be nice. I'd sleep until ten every day if left to my own devices."

"Yeah, but according to Google you've got a booming physical therapy practice, and"—she motions in the general vicinity of my chest—"you get to look at that in the mirror every morning. It's worth getting up."

I don't know what feels more incongruous: the mental image of Hazel using a computer, or the idea that she used it to look me up. "You Googled me?"

She huffs out a little breath. "Don't get an ego. I Googled you sometime between Googling beef Wellington and chicken coops."

At my questioning look, she adds, "The chicken thing should be pretty self-explanatory. Spoiler alert: you can't raise chickens in a nine-hundred-square-foot apartment." She gives a dramatic thumbs-down. "And I was going to make something elaborate for lunch today but then remembered I'm lazy and a terrible cook. We're having sandwiches. Surprise!"

Being near Hazel is like being in a room with a mini cyclone. "That's cool. I love sandwiches."

"Peanut butter and jelly." She makes a cartoonish lip-smacking sound.

I burst out laughing, and have a strange urge to ruffle her hair like she's a puppy.

She turns back to the kitchen and pulls out a baking sheet with supplies: a stack of small bowls, a few innocuous baking ingredients—including cornstarch—and some bottles of nontoxic paint.

Peering over her shoulder, I tell her, "I've never made peanut butter and jelly sandwiches like this before."

Hazel looks at me, and this close up I can see that her skin is nearly perfect. Dating Tabby makes me notice things like this—hair, and lipstick, and clothes—because she's always pointing them out. Now that she's made me aware of it, I hardly ever see women without makeup on, and it makes me want to stare a little bit at the smooth, clean curve of Hazel's jaw.

"This isn't for the sandwiches," she says. "We're making clay."

"You—" I stop, unsure what to say. Now that I know what we're going to be doing, I realize I had no idea what to expect, and it seems pretty obvious that, of course, we'd be doing some random art project. "We're having a playdate?"

She nods, laughing. "But with beer." Handing me the tray, she lifts her chin to indicate that I should take it to the living room. "Seriously, though, it looks fun and I wanted to try it out before attempting it in front of twenty-eight third graders."

Hazel brings us sandwiches and we mix up a couple of bowls of clay, adding paint to make a variety of batches in a rainbow of colors. She gets a smear of purple on her cheek and, when I point it out, reaches over to put her entire paint-wet green palm on my face.

"I told you you'd have fun," she says.

"You actually never said that." When she looks up, feigning insult, I add, "But you're right. I haven't made clay in at least two . . . decades."

My phone chimes with Tabby's text tone, and I apologize under my breath, pulling it out carefully with my clay-covered hands.

> I'm not going to make it tonight. Trish has me here late and I'm so bummed. I've been thinking about your cock all fucking day. And fucking your cock all day . . .

I stare at the screen, looking up at the name again to confirm it's from Tabby, and not a wrong number.

But it's Sunday.

Was Tabby planning to come up today? Was she going to make up for flaking on Friday . . . and skip work tomorrow?

Confusion slowly cools into dread, and it drains all the blood from my heart into the pit of my gut. Not only am I fairly sure she wasn't planning on coming to Portland tonight, she's also never said anything nearly that filthy to me before.

I wipe away most of the clay and with shaking hands, I type:

> I didn't know you were planning on flying up.

The three dots appear to indicate she's typing . . . and then disappear. They appear again, and then disappear. I stare at my screen, aware of Hazel's eyes on me occasionally as she works a blob of bright blue clay.

"Everything okay?" she asks quietly.

"Yeah, just . . . got a weird text from Tabby."

"What kind of weird?"

I look up at her. I like to keep my cards pretty close to my chest, but from the expression on Hazel's face, I can tell I look like I've been punched. "I think she just sent me a text that was meant for . . . someone else."

Her brown eyes pop wide open and she uses a blue-green finger to pull a strand of hair from where it's stuck to the purple paint on her cheek. "Like, another *guy*?"

I shake my head. "I don't know. I don't want to go out on a mental ledge right now, but . . . sort of."

"I'm gonna guess it wasn't, like, a 'Can I borrow a cup of sugar?' type of text."

"No."

She goes quiet, then makes a little choking noise in the back of her throat. When I look up at her, it's almost like she's in pain.

"Are *you* okay?" I ask.

Hazel nods. "I'm swallowing down my terrible words."

I don't even have to ask. "What, that she was destined to screw up because her name is Tabitha?"

She points an accusing finger at me. "I didn't say it. *You* said it!"

Despite the hysterical thrum of my pulse in my ears, I smile. "You can't hide a single thought you have."

There's still no reply, and my thoughts grow darker with every passing second. *Was* her text meant for someone else? Is there any other explanation for her silence now? The thought makes me want to vomit all over Hazel's chaotic living room floor.

Hazel drops the clay into a bowl and uses a wet wipe to clean her hands. I half wonder how I look right now: bewildered, with a giant green handprint on my face.

"How long have you been together?" Hazel asks.

A tiny montage of our relationship plays in front of me: meeting Tabby at a Mariners game in Seattle, realizing we were both from Portland, having dinner and taking her home with me. Making love that first night and having a feeling about her, like she could be it for me. Introducing her to my family and then, unfortunately, helping her pack up her apartment, and all the promises that her move to L.A. wouldn't change us. "Two years."

She winces. "That is the *worst* amount of time when you're our age. Two of your hot years, gone. *Invested*." I'm barely listening but she doesn't even notice. Apparently when the Hazel train gets going, it doesn't stop until it's gone completely off the tracks. "And if you've been living together or engaged? Forget about it. By then your lives are all crisscrossed and overlapping and like, what are you supposed to do? Do you get married? I mean, generally speaking, but obviously not in your situation. You know . . . if she's cheating on you." She covers her mouth with her hands and mumbles from behind them, "Sorry. It's a curse."

In my lap, my phone lights up with a text.

> Yeah, I was going to surprise you!!!!
> I'm so bummed I can't!!!!

I groan, rubbing my face. This reply makes me feel infinitely worse. I mean, she's lying. Right? That's what's happening right now? One exclamation point means enthusiasm. Four means panic. There's a car inside my veins, driving too fast, no brakes.

"This is not good," I mutter.

I feel more than hear Hazel crawl over toward me and when I uncover my eyes, she's so close, sitting cross-legged beside me and staring at the mess of clay on the floor. I don't know why I do it—I barely know her—but I wordlessly hand her my phone. It's like I need someone else to see it and tell me I'm misreading everything.

It's Hazel's turn to groan. "I'm sorry, Josh."

I take the phone back and toss it behind us onto her couch. "It's okay. I mean, I could be wrong."

"Right. Sure. You probably are," she agrees, half-heartedly.

I let out a slow, controlled breath. "I'll call her tomorrow."

"You could call her now, if you need to. I would be going insane. I can leave the room and give you some privacy."

Shaking my head, I tell her, "I need to sleep on this. I need to figure out what I want to ask her."

She goes still beside me, lost in thought. Traffic passes by, unhurriedly, on the street outside. Hazel's fridge gives off a metallic rattle, almost like a shiver, every ten seconds or so. I stare at her every-colored toenails and notice a tiny tattoo of a flower on the side of her left foot.

"Do you have a comfort movie?" she asks.

I blink up, not sure I've understood. "A what?"

"For me, it's *Aliens*." Hazel looks at me. "Not the first one, *Alien*, but the second, with Vasquez, and Hicks, and Hudson. Sigourney Weaver is so badass. She's a warrior, and a quasi–foster mother, and a soldier, and a sexy *beast*. I would do her so fast. It's the first movie I saw where a woman demonstrates how easily we can do it all."

I let her odd brown eyes steady me; it's almost like I'm being hypnotized. "That sounds pretty great."

"I still can't believe Bill Paxton died," she says quietly.

I think Tabitha and I are done. I'm not even sure what to feel; it's a weird no-man's-land between sad and numb and relieved. "Yeah."

Her eyes soften and I'm finally able to give the name a color: whiskey.

Very gently, she asks, "Wanna watch *Aliens*?"

FIVE

HAZEL

I can forgive Josh for never having seen *Aliens*—because no one is perfect—and in his favor, he tried to pretend he wasn't terrified in the opening scene when the dream alien rips out of Ripley's torso. If he thought that was bad, imagine his reaction when Hudson, Hicks, and Vasquez find all the cocooned colonists in the corridors. Boom! Aliens everywhere!

In the end, he wouldn't go so far as to agree with me that it's the best movie ever made, but before he left he managed to work in the phrases *Game over, man, game over* and *They mostly come out at night. Mostly.* Clearly I'm a stellar influence.

I spend some time the next morning with Winnie at the park. While she lounges in the grass next to me, I stare up at the clouds, trying to find animals in them and wondering what it is about Josh Im that I'm so drawn to. It isn't just that he's good-looking. It isn't only that he's kind. It's his calm center that's a gravitational pull to my chaotic one. Every time I've met his eyes—from that first puke-filled night to now—I've felt a gentle hum inside my breastbone: I'm a satellite that's found its safe-space beacon.

A few days after our friend-date, I ambush Josh at work to take him on an ice cream break. Partly it's because deep down I really want to have ice cream for lunch every day this summer, but partly, too, it's the memory of Josh's expression while he was reading the texts from Tabby. He looked like he'd been kicked. I'm still waiting for him to update me, to tell me what happened with her, but despite the display of emotion he shared with me at my place, he's gone back to his even-keeled, dry-humored self.

I'm afraid to tell Emily what the text said because I get the distinct impression she does not like Mistress Tabitha, and I also sense that the last thing Josh needs is an opinionated sister telling him how to feel about this. I'm just going to have to woman up and ask him about it myself.

"*So.*" I smile over my cone at him.

He knows exactly what's coming and just stares at me flatly.

I must be pretty easy to read because it feels like Josh is never surprised by anything I say. "Do you love or hate the way I've already insinuated myself into your life?"

He takes a bite of his mint chip and swallows. "I remain undecided."

"And yet you're here." I sweep my hand over the outdoor

table, gesturing to the beauty before us: his little kid-size cup and my enormous, dripping two-scoop cone. "Enjoying a magnificent break from work."

Josh arches an eyebrow. "I wouldn't turn down ice cream."

I acknowledge this with a sage nod. "Well, regardless, Jimin, I like you."

"I know you do."

"And as someone you would never date, but who will soon be your best friend, I can say with no ulterior motive that I don't like that you're in a relationship with a potentially trea- sonous skank."

His eyes go wide. "Wow. Let's jump right in."

"Ha!" I smack my thigh. "So that came out a little balder than intended. What I meant to say"—I clear my throat delicately—"is have you talked to Tabby since Sunday?"

"We've been playing phone tag." He gives me a wary look before dropping his attention to his cup again, scraping around the edge. "And yes, I realize that seems odd given that we're in the same time zone. She's avoiding this conversation. Maybe I am, too."

Wait. It's been five days since that weird text came in, and they haven't even spoken to each other? I would feel like a grenade with the pin pulled free. Granted, I probably tend to overprocess things rather than under-, but to be in a rela- tionship and wondering whether infidelity is happening and not need to know ASAP?

"Are you both dead inside?"

He doesn't miss a beat. "We might be."

"Why don't you go to L.A. and do this in person?"

He looks up at me, dropping the tiny spoon into his empty cup. "So here's where I keep getting stuck. She's not moving back. I get that now. So, if we work through this, either I move to L.A.—"

"Gross." I scrunch my nose.

"Exactly, or she and I . . . what? Have a long-distance relationship forever?"

"If you go that direction you are going to get tennis elbow because that is a lot of phone sex." I lick a drip of chocolate from my cone and as an afterthought add, "Good thing you're a physical therapist."

Josh gazes at me impassively.

"Maybe she could get a job somewhere more appealing to both of you—"

He shakes his head. "I have an established practice here, Haze."

"*Or*," I continue, feeling the warm glow fill me when I realize he's shortened my name out of familiarity, "she could decide L.A. isn't for her. Geography is just space; you can't let that come between you if it's good."

Josh eyes me, unblinking. "I thought you didn't want me to be with a 'treasonous skank'?"

"Of course I don't. But do we actually know whether she's treasonous?" I take a long lick of my ice cream. "You haven't *talked* to her."

He grumbles something and stands to throw his cup away in a nearby trash bin. "I need to get back to work."

Hefting up my cone I stand, following him down the block. He's walking back all stiff and soldierly, and I have to jog to keep up. The top scoop of my ice cream slides off and lands on the sidewalk with a sorrowful splat. I stare at it, forlorn.

"I can see you working out whether it's okay to pick that up and put it back on." He rests a hand on my arm. "Don't do it."

The chocolate and peanut butter begin to melt, and a whimper tears out of me. "It was so delicious. I'm blaming you for walking so fast and angrily."

His hand stays there, and I look up at him with a pout that slips away as I realize he's working this Tabby thing around in his thoughts like a Tetris piece.

"You should go to L.A.," I tell him. "Whether it's to fix things or end them, it can't be done over the phone, and definitely not over text."

"Zach and Emily think I should end it, and they don't even know about the text." He drops his hand back to his side. "My mom and dad don't like her, either. Thanks for at least considering the possibility that she's not a treasonous skank." He pauses. "I'm worried she is, though."

"Why don't they like her?" I ask.

Straightening, he turns to start walking again. I give a fond farewell to my melting ice cream before reluctantly following. "They don't know each other very well."

"How is that possible? You've been together for two years!"

"Tabby never really went out of her way to build a relationship with Umma—my mom—and my dad is quiet to everyone, but I'm not sure she's even tried to have a conversation with him. Especially to my parents, that's a pretty hard thing to overcome."

He digs in his pocket for his phone when it chimes with a tone I've come to understand is Tabby's. I watch as he reads the text a few times and then looks up at me.

"Seems like you and Tabby are on the same page." He shows me the text.

> Will you take some time off and come to L.A.?
> I can't get away, but want to see you.

....

Josh heads back to the office, and I watch him leave, feeling protective. He's built like an athlete—all lean muscle and definition—but there's a vulnerability in him somewhere, the back of his neck, maybe, the small downward tilt of his head. We've only been friends for a week now, but I don't want him to get his heart broken. I'm also bummed there won't be anyone around to give me shit in the way he does—so straight and somehow, beneath it all, entertained by me anyway.

To make matters worse, when I return to my apartment, I hear Winnie barking maniacally from inside. Panicked, I rush in and my first step is a sodden one. With a gasp, I register that my apartment is completely flooded. The carpet squishes under my feet. Winnie barks from the bedroom, and between her hollers, a quiet hiss comes from somewhere deeper inside; water gushing happily everywhere. A pipe must have burst because a miniature lake spreads across the living room and kitchen, down the hall. I slosh through it, scanning for the source before realizing that it's the sink in the bathroom.

I find Winnie standing on the safe island of my bed, yelling at me. Vodka squawks angrily from his perch when he sees me and Janis hops around her cage like a maniac. It's such an oddball sitcom moment that I actually laugh, but the sound quickly dies into a tiny whimper.

It takes only a few twists of the valve to shut it off, but the damage is done. I collapse back on my butt in the deepest puddle and stare out through the bathroom door. The carpets are ruined. The furniture also probably ruined. Piles of papers I'd left on the living room floor have disintegrated. Books, clothes, shoes, dog toys, everything.

For a few minutes, I'm only stunned. I have no other thought but

Oh shit.

Oh shit.

Oh shit.

I hate having to be the grown-up in situations like this. I know it's not my fault, but my landlord is going to freak out anyway and I'm going to have to work really hard to not feel the need to apologize. He'll blame this on Winnie or Janis somehow because I had to charm his pants off to let me have them here in the first place. (I didn't *actually* charm his pants off—gross.) I'll have to clean out everything in the apartment, and move—at least for a while. I'll have to find somewhere to stay with my animals, so most hotels are out of the question. I can't stay in Mom's tiny apartment with the dog and bird and rabbit *and* possibly permanent Glenn. Emily has a spare room, but her house is so obsessively clean that just being there for dinner sometimes stresses me out.

Pushing up, I find my purse on the kitchen counter and make the first call to the landlord. Perhaps not surprisingly, he just got off the phone with my downstairs neighbor, whose ceiling started dripping, so I'm relieved to not be the one to break the news. He lets me know he'll cover the cost of my rent elsewhere until this is fixed, and I know my insurance will replace anything ruined by the flooding. It's a relief, but this still sucks because there's no one but me to pack it up, to figure it out, to find somewhere to sleep in the meantime.

I'm sure Mom will take Janis, Vodka, and Daniel. Winnie has to stay with me. I shove everything I can into a couple of suitcases and pack up my animal family into the car before sitting and staring out the windshield. Daniel swims winningly in the small cup in my cup holder. Vodka repeats the word *cookie* about seven hundred times in the back seat. Winnie leans over the console and licks my ear. I can hear Janis burrowing in some newspaper in her cage.

"We're homeless, guys."

Winnie looks at me like I'm being melodramatic, so I call Emily for sympathy.

"*Flooded?*" she repeats. "Seriously?"

I feel my lip wobble and the wobble spreads to my chin and then I'm crying into the phone, babbling about all the ruined art projects and carpet and my favorite blue espadrilles and how I'm not going to live with my bird and bunny for the next few weeks and I liked that apartment because it was sunny and my neighbor baked cakes a lot so it always smelled good and—

"*Hazel, shut up,*" Emily yells into the phone. "I'm trying to tell you. I think you can stay at Josh's."

I sniffle. "If Josh is anything like you about laundry and vacuuming, he would murder me in my sleep."

"He's going to be in L.A. for a couple weeks."

I pause. So he booked the ticket, then. I'm both happy for Josh and sad. I want someone better for him than Tabitha, even though I barely know him·and I've never met her.

"Let me add him in real quick." Emily disappears before I can protest, and when she comes back, she makes sure we're each on the line.

"I'm here." Josh sounds tired and bored, and I can't tell if it's his usual lackadaisical manner or he's upset . . . or both.

"So, Hazel's apartment flooded," Emily begins.

Josh sounds significantly more alert when he says, "Wait, seriously? While we were out just now?"

"You two were out just now?" Emily asks.

I ignore the strident interest in her voice and explain, "A pipe burst, and normally I'd be making lots of terrible sex jokes about that, but really, it just sucks." I fidget with my car keys in the ignition. "I'll be out for at least three weeks."

Emily hops in: "Josh, I was thinking she could crash at your place until she finds somewhere to stay longer term. You'll be gone and there's plenty of space. She'll even keep the tornado confined to the guest room."

"I will?" I wonder whether Emily really believes this.

"No pets," Josh says immediately.

"Winnie?" I counter. "I can pay you rent."

"Is she housebroken?"

I press a hand to my chest, genuinely offended. "I beg your pardon, sir, my canine has impeccable manners."

Josh laughs dryly. "Okay, sure."

"Really?" I dance happily in my seat. "Josh, you are the best."

"Whatever."

His tone makes my heart wilt a little. "You sound so sad, best friend."

"*I'm* your best friend," Emily reminds me.

I can't help the giddy lean to my words. "It's been my plan all along to have you two fighting for my love."

Josh sighs. "I'm hanging up now. I'm at work, and leave for L.A. at seven. Emily will give you her spare keys."

"You doing okay?" I ask.

"Wait," Emily says. "Why wouldn't he be okay?"

I blurt out the first thing that comes to mind. "He was having some intestinal distress earlier."

Josh groans across the line. "I'm *fine*." He pauses, and when he speaks again, his voice is a little gentler. "Call me if you, you know, need anything, Hazel."

My heart squeezes so tight. "Thanks, Josh."

He doesn't say anything else, but I hear when he disconnects from the call.

Emily falls completely silent.

"Hello?"

She clears her throat. "I'm still here."

"So, can I swing by for the keys? That's so insanely nice of him, I can't—"

"What is going on with you and Josh?"

I make a frantic *time-out* gesture, but Emily can't see it. "Nothing, *gah*. Josh and I aren't romantic, like at all. I just really, really, really like him. He's like a Hazel magnet. I love his dry humor and sarcasm and that he seems to *get* me. I think we're just becoming really good friends and it makes me really happy."

"*Really?*" she says, and I start to answer before realizing that she's making fun of my tendency to be superlative.

"*Really,*" I say. "Seriously. There is zero attraction there."

Emily snorts. "Okay."

SIX

JOSH

*T*wo days, two flights, more drama than a drunken night in a freshman dorm, and here I am: back home again. So of course my door won't open.

Jiggling the key free, I kneel down until I'm level with the lock. I replaced both of the doorknobs when I refinished the front and back porches only a year ago, and can't think of a single reason why the front door would be jammed.

Unless, I think, leaning in to get a closer look, someone tried to pry it open.

Hazel.

I straighten, looking down at my watch as I debate what to do. This day has been nothing but a nightmare, and even though I know I should go to my sister's place and sleep on the couch, the only thing I want right now is to take my clothes off and climb into my own bed. It's after two a.m., which means Hazel is most likely inside and asleep in the guest room, so there's no harm in letting myself in and explaining it all in the morning, right?

With this decided, I reach for my bag and turn down the stairs, headed toward the backyard.

The light from the street doesn't make it to this side of the house: it's damp, and shaded by trees even in daylight. Right now, it's pitch black. I pull my phone from my pocket, shining the flashlight along the ground until I reach the gate. I haven't been back this way for a few weeks; the hinge protests as I swing it open, and my footsteps squelch in the wet grass as I make my way up the back stairs and to the door. Thankfully, this lock seems fine. I unlock it quickly and silently, only to trip on something as soon as I step inside. A shoe—one of at least six random pairs piled haphazardly in the corner and spilling out onto the rug. Exhausted and too tired to care, I kick them out of the way.

A shower will have to wait.

I'm shuffling toward my bedroom when a flash of movement catches in the light of my phone. I swing it around to see a bag of chips on the counter, a trail of crumbs leading to an empty pizza box, and a sink full of dirty dishes. Inside my chest, something itches to clean it all up now, but I'm distracted when I hear a gasp behind me. Turning, I throw my arms up just in time.

"Shi—" is all I get out before there's a searing bolt of pain and everything goes black.

....

When I come to, it's to find Hazel standing over me. She looks like something out of a cartoon: crazy wide eyes and an umbrella brandished threateningly over her head. She's dressed only in a tank top and the smallest pair of shorts I've ever seen. If I didn't want to murder her right now I might actually take a moment to appreciate the view.

"Did you hit me with an *umbrella?*"

"No. Yes." She drops it immediately. "*Why are you sneaking in your own back door?*"

The pain in my head intensifies at the volume of her voice. "Because someone broke the front lock and my key wouldn't work."

"Oh." She bites down on her bottom lip. "It's not broken, exactly. I locked myself out and tried to pick it with a bobby pin. Technically it's the bobby pin that broke. Not the lock."

She rests a hand on each hip and looks down at me. The problem with this is that it pushes her chest out and even in this light I can tell that I should turn up the thermostat. Hazel is definitely not wearing a bra.

"I thought you were a murderer." She points to her dog, who is half lying on me, licking my face. "Winnie started growling and then I heard someone banging around the side of the house. You're lucky I didn't smash your brains all over your Clean Room–level kitchen floor."

I squeeze my eyes shut. Maybe if I keep them closed long enough I'll open them again and realize none of today even happened. No luck. "Right now it looks like a family of raccoons has been living here."

Hazel has the decency to look at least a little guilty before she waves me off, walking to the refrigerator to open the freezer drawer. I shift my eyes away just before she bends over.

"I was going to clean it up," she says, bag of frozen peas in hand. "Why are you home?" She kneels down, handing them to me. "Things didn't go well?"

"An understatement." I sit up and place the ice-cold peas against my forehead, where I can tell there's already a lump. In some ways, this is a fitting end to the trip from hell. Day one, Tabby admitted she's been sleeping with someone else. I spent the rest of the afternoon on the beach, staring out at the ocean and not feeling surprised, exactly, but working to give genuine thought to her insistence that we could work it out. But on day two, she admitted they started sleeping together before she moved to L.A., that she moved to be closer to him, and that he'd helped her get a job. The cherry on top was when she told me she hoped she could keep seeing us both.

Day two also happens to have been today.

"Do you want to talk about it?"

It's all starting to sink in that Tabitha and I are over. I stare straight ahead, eyes locked on that single freckle on Hazel's shoulder. What does it mean that I'm more interested in asking when she first noticed that freckle than explaining what happened with Tabby? Is it shock? Exhaustion? Hunger? I drag my eyes back to her face.

"I'm okay." I look down at my socks. They're gray with tiny pineapples and cups of Dole Whip on them—a gift from Tabby on one of my first visits down there after the move. She'd taken me to Disneyland and I remember standing in line thinking, *I'm going to marry this woman one day.* What an idiot.

Two years we were together—with her in L.A. for half of it—and all I feel now is duped and pathetic.

Hazel sits down next to me on the dark floor. "I take it you ended things?"

"Yeah." I adjust the peas and look over at her. "Turns out, she *is* a treasonous skank."

Hazel makes a grumpy face.

"And has been since before she moved."

To this, Hazel adds a feral growl. "Wait. Seriously?"

"Seriously. She's been sleeping with him since before she left. She moved to be closer to him."

"What a *dick.*"

"You know," I say, "the worst thing isn't even that I'm going to miss her. It's how stupid I feel. How blindsided. This other guy knew all about me, but I had no idea." I look at her, and—because I know she'll understand why this kills me—tell her, "His name is *Darby.*"

"She's been having sex with a dude named Darby?"

Anger twists hotly inside me. "Exactly."

She lets out a bursting cackle. "Tabby and Darby. That's too dumb, even for Disney."

A single sharp laugh escapes. "But why wouldn't she tell me about him? Why drag me on?"

"She probably wanted to keep you because you're the blueprint for Perfect." A pause. "You know, except for the *Aliens* thing."

Her hair is a disaster on top of her head. Her eyes are puffy from exhaustion. But still, she's smiling at me like I've been gone for months. Does Hazel Bradford ever stop smiling?

"You're trying to make me feel better," I accuse.

"Of course I am. You're not the asshole here."

"That's right, you are, because you broke my face."

"Your face is fine." She pushes up to stand and holds out a hand. I let her help me up, and she pats my chest. "But how's your heart?"

"It'll recover."

She nods, and leans down to pet a sleepy Winnie. "Don't ever sneak into a house when a woman is there alone, or you'll risk getting an umbrella to the face."

"It's *my* house, dumb-ass."

"A text letting me know you were coming back would have saved your face, *dumb-ass*." She turns to head toward the guest room. "Get some sleep. We're going miniature golfing with my mom tomorrow."

....

I'm so tired and sleep so soundly that I forget her last words until I wake up and shuffle into the kitchen to find Hazel in shorts, knee-high argyle socks, a polo shirt, and a beret. I know her well enough now to realize this must be her Goin' Golfin' costume. She's also wearing my apron and standing at the sink as a cloud of black smoke balloons around her.

"I'm not used to your stove," she says by way of explanation, trying to angle her body to hide whatever is happening in front of her.

"It's just gas." I bend to retrieve a towel and use it to wrap around the handle of the still-smoking cast-iron pan. The aroma of burnt bacon quickly saturates my T-shirt. Walking the pan to the back door, I set it on the painted concrete porch outside to cool.

"I have gas at home but it doesn't do *that*."

"Doesn't do what?" I say over my shoulder. "Make fire?"

"It doesn't make it so hot!"

Closing the door behind me, I toss the towel to the counter and survey the damage. I *think* she's been making pancakes. Or at least that's what the beige liquid running down the front of the lower cabinets indicates. There's a torn bag of flour and what has to be the contents of my entire pantry scattered across the countertop. There are dishes *everywhere*. I take a deep, calming breath before continuing.

"It's a professional-grade range." I pick up the garbage can to swipe a handful of broken eggshells inside. "It has higher BTUs, so it gets hotter faster and can generate a larger flame."

She puts on an affected British accent. "Riveting, young sir."

Winnie sits obediently just outside the kitchen and watches with what I swear is a look that can only mean *Do you see what I put up with?*

Yeah, Winnie. I do.

"Hazel, what are you doing?"

She holds up both hands. In one there's a Mickey Mouse spatula she must have brought from her place; the other palm is stained purple. I don't even want to know. "I'm making breakfast before we go golfing."

"We could have just gone out for breakfast." By the looks of things, we'll have to do that anyway.

"I mean, obviously the bacon is a bit . . . *ashier* than I normally like," she says, "but we still have pancakes." At the stove, she plates up two of the saddest flapjacks I've ever seen. Turning back to me, she holds the plate proudly. "How many do you want?"

I'm surprised by the wave of fondness that angles through my chest. Hazel nearly created a fire in my kitchen, I have a bruise on my forehead from her umbrella—and a lock to fix—but I'd still rather choke down a plateful than hurt her feelings while she's wearing argyle and a beret. "Just the two."

"Good," she says brightly, setting the plate on the counter and depositing a bottle of syrup next to it. Ready to start another batch, she reaches for a pitcher of batter and pours it into what I can tell from here is a too-hot pan. "I talked to your sister this morning."

I look up from where I'm delicately scraping off some of the burnt bits. "Already?" I glance to the clock on the stove. "It's barely eight."

"I know, but I texted her last night when I thought someone was breaking in. I had to update her that I wasn't being murdered in bed, which led to me having to tell her you're home."

Great. If there's anyone who's going to gloat over this, it's Emily. She might even throw a party. I return to my pancakes. "What did she say?"

"I didn't give her any other details. She wants you to call when you're up."

"I'm sure she does," I say, barely loud enough for her to hear, but she does.

"You know, you don't have to tell her everything. Saying you ended things is plenty."

"How do you think that'll work?" I look up as she tucks a strand of hair behind her ear, exposing the long line of her neck. "You'd be able to keep from spilling that Tabby was cheating for over a year?"

Hazel looks at me quizzically. "It's not my story to tell."

The idea of not having to share the specifics makes relief rush through me, cool and limber. Emily would never run out of *I told you so*s.

I look down to see a mournful Winnie staring up at me, her brown eyes pleading for me to drop something. I tear off a chunk of pancake and carefully feed it to the dog.

"Don't spoil her," Hazel tells me over her shoulder.

"Hazel. The dog you don't want me to spoil is wearing a Wonder Woman T-shirt."

I hear the click of the burner being turned off, and then she's there in front of me, leaning on the other end of the counter. "Your point?"

"I don't have one." I feed the dog another bite of pancake. "But do I really have to go miniature golfing?"

She tears off a bite of too-hot pancake and eats it. "You don't *have* to. Mom and I were going to go, and I didn't think you'd want to be alone."

As soon as she says it, I know she's right. But I should also check in at home. It's been a couple of weeks since I spent any time with my family. "I was going to head to my parents' place later."

She shrugs. "Up to you. If you want to come with us, I can go to your parents' with you after. I haven't met them yet."

"You don't have to babysit me, Hazel."

She pushes away from the counter and gives me a guilty smile. "Okay. Sorry. I'm being too Hazel-y."

I watch her wash the dishes and manage to clean up the kitchen quite capably while I pick at my breakfast. She isn't pouting, and it doesn't seem like I've hurt her feelings—she honestly just seems to have heard something in my tone that

I didn't intend. "What does that mean," I ask, " 'being too Hazel-y'?"

Turning with a dish towel in her hand, she shrugs. "I tend to be too chatty, too silly, too exuberant, too random, too eager." She spreads her hands. "Too Hazel-y."

She is all of these things, but it's actually why I like her. She's entirely her own person. I reach for her wrist when she moves to leave the kitchen. "Where are we going mini-golfing?"

....

Hazel looks nothing like her mother, but genetics work in wild, mysterious ways, because I would never doubt for a second that she came from this woman, Aileen Pike-not-Bradford, as she's introduced to me. She's wearing a flowing skirt decorated with embroidered peacocks and a bright blue tank top, and not only does she have rings on every finger, her earrings brush the tops of her shoulders. She and Hazel dress nothing alike but they both silently scream *Eccentric Woman*.

Aileen hugs me upon greeting, agrees with Hazel that I'm adorable but not her daughter's type, and then apologizes for Hazel's painkiller email all those years ago. "I knew I should have typed it for her."

"I still have it printed out." I grin at Hazel's complete lack of self-consciousness. "I may actually frame it for the duration of Hazel's visit in my house."

"A constant reminder of my charm?"

I take the golf club and a bright pink ball from the guy behind the counter. "Yeah."

"Speaking of your home," Aileen begins, "is my daughter trashing it?"

"Mildly."

Hazel tosses her blue golf ball from hand to hand like she's juggling it. A single golf ball. "I knocked him out with an umbrella last night."

At her daughter's proud tone, Aileen slides knowing eyes to me. "Be glad it wasn't a frying pan, I guess?"

Given that the umbrella gave me a bruise the size of a baby fist on my forehead, I can't really disagree. "She's got quite a swing."

We make our way to the windmill at the start of the course, and out of courtesy for our elder, let Aileen go first. She easily makes a hole in one: through the sweeping windmill, up and over a tiny hill, and down into the hole in the back corner.

It takes me ten shots to make it—so long that Hazel and Aileen are sitting on the bench by the little creek, waiting for me when I approach. Hazel has a handful of pebbles from the path and is trying to get one into the guppy statue's waiting mouth.

"Are you a mini-golf shark?" I ask.

"If only it got me something useful." Aileen laughs, and again, I'm reminded of Hazel. She has the same husky belly laugh that seems to come out of her as naturally as an exhale. These two women: laugh factories.

"Mom used to bring me here every Saturday," Hazel explains, "while Dad watched college football."

They exchange a knowing look, which morphs into a smile, and then Aileen asks her daughter for an update on the apartment. It's a few weeks away from being move-in ready. I listen to them speak and marvel over how they seem to communicate in half sentences, finishing thoughts with a nod, an expression, a dramatic hand gesture. They seem more like sisters than mother and daughter, and when Hazel gives her mom crap about her boyfriend, I look over in shock, expecting Aileen to be scandalized, but instead she just grins and ignores Hazel's needling.

Hazel and Aileen have the same wackiness with an undercurrent of unshakable confidence; people look at them as they pass, as if there is something ultimately magnetic about the two of them obliviously dancing their way through the course. I follow behind, registering how quickly I've become the straight man to Hazel's clowning.

I end up being glad we didn't put any money on this outing; Aileen cleans the floor with us. To make up for our bruised egos, she buys us coffee and cookies, and I'm treated to several amazing Hazel stories, such as the time Hazel dyed her leg hair blue, the time Hazel decided she wanted to play drums and entered the high school talent show after only two weeks of lessons, and the time Hazel brought home a stray dog that turned out to be a coyote.

By the time we get back to my car, I realize I haven't really thought about Tabby for more than an hour, but as soon as the awareness hits, the sour twist works its way back into my gut and I close my eyes, tilting my face to the sky.

That's right. My girlfriend was sleeping with another dude for most of our relationship.

"Oof," Hazel says, looking over at me across the top of my car. "You just left the happy bubble."

"Just remembered I'm an idiot."

"So here's the thing." She follows after me, climbing into the car. "I know this Tabby thing sucks, but *everyone* feels stupid in relationships at least some of the time, and you have a better excuse than anyone. Me, I work to not feel stupid most of the time. I don't always understand the best way to interact with other humans."

I grin over at her. "*No.*"

She ignores this. "I tend to get too excited, I realize that, and I say all the wrong things. I have zero chill. So yeah, guys have made me feel stupid about a *trillion* times."

"Seriously?"

She laughs. "This can't surprise you. I'm a maniac."

"Yeah, but a benevolent one." I turn the key in the ignition, and we both wave as Aileen pulls out of her spot, a bumper sticker that reads NEIL DEGRASSE TYSON FOR PRESIDENT clinging proudly to the back of her battered Subaru.

"I realize that finding the perfect person isn't going to be easy for me because I'm a lot to take," she says, "but I'm not going to change just so that I'm more datable."

Shifting the car into drive, I chance a glance over at her. "You're awfully hung up on your position on the datable scale."

"I've learned to be," she says, and then pauses for a moment. "Do you know how many guys like to date the cute wild girl for a few weeks before expecting me to chill a little and become more Regular Girlfriend?"

I shrug. I can sort of imagine what she's saying.

"But at the end of the day," she says, and puts her hand outside the open window, letting the wind pass through her fingers, "being myself is enough. *I'm* enough."

She's not saying it to convince me, or even herself; she's already there. I watch her pick up my phone and choose some music for the drive to my parents' place and wonder whether that's part of my problem: I used to think I was so together, but now the only thing I feel is a hollow sense of *not enough*.

SEVEN

HAZEL

*I*t never occurred to me that meeting Josh's parents might be something I'd need to prepare for. They're just people, right? Emily's mentioned that they're super protective (particularly of Josh, since he isn't married), but . . . whose parents aren't? I know his mom is always filling his fridge with food, but that's not unusual, either. Seriously, if it weren't for my mom and her thriving garden, I'd probably have scurvy by now.

I remember Josh saying it was family tradition to bring fruit, so I make him stop at the store on our way, where I put together the largest, most fantastic fruit basket I can manage.

"You know, a couple apples would have been more than enough," he says, closing his car door and meeting me in the middle of the narrow driveway.

I peer at him over the top of a particularly high pineapple shoot. "I want to make a good first impression."

"You're nuts. You know that, right?"

The basket starts to slip and I adjust it, sidestepping him just as he's about to take it. "Listen," I tell him, "I plan on giving the best man's speech at your wedding one day. This is no time to take chances."

He laughs, leading me up the steps to a small porch filled with potted ferns and a tinkling wind chime.

The door is unlocked and Josh steps inside. "Appa?" he calls out, waving me in. "Umma?"—followed by a stream of words I don't understand.

I trip on the sexual speed bump that is the sound of Josh speaking Korean, but my attention is immediately snagged by a voice from the other side of the house.

"Jimin-ah?"

"My mom," he explains quietly, and proceeds to toe off his shoes and place them neatly just inside the door. "Umma," he calls out, "I brought someone."

I follow suit, managing to slip off my sandals just as an adorable dark-haired woman turns the corner into the living room.

I'm not sure I fully appreciated exactly how much Emily and Josh look alike until now, when I see the amalgamation of their features standing in front of me. Josh's mom is petite, just like her daughter, with chin-length dark hair that flips up rebelliously at the ends on the left side. She's not smiling yet, but there seems to be one permanently residing in her eyes.

Josh places a hand on the center of my back. "This is my friend Hazel."

"Yujin-ah's Hazel?"

I sense a hint of sibling rivalry as his brows come together. "Well . . . my Hazel, too," he says, and I don't have to tell you that I am freaking delighted by this. "Haze, this is my mom, Esther Im."

"It is nice to meet you, Hazel." Her smile spreads to her mouth and it takes over her entire face. It's Josh's unexpected, sun-coming-out smile. I love her already.

My first instinct is always to hug, to glom all over people as if there's some direct line that leads from my heart to my extremities. Fortunately I happen to be holding the world's largest fruit basket and my arms are otherwise occupied.

Unfortunately, every K-drama I've ever seen chooses this exact moment to shuffle through my brain and I bend, bowing deeply at the waist and sending apples and oranges sailing across Mrs. Im's spotless entryway floor.

A few things happen in rapid succession. First, I let out a stream of curse words—something I shouldn't be doing in front of anyone's mother, let alone my new bestie's sweet Korean *umma*. Next, I throw the rest of the basket at a very surprised and unprepared Josh and dive for the floor, scuttling across the rug on my hands and knees.

Josh doesn't even sound horrified by my antics anymore: "Hazel."

"I've got them!" I say, frantically scrambling for the bruised fruit and making a basket out of the front of my shirt for safekeeping.

"*Hazel.*" His tone is firmer now, and I feel his hands on my waist as he drags me back toward them and helps me to my feet.

Hurricane Hazel strikes again.

"I'm so sorry," I say, smoothing my hair and twisting my skirt so it's facing the right direction. "I've been so excited to meet you and of course that means that I do something like launch a fruit basket." With as much grace as I can muster, I pull a couple of clementines from the vicinity of my cleavage. "Can I put these in the fridge for you?"

....

Seated at the kitchen counter, I glare down at the glass of water Josh sets in front of me, muttering, "At this rate I won't even be invited to the wedding."

Josh's mom is at the stove, dropping onions into a pot that looks like it is at least as old as Josh.

"What are you talking about?" he whispers, and kneels down at my side.

"She started speaking in Korean. Was she saying she hated me?"

"Of course not. She thinks you're a pretty funny girl."

Pretty funny? Or pretty, funny? Is that a half compliment, or two solid ones? Either way, my eyes widen and I grin. "Your mom is pretty comma smart."

Without expecting me to translate this, Josh taps me on the nose and moves to the counter, reaching for something in a cupboard too high for his mom to reach. He isn't exactly what you would call redwood tall, but he's got at least a few inches on me, and looks like a giant standing next to her.

Mrs. Im glances over at me. "So, Hazel, where does your family live?"

"My father passed away a few years ago, but my mom lives here in Portland."

"I'm sorry to hear that." She turns again to give me a sympathetic smile. "Josh's grandmother died last year. We still miss her very much." She scoops rice into two bowls, handing one to Josh, who immediately tucks into it. "You have no brothers or sisters?"

"No, ma'am. Just me."

She crosses the room to set the other bowl in front of me. It smells amazing. "And you're a teacher?"

I pick up my chopsticks—metal, not wood—and manage to scoop the first bite into my mouth. It's delicious—fried rice and vegetables. I may marry Josh myself if it means I can eat like this every day.

"She teaches with Emily," Josh offers.

"Oh, that is nice," she says. "I like Yujin-ah having good friends at work."

Good friends. I manage to tear my face from my food and give him a thumbs-up, right as the bomb drops.

"And Tabby?" Mrs. Im asks. "It's been a long time since we've seen her."

My eyes dart to Josh's. Like the soul mate I always knew he'd be, Josh is already looking my way. I give him an encouraging nod, one meant to remind him that this is his life and he only has to tell people as much—or as little—as he wants.

Even if those people are his family.

Clearing his throat, Josh pretends to be super engrossed in his empty bowl. He is a terrible actor.

"Actually, I wanted to talk to you about that." He clears his throat again. "Tabby and I broke up."

Now, obviously I am an outsider and privy only to the things that I've been told, but I don't think I'd be off base in describing his mom's immediate reaction as fucking elation.

She does her best to look casual, though, pinching his waist with a frown before depositing another scoop of fried rice into his bowl, but the terrible acting gene is obviously genetic. "So Tabby is not your girlfriend anymore."

"No." Her gaze slips to me and Josh reads the silent question there. *"No,"* he tells her meaningfully, and I might be offended if I didn't have this delicious bowl of rice keeping me joyful.

"Tabby never visited," she dramatically stage-whispers to me, and then moves to the fridge. "We should have a big dinner to celebrate."

....

If my current life were a movie, I would (1) be much better groomed, and (2) co-star in a montage of scenes in which Josh sits on the couch in his sweatpants and I dance around in front of him, trying to get him to laugh. Since he cleared his schedule and took the time off work anyway to go see Tabitha, he's decided he wants a staycation for the remainder of the two weeks, which I insist is *super lame*. I'm on summer break. We could go to Seattle! We could go to Vancouver! Let's go canoeing, or hiking, or biking, or even to a bar to get hammered and topless!

Nothing. He's not into it. Instead, he's watching Netflix with one hand tucked in the elastic waistband of his sweats. Even telling him that I can practically see his abdominal muscles atrophying—and it is a sad prospect, indeed—doesn't rouse him from his slouch.

I don't really know how much he's told Emily. When we were over there for dinner the other night, she seemed as annoyed at her brother's ex as she ever was, but there doesn't seem to be any specific direction to her ire. It was more *How could my amazing brother have wasted so much time with that woman* than *How could that whore have cheated on my amazing big brother for so long?*

And I sort of understand why he doesn't want to tell her. Aside from fanning her protective-sibling fire, being cheated on is obviously humiliating, and I realize that's ninety-nine percent of why Josh is glued to his couch. It would suck to have his girlfriend choose a job over their relationship, but it must suck even more to realize that Tabby actually chose another dude (Darby!!) who helped her get that job, and she happily strung Josh along because he's Perfect, and, who knows, maybe because he's also really amazing in bed.

That sort of understanding—that someone treated him so carelessly and he had no idea—would not only make others see him differently but probably make Josh see himself differently, too.

So I get the couch potato inclination, but it also bums me out. Here's the thing: Josh is hot, as we've established, and not only that but he's incredibly tenderhearted, despite his sarcastic exterior. He's still letting me stay with him—even though he's home. He makes a point to thank me when I clean the dishes once for every ten times he does them, and he always brings me a coffee back from his morning run. We talk in a straightforward, honest way: the dreams we had the night before, political drama, stuff that bums us out or makes our goddamn day. It's like living with a best girlfriend who is actually male and very nice to look at. It's not that I want to live here forever, but it hasn't exactly sucked being with Josh Im for the past couple of weeks.

Still, with two days left of his staycation, I'm about to blow. I've gone out every day to do something new. One day, Dave and I went hiking in Macleay Park. Another afternoon, Emily and I found a new farmer's market and Dave cooked up an amazing dinner. Josh sat on their couch, too, staring at whatever was on TV—a summer softball tournament. Today, I went to play with dogs and cats at the Humane Society, and the only thing Josh says when I walk back in the house is that I need a shower.

"Don't you want to have sex?" I yell.

He stares up at me, slowly pulling his hand from the front of his pants.

"Look at your body!" I gesture to the splendor of it with my hand. "You're amazing. And your face? Pretty fucking great, too. Come on, Josh, where is your sex drive?"

His eyes slowly widen, and I realize he thinks I'm propositioning him while I smell like a barn.

"Not with *me*, Jimin, I mean with someone in *your* league! Don't you want a companion—not even just for sex, but for hanging out and talking and enjoying life? Getting your dick played with would just be a bonus!"

"Hazel."

"*Josh*."

He does a dramatic sweeping gesture with one hand. "I'm here, aren't I? Hanging out and talking with you." He turns back to the *Law & Order* rerun.

"Joossssh," I whine.

He mutes the television and looks up at me with a deep sigh. "I hate dating and I don't want to be in a relationship."

"But sex?"

"I like sex," he concedes, "but what comes with it isn't appealing right now." He groans and repositions himself on the couch. "The games? The getting-to-know-you dance? The putting on of actual pants? No, thank you."

Sitting next to him, I take his hand. It's nice and warm, but remembering where it's been, I put it back on his thigh. "Look. I realize Pussycat did a number on your head, and you think that all women are jerks. We aren't."

"*You* aren't," he says. "You're just annoying."

"Right. But you don't want to fuck me."

"And you don't want to fuck me," he agrees. "But Hazel, it's not like you're getting out there and dating left and right, either. When was the last time you were with someone?"

"With, as in dating? Or with, as in sex?"

He scrunches his nose. "They're different answers?"

I look at him as if he's crazy. "I've had sex with guys I haven't dated, and dated guys I haven't had sex with."

It's his turn to look at me like I might be crazy.

"What?" I say. "You've never just . . . boned someone?"

He hides his blush by pretending to be grossed out by me. "That's the worst word."

"Bone. Bone. Boner. Booooones."

He leans his head back against the couch. "God, would you just go away?"

I ignore this. "What if I set you up with someone?"

"No."

"Just listen," I tell him, pushing up onto my knees and invading his space. "What if I set you up with someone, and you set me up with someone, and we went out together?"

"Seriously?"

"Seriously. No games, no expectations. Double blind date. Just for a laugh."

"No."

"Come on, Josh, just one time."

He rolls his head to look at me. "If I say yes, will you leave me alone for the rest of the day?"

"Yes."

"And if I hate it I never have to do it again."

I nod, reaching up to scratch his scalp. His eyes fall closed. "If you hate it, *we'll* never have to do it again. You can die in peace and will never have to take your hands out of your pants."

He's quiet for a minute. Is he considering it? Was it really the hands in his pants that sweetened the deal? He opens his eyes again. "Fine."

I sit up straighter. "Fine? Really?"

"Yeah. But make sure she isn't a jerk."

EIGHT

JOSH

We set the date for a Friday night, almost four weeks from our original deal, and agree to spend the evening at the Rumrunner's Tree House, a kitschy little bar Hazel found downtown. The location should have been my first clue.

Adam—a defensive lineman for an arena football team—shows up at the house while Hazel is still getting ready. I let him in, keeping my face neutral as we both pretend not to hear the horrible sound of her singing from the other end of the house.

The repairs on Hazel's apartment are taking longer than expected, but we've managed to find a happy medium between my need for order and the trail of chaos that follows her everywhere she goes. Since the house looks presentable for the first time in days, I lead Adam back to the kitchen for a beer.

He follows with Winnie right on his heels and takes a
seat at the kitchen bar.

"The place is looking great." He nods, glancing around.
"I think the last time I was here you were just finishing the
floors."

"I did the floors in the spring, and just got the new window casings in. I'll let you know the next time I have a barbecue. Zach would like to catch up."

"Cool."

I met Adam at a youth event we were both doing a couple
of years ago. We had just started the practice, and Adam was
there with the team he played on at the time. He's a nice
enough guy—I mean, obviously, or I wouldn't have set him up
with Hazel—and at six foot four and 235 pounds of muscle
he's definitely good-looking, but he's a little on the quiet side.
My first instinct was that it would be a nice contrast in per-
sonalities, but now I'm wondering whether Hurricane Hazel
might eat him alive.

"So this is kind of weird, right?" he says, reaching down
to scratch Winnie behind her ears. "I mean, picking her up
here? The two of you living together? I wouldn't want to . . ."

I follow his eyes back down the hall to where Hazel is
belting out an operatic version of Quiet Riot's "Cum On Feel
the Noize" and realize what he means. "Oh no. No." I hold my
hands out in front of me. "Hazel and I have never been, and
are not, together."

"So you're just roommates, then?"

"*Temporary* roommates," I correct. "She has her own place, but they're doing some work on the building and she needed somewhere to crash for a few weeks. Or months, I guess."

"I wondered what was going on when you called because you're the last person I expected to want a roommate." He chuckles as he brings the bottle to his lips, pausing to add, "No offense, man."

My smile is wry as I take a sip from my own bottle. I turn my attention to the dog. "Winnie? Potty?" She bolts to my side. Bending, I stage whisper, "You stay away from him, okay? He's a dick."

Adam laughs, and Winnie barks in what I take as agreement before following me to the back door and bounding down the steps into the yard.

When I return to the kitchen, Adam is eyeing a drawing of a unicorn Hazel doodled while I cooked dinner last night. It has two horns, a purple mane, pink fur, and a giant yellow penis.

Adam looks up at me with his beer paused midway to his lips. "She's not like . . . crazy or anything, is she?"

There's a twinge in my gut at this, a protective aversion to that word, but I refrain from asking him to define *crazy*. I wave him off instead. "Definitely not *crazy*."

Of course it's this moment she decides to make an appearance, bursting into the kitchen in a bright yellow sundress. "Who's crazy?"

"Winnie," I say quickly. "She's been chasing squirrels

again." Placing a hand on the small of her back, I usher her closer. "Hazel, this is my friend Adam. Adam, this is Hazel. You two might actually see each other this year because Hazel just got a job at Riverview, and Adam's team participates in the youth program there."

Adam stands to greet her, and I watch as her eyes widen and visibly travel the entire length of him. Subtle, Haze.

"It's so nice to meet you," she says, vigorously shaking his hand. "Be sure to stop by and say hi if you're ever in the school." Leaning in, she puts a hand to the side of her mouth and adds conspiratorially, "Unless of course this sucks, then never speak to me again. Oh my God, Josh. Your face. I'm kidding!"

"Definitely not crazy," I mumble, moving to let Winnie back inside before clapping my hands. "Let's go."

....

Hazel's friend Cali—an admin at the school where she used to work—plans to meet us at the bar, so we pile into my car, with Adam crammed into the front and Hazel in the back seat, poking her head between us.

She leans farther forward to see out the windshield when we park. "Isn't it great?" she says, halfway in my lap. "I didn't even know this place existed until Google sent a message to my soul."

Out on the street, I look up at the flashing marquee that

announces it's trivia night. The other businesses in the area are glass and modern, or retro hipster and painted in glaring colors. They bear no resemblance at all to the dark brown building in front of us, its A-frame roof lined in humming neon lights.

The sidewalk leading to the entrance is faded and cracked but bordered by buckets of glossy ferns and bright purple flowers. The sounds of Elvis Presley and steel guitars can be heard from outside. Hazel nearly skips to the door.

"We can always go somewhere else," I hedge, and reach for her hand to reel her in, pulling her back toward me.

"Are you kidding?" She points to a string of umbrella lights and fake roof thatching tacked just above a pair of glass doors. "I mean, *look* at this place."

"Oh . . . I'm looking."

She gives me a playful poke to the stomach before tugging me forward. "Come on. Cali is already here and I promise you'll be impressed. She does yoga," she adds, and wiggles her brows suggestively.

I pay our entry fee at the door and follow her inside the dimly lit bar. It's early but the place is already packed. The main room is reflected in a smoked mirror that serves as backdrop to a small stage. Paper lanterns sway overhead and waitresses in grass skirts wind their way between crowded tables, trays held aloft and filled with everything from bottles of lime-corked Corona to tiki-shaped glasses with colored smoke rising above the rims.

Hazel and Cali spot each other from opposite sides of the bar and Cali waves us over to where she's been saving a table.

Hazel must see the way my eyes widen, because she pushes up on her toes and whispers, "Told you."

Adam leads the way, with Hazel and I close behind. "I know you did," I say, leaning down to talk above the noise, "but you also described her as an avid knitter with a great personality and three cats. Forgive me for being cautiously optimistic."

Cali is about Hazel's height with strawberry-blond hair and light eyes. When she stands to hug Hazel, I'm treated to a view of long legs in a pair of little red shorts, and curves in all the right places. I catch Adam noticing, too.

Hazel makes the introductions and nearly as soon as we sit, our waitress materializes, tossing coasters down in front of us.

"Game's about to start," she says, pulling a pencil from her hair and pressing it to a lined notepad. "Anything I can get you beforehand?"

We place a drink order, select a mix of different appetizers, and she leaves us with our scorecards.

"So how do you two know each other?" Cali motions between me and Hazel.

"The short version is that we knew each other in college," Hazel says, "and then met up again recently. I'm friends with his sister."

"You dated in college?" Cali asks.

I'm not sure which of us jumps to correct her first, but there's a lot of head shaking and at one point Hazel is doing a comedic reenactment of someone choking. "More like casual acquaintances," I say evenly.

Cali points to Adam and dials up her smile. "And how do you know Josh?"

"We met at a youth sports event."

Her interest is definitely enhanced. "Are you an athlete?"

"Football." He gives her a proud smile that's all straight white teeth and just a trace of dimple. It's an all-American smile, the type you expect to see on cereal boxes and stadium jumbotrons. Unfortunately I've seen that smile at least a dozen times before, only usually it's directed at cheerleaders and groupies at after-game parties. My eyes flash to Hazel and only now does it occur to me that I've set her up with Adam the Panty Dropper, and she's staying at my place.

Brilliant move, Josh.

"I tore my PCL two winters ago," he continues, "and Josh got me back on the field in time for spring training."

The conversation slows when our waitress returns. Hazel's drink is a literal fishbowl filled with some kind of blue alcohol and gummy fish. When Adam and Cali's attention is drawn by a loud crash behind us, Hazel mimes that it's my job to make sure her shirt stays on.

We dig into our appetizers just as a middle-aged guy in a blazer and jeans—our emcee for the night—steps out on the stage.

"Hello, everyone!" he shouts, to surprisingly lively applause. "Some of you may recognize me from *Channel Four Weekend News*. My name is Richard Stroker, and I am your host for tonight's game."

"Richard Stroker?" Hazel gapes at me from over the top of her drink. "His name is *Dick Stroker*? I knew tonight was going to be awesome."

Adam blinks at her side, confused. "I don't get it."

There are about a hundred unsaid things in the look she gives me before she returns her attention to Dick.

"We'll play seven rounds tonight," Dick says. "Pop culture, music, math and science, world history, sports"—Adam does a little fist pump here—"wildlife, and grammar." A collective boo moves through the crowd at the last one, but he continues. "You'll notice several large television sets around the bar—courtesy of Bob's Sports, thank you, Bob—where the questions will be displayed. Everyone should have seven scorecards, each one labeled with its respective category. We'll score each category individually and then tally them for a cumulative winner at the end. Who wants to know what we're playing for?"

I laugh when Hazel's arm is the first to shoot up.

"Third place will receive a set of new steak knives from Kizer. *Kizer: Because Chinese knives can be awesome, too.* Our second-place team will win a year's subscription to Omaha Steaks, valued at over three hundred dollars." The room fills with the collective ring of *ooohs* and *ahhhs*. "Our last prize is the big one, folks. Because all the proceeds of tonight's game go to the Children's Cancer Fund, Budget Cruises has generously donated a three-day Pacific Coast cruise!"

While Cali and Adam are listening to the rules, Hazel leans across the table. "You have to be on my team."

"In case you haven't noticed," I remind her, "we're supposed to be on dates. With other people. Play with Adam." I straighten, but she reaches out, grabbing my shirt.

"I want that cruise, Josh, and you're smarter."

"Why do you think I'm smarter?"

"I saw Adam flexing in the windows outside the car. Call it a hunch."

"Hazel, a normal cruise is bad enough. You really want an all-you-can-eat buffet on a *budget* cruise?"

"It's *free*."

"Diarrhea is never free."

She drops back in her chair and I know I'm going to regret this.

"*Fine*," I say. "But you owe me. Next time we do this, *I* pick what we do."

She immediately perks up. "Next time?"

I quickly clarify. God, it's been two seconds and she already looks smug. "*If* we do this again. Look, I can admit it's been good to get out of the house. I was spending too much time at home and—"

"—wallowing."

"No."

"Playing with yourself because nobody else wants to?"

I give her a warning look. "It's possible you were right—about the *wallowing*."

"Possibly," she says with a small smile.

"Plus—and I can't believe I'm saying this—I just really like to win."

"I *knew* it! I knew you were as competitive as me." She points to my stomach. "I mean, a person doesn't get abs like that without a lot of drive—"

"Everything okay?" Adam asks.

"Of course!" Hazel leans closer, reaching for his arm and lowering her voice, but I can still hear her. We can *all* still hear her. "Hey, would it be okay if I was on Josh's team? He's not very good at this kind of thing and I don't want him to feel bad. Shaky confidence, you know."

"I'm right here," I deadpan.

"Of course," Cali volunteers with a sympathetic nod. "Adam and I can team up!"

With that settled, a grinning Hazel hands out the cards. By the time I get mine, she's already written our team name across the top: *Stephen Hawking's School of Religion.*

The first round is pop culture, and at the opening question—*The character Jar Jar Binks first appeared in which Star Wars movie?*—she immediately scribbles down the correct answer.

The questions fly out, and by round five, we've somehow managed to get all of them right.

"Wow," Cali says, looking across the table to our total, and then frowning down at their own. "Who knew you guys were so smart? Guess poor Josh didn't need that much help after all . . ."

"What can I say, I'm an encyclopedia of useless information." Hazel gives her an innocent shrug before quickly pointing to the stage. "Oh look, Dick is back."

"Our next category—and judging by the number of Budweiser cans in the recycling bin, one a lot of you have been waiting for—sports!"

"Yes!" Adam slams a hand on the table, knocking over his beer just as Cali groans. "Fucking *finally*."

"Now, this one's a little tough," Dick says, looking out over the room.

"Bring it!" Adam yells, full of confidence and beer.

"ESPN analyst Lee Corso played football in college. He attended Florida State in the midfifties and roomed with another player who would eventually go on to find further success on the silver screen. Who was Lee Corso's soon-to-be-famous roomie?"

Adam looks absolutely stumped. Cali looks about two seconds away from walking out. I have zero idea who Onetime Football Player Turned ESPN College Football Analyst's Eventually Famous Roommate could be, but when I glance at Hazel, her eyes are wide, glazed over with what I'm beginning to understand is recognition.

"I know this . . ." she mumbles.

"How could you possibly know that?" Cali asks. "You don't even like sports."

Leaning across the table again, Hazel pulls me close. "My dad loved Dolly Parton and any time she was on TV, he'd record it. He used to watch reruns of her show."

I wait, confident she's leading us somewhere useful. "Okay?"

"The answer is Burt Reynolds. I know it."

I sit back in my chair. Burt Reynolds played halfback at Florida State University. She's fucking right. Hazel Bradford is a genius.

By the time we get to the last round I can't believe how much fun I'm having. Adam is talking to a girl at the next table and I have a pang of guilt when Cali starts playing on her phone, but Hazel and I are practically on the edge of our seats. According to the scoreboard—and with the final card to be tallied—the top two teams are tied and we need the next question to win. I've never wanted a terrible cruise more.

Dick has taken off his sports jacket, and shuffles a set of notecards in front of him, building up the suspense as he prepares to ask the final question.

"All right," he says, speaking solemnly into the microphone. "This is it. It's sudden death so we're going to do this one a little differently. When you have completed your answer, please send a team captain to the stage so we can see if you're correct and, indeed, the winner. Good luck, everyone." He takes a deep breath before dropping his eyes to the card.

"The term *pronoun* covers many words in the English language. For the final question, name eight types of pronouns."

Hazel puts her pencil to the paper and hesitates for only a beat.

"I only know two," I whisper, but she's already writing. A second later, she tears off her sheet, stands from the table, and races up onto the stage.

"Okay, okay." Dick takes the paper from her hand. "What's your name?"

"Hazel," she squawks breathlessly into the microphone. She waves to the crowd and I shake my head, laughing.

"Okay, Hazel, captain of . . ."—he squints at our card—"Stephen Hawking's School of Religion? Read me your answer."

"So, Dick—can I call you Dick?"

"Many women do," he says with a lecherous wink.

"You see, Dick, I'm an elementary school teacher, but I also have a really crummy memory."

"That's gotta be rough, Hazel."

"You're telling me. Because of this I'm always looking for ways to trick my brain." Hazel holds up a finger and counts off as she recites, "Getting Pretty Panties Ripped Requires Real Damn Initiative. *Or*—general, personal, possessive, reflexive, reciprocal, relative, demonstrative, and interrogative!"

Dick pauses to check the answer before taking Hazel's hand and lifting it over her head in victory. "What a correct, and yet totally inappropriate, response! Hazel the elementary school teacher and her partner win! We have a winner!"

....

"I don't know how you did it." Emily walks into the living room with a bowl of popcorn in one arm and a bottle of wine in the other. "Not only did you get my brother to a dive bar for a blind date, but you won a shitty cruise, *and* he had a good time. Clearly you're the Prude Whisperer."

"Hey." I glare in my sister's direction.

"Actually, I didn't talk him into anything."

I turn to where Hazel is curled up on the couch behind me and smile. Hazel: defending my honor like good friends do.

"I didn't even *have* to. His competitive nature made manipulating him far easier than I'd have guessed."

"*Hey.*" I glare at Hazel now.

Emily barks out a laugh, which in turn makes Winnie bark from where she's lying across my feet.

"You too?" I ask the dog, bending to ruffle her fur. She's as bad as her owner, a total nuisance, and yet . . . somehow endearing.

"My fussy brother on a budget cruise. I never thought I'd see the day."

"Oh, don't start worrying about him yet." Hazel stretches her long legs just enough to encroach into my space. "The cruise isn't until next spring. I'm sure he'll figure a way to weasel out of it by then."

With the movie set to play, I toss the remote to the table and turn to face her. "With that attitude, good luck asking me to send you Imodium from the mainland."

Dave joins us in the living room. "Are you two sure you're not married?"

Hazel scrunches up her face before lobbing a piece of popcorn at him. Winnie immediately wolfs it down.

"The only person I bicker that comfortably with is my wife," he says, "and it's a skill that's taken years to perfect." Rounding the couch, he drops down onto the cushion next to my sister. They look so easy together. It's hard not to wonder whether *I'll* ever have that. Judging by my results with Cali, it does not look good.

Fortunately, I get little time to wallow because Hazel shoves her foot into my kidney, attempting to make room for Winnie under the blanket. I push her foot away. "You know there's another side to this couch, right?"

Dave looks at us, smug. "See?"

"David, gross." Hazel pulls up the blanket. "We just ate."

Emily reaches for a handful of popcorn and sits back against the couch. "So, back to the double date of doom, what happened to those two? I assume they don't want to see either of you again since you were basically trivia nerd besties who plan to never get laid."

"Oh, we haven't told you the best part—" I start, but Hazel interrupts me.

"The *cruise* is the best part, Jimin."

I push her off the edge of the cushion and continue. "They went home together."

Emily's mouth falls open. "They did not."

"They did." Hazel nods happily from where she's landed on the floor, as if she's thrilled for them. "I stopped by my old school to drop off a box of supplies yesterday and saw Cali in the faculty room touching up the concealer on a giant hickey. Who gives hickeys anymore? Honestly."

"But you are going to do it again, right?" Emily asks, watching as Hazel climbs back onto the couch, roughly inserting herself into my space again. "Please don't let my brother go back to the sweatpants."

Hazel tosses a piece of popcorn in her mouth and gives me a little shrug. "I don't know, what do you think?"

"Off the top of my head," I say, "I can't think of any friends I want to alienate. But I'm not opposed to trying."

Hazel considers this. "Yeah, nobody else at my new *or* former place of employment—I have to maintain my thin veneer of a professional demeanor. And most of my friends are married or gay, or even weirder than I am."

I frown at her. "That's hard to believe."

"We know tons of people!" Emily chimes in, scooting

to the edge of the cushion and turning to face her husband. "What about that adorable girl at your chiropractor?"

Dave searches his memory for a face. "The redhead? She's a lesbian."

"There's no way Josh is getting lucky anytime soon," Hazel says, "so that won't matter."

Emily straightens. "Oh! What about your brother? He'd have so much fun with Hazel."

"My brother is engaged."

Emily levels him with a flat look. "David, we all know that's not going to last."

"We might want to let it run its course regardless."

Hazel reaches for the bottle of wine and mutters to me, "I think we're going to need this."

"What about that guy at the dentist's office," Dave says, "the one who does the scheduling?" He looks around the couch. "We should find a notebook to write all these down."

Emily rummages through an end table drawer and I hold up my glass for Hazel to refill.

Pencil in hand, Emily starts making notes. "The guy who does your lawn is always playing with Winnie, Josh. And he's really cute."

Dave looks at her from where he's reaching for a cookie. "Isn't he, like, nineteen?"

"You might be right." She turns to Hazel. "Haze, do you have a problem with younger men?"

Hazel burps before answering. "Nope."

"Joshy, what about you?"

"I think younger men are fine but I'd prefer a woman. And at least old enough to vote, please."

David's eyes light up. "What if we made them dating profiles on Grindr or eharmony or one of those?"

Emily's brows come together. "I don't think Grindr is the right one. Let me Google it."

Hazel leans against my shoulder, staring at them. "They don't even need us here for this."

I take a sip of wine. "I think you're right."

"You know . . . my hairstylist is pretty cute," Hazel says thoughtfully. "And funny, too. You might like her."

"Really?"

She looks up at me. She's so close, her whiskey eyes seem lighter tonight. "Mm-hm. She likes to fish. Do you like to fish?"

"I do."

"I have an appointment next week." With one hand, she pulls her hair up on top of her head. "Maybe I'll talk to her?"

"But what about you?" I ask. "If we're going to do this, I still want to do it together." Hazel opens her mouth to answer, but stops. I follow her gaze to where Emily and Dave are both watching us. "What?"

"Nothing." Emily bends to write something down, and I'm guessing it's just a scribble because we've caught her ogling us. "You're just cute together."

Hazel sits up, preening. "That's because we're both insanely attractive." She looks back at me. "I think Josh might like my hairdresser, though. But he can't screw it up because I really love my hair right now."

I lift my glass. "Scout's honor."

Dave reaches for Emily's arm. "You know that barista at Heavenly Brews? The one you think is always flirting with you?"

Emily holds up her hands in defense. "All I'm saying is he never charges me for a double shot."

"Anyway, I could talk to him about Hazel." In Hazel's direction he adds, "He's pretty cute—as far as guys go. Dark hair, athletic. No obvious psychotic tendencies that I've noticed, and he makes a kick-ass cappuccino. I think he's in graduate school or something."

Hazel tilts her head side to side. "I'm interested. Baristas tend to like the peculiar girls."

Something pulses in me when I hear her describe herself that way.

"So we have a plan then?" Emily asks. "Hazel will talk to her stylist and Dave can talk to the hot barista. We'll meet back here to finalize the details?"

Hazel offers a hand and I reach over to shake it. This is all becoming very . . . communal. I just hope no one gets invested in someone for me before I do.

NINE

HAZEL

Unfortunately, I spend the Saturday morning after date number two searching for a new stylist.

I'm scrolling through Yelp reviews when Winnie starts to bark, her wet nose pressed against the front room window. Poor Josh and his once-spotless glass.

Winnie can barely contain herself and races back and forth, tail wagging furiously and feet slipping along the wood floors. There are only two people who get that kind of reaction. One of them woke up with a headache and has gone back to bed, and the other is my mom.

"Calm down," I say, pulling her back by her collar so I can open the door. "You'd think nobody pays attention to you."

"There she is," my mom croons. "There's my pretty, good girl."

I'm shocked—*shocked*, I say—to find that she's not speaking to me.

Winnie dances around Mom's legs as she comes inside,

and I close the door behind her. "I'm so happy to see you, too, Mom!"

"You hush," she says, and hands me a white paper bag that smells suspiciously like blueberry muffins. All is forgiven. Doing a quick glance toward the kitchen she adds, "I see you haven't burned the place down."

I deliver a thumbs-up over my shoulder. "So far so good!"

Thank God my apartment should finally be ready soon. I'm excited to be back in my space with my rabbit and bird and fish. Still, I'll admit I'm going to miss cohabitating with my new best friend.

Winnie follows Mom as she crosses the room, settling comfortably at her feet beneath the kitchen table. "Where's that captivating boy?" Mom asks.

I pull a couple of plates from the dishwasher and put a muffin on each one. "You know, most moms would have more to say about their daughter living with a random dude than how *captivating* he is."

"Are you saying I'm wrong?"

"Oh, not at all. But don't let that face fool you, he's a captivating pain in the ass."

"Must be why you get along so well," she says with a winning smile.

"Ha, ha."

"So where is he?"

The coffeemaker gurgles in the background and I carry the plates to the table. "He went back to bed."

She looks at her watch and then back up to me, lips turned up in a knowing smirk. "What did you do to him?"

"*Me?*" I do my best to look innocent. She isn't buying it. Busted, I set her muffin down in front of her and turn back to the kitchen. "Let's just say date number two was a doozy."

"Remind me again? The coffee guy and—" She pauses when she sees me nodding. "Oh dear."

"Yeah."

"You guys were excited for that one. It wasn't fun?"

I'm not sure I'd describe it as fun, but it was definitely *something*.

Going off what little I'd told him about McKenzie, Josh had arranged for us to spend the day fishing on the Columbia. I'd been so excited I was up and dressed and in the kitchen making sandwiches before he was even out of bed.

We were set to meet and check in at the dock before sunrise. Hot barista—aka Kota—was already there, a drink tray with four coffees in hand. Points for the boy. I made a mental note to thank Dave, because looking at Kota? Dave did *not* oversell.

The sky was sherbet-colored and blurry, the air still dawn-cold while we introduced ourselves. Kota had dark hair that was shaved over his ear and dyed red at the tips. He had earrings, and a tattoo that peeked out the back collar of his shirt. I'm not even going to lie, I was smitten.

Then McKenzie pulled up.

We'd been standing at the side of the boat, conversing easily as we warmed our hands on the cups of coffee, when a red Honda Civic pulled into the lot. I noticed the way Kota stumbled in his story about the time Dave ate a bad egg salad sandwich at the shop. But he was still talking, and he was still pretty, so I didn't let it distract me too much.

I heard a car door close and then the sound of boots crunching across gravel echoed through the early morning. I turned to McKenzie and smiled, waving an arm over my head. As she waved back Josh quieted, obviously checking her out. I assume it went something like this: *Hot, good body, not immediately crazy. I owe Hazel big.*

At least it should have.

But next to me, I felt Kota stiffen, and watched as recognition straightened his easy smile. As McKenzie neared, I saw it flicker across her face, too.

Huh.

Shrugging it off, I rushed forward to meet her.

"You're here!" I said, wrapping her into a tight hug. She smelled exactly like the salon I'd grown to love and I hoped Josh was paying attention as I subliminally threatened his balls if he somehow screwed this up. I stepped away, bouncing a little on my feet and clapping. "I'm so happy you came."

"Of course!" Her eyes flickered over my shoulder, her spine stiffening.

I turned, looping an arm through hers as I led us back toward the guys. "Everything okay?"

She fell into step at my side, covertly looking at me from beneath her lashes. "What's that guy's name?"

The waves crashed against the pier as the tide came in, and a seagull squawked overhead. "That's Josh! The friend I told you about. I swear you're going to love him, he—"

"No, the other one."

I glanced up at them, and then back again. "His name's Kota. Do you know him?"

"Sort of," she said under her breath, just as we reached the others.

"Josh, this is McKenzie." Josh reached out to shake her hand and—*huh*. He gave her his pretty-boy smile. Not the small, sweet version he saves for the cashier at the grocery store, but the one I love—the one that reaches his eyes and carves a dimple into his cheek.

His unexpected, sun-coming-out smile.

Easy, Josh, let her settle in before you hit her with both barrels.

"And Kenzie," I said, "this is—"

"Hey, McKenzie," Kota cut in, a muscle twitching in his jaw.

Josh glanced to me, and then back at them. "You two know each other?"

"We went out a few tim—" Kota started to say, before Kenzie held up her palm.

"Fucked. We *fucked* a few times—and then he didn't call me back."

"*Euuusssh*" was pretty much the only sound I could make as the awkward ballooned around us. I looked to Josh for help.

He clapped his hands in front of him. "Maybe we should split up and do something else?"

McKenzie took a step forward, hooking her arm through Josh's. "Not necessary." Her smile was aimed at him but the venom in her voice was all for Kota. "I'm here with you." A meaningful pause. "He doesn't matter."

"Mmokay?" The plea for help in Josh's eyes was as clear as a flare shot up over his head.

We turned at the sound of our guide descending the plank that led to the dock, clipboard in hand. We checked in and were welcomed aboard and given slickers and boots. Introductions were made before a brief spiel about life preservers and where we were allowed on the boat, and where we weren't. We were told to watch for ropes on the deck because they're everywhere and dangerous and easy to trip over. The words *death trap* were definitely used. We talked about motion sickness and were told exactly where we could barf. I met Josh's eyes over Kenzie's head and was almost giddy to see him already smiling in my direction and mouthing the words, *Not on my shoes.*

Inside jokes, the sign of a true bestie.

Things seemed fine as we headed out on the water and started to fish.

I listened to everything our guide said, and did as the deckhand instructed. Kota was at my side, working his hot-dude charm. Despite the awkward start to the date, he was actually pretty funny. Even so, it was hard not to let my attention wander to where Kenzie—clearly putting on a show for Kota's benefit—was laughing and clinging to Josh's arm like he'd just proposed to her.

At one point my line pulled and began to disappear off the reel; whatever was on the other end was really trying to get away. The deckhand came over to help, as did Josh, but Kota and McKenzie sort of disappeared into the background. By the time I had my fish held in front of me, they were off on their own.

Josh eventually caught a fish and we took a few photos, but when an hour had gone by and our dates still hadn't returned, we dug into our lunches and started to just . . . talk. Josh told me a little more about the kids they mentored down at the office, about Emily's wedding and how he never worried about her, even for a second, because Dave was exactly who he would have picked.

I talked a little about my mom and Winnie and being excited for school to start again. I told him about the time I ran into my gynecologist at parent-teacher night and he pretended not to recognize me.

"That doesn't exactly seem odd," Josh said, leaning over to check his line. Occasionally a sturgeon would make itself known by jumping off in the distance, but nowhere near the hooks. At least, not yet.

"Why do they do that?" I asked, watching the shiny body

flip through the air before landing with a splash. "I get why they do it when they're hooked—I'd put up a fight, too. But this seems counterproductive. Like, you're a fish and people are trying to find you. Hide!"

Josh laughed and rested his elbows on the edge of the boat. He was so handsome. Once he got over this Tabby thing he was going to have women lining up. But now, I could still see the reserve pinching his shoulders in, making the hesitation he felt spread across every one of his features. "I don't know if anyone has asked the sturgeons directly, but I think it's to clear their gills? Or maybe avoid predators."

I squinted off into the distance. "Maybe it's just fun."

Josh grew quiet and I looked over to see him watching me. "I never thought of it that way before." He turned back to look over the river; the water had turned a little rougher and we leaned into each other, bracing instinctively. "I can't believe I'm encouraging this conversation, but you were telling me about your gynecologist snubbing you and I'm actually curious to hear how it turned out."

"So I stopped in the middle of the gymnasium and smiled at him—not my courtesy smile, but my real one—and he just walked by."

"Maybe he didn't see you."

"He definitely saw me—and don't get me wrong, I run into guys all the time who've seen my vagina and pretend not to know who I am. Things don't work out and that's fine. But I *paid* this guy."

Josh's mouth turned up at the corners. "Maybe he was busy. Maybe he didn't want to mix business with pleasure. I've seen you avoid students when we're out."

"That's different, and I only ignore the brats, or their fathers if I'm not wearing a bra." Josh shook his head but I pushed on, eager for him to see my point. "Shouldn't there be a certain level of public acknowledgment when you've seen a person's genitals?"

Josh looked at me with the expression he uses when he's hoping I didn't just say something but he's pretty sure I did. "Oh my God, Hazel." But this time his smile was too big to bite back. "So what did you do?"

"Nothing," I said, shoulders slumping. "I guess that was a pretty anticlimactic story."

"Not really. At least I know next-day protocol if we ever see each other's genitals."

"Which we won't."

"Which we definitely won't," he agreed, and then turned toward the sound of raised voices.

Kota was walking toward us, hands in front of him as he finished zipping up his pants.

You have got to be kidding me.

"So that's it? You're just going to walk away again?" Kenzie stumbled a little as she crossed the deck behind him, the boat lurching on the uneven water. Her hair was a mess, her life vest unfastened and twisted around her torso. It didn't take a genius to figure out what they'd been up to. "By the way, I faked it."

Kota stopped, slowly turning to face her.

I gasped.

Josh let out a low, sympathetic whistle.

"Didn't sound like it back there," Kota said.

Josh stepped away from the railing. "Everything okay here?"

Kenzie looked ready to spit fire, and got close enough to poke Kota with a finger to the chest. "Like I said, *faked*. You probably couldn't tell the difference because you're so used to hearing it."

Kota knocked her finger away. "This is exactly why I stopped calling. You're way too much work."

The next part happened kind of fast. McKenzie lunged for Kota and Josh tried to step between them. It was a blur of life jackets and me shouting about rope and death traps, just as the boat lurched upward. I ended up on my ass and when I stood again and looked around, Josh was gone.

....

"He fell in the river?" Mom stares up at me, her breakfast abandoned on the plate.

"Yeah. He was wearing his life jacket and they were able to get him out, but he hit his head on one of the steel poles as he went in."

"Oh my God. Is he okay?"

"I'm fine." Josh walks slowly into the kitchen, a new angry

bruise the size of a strawberry across his forehead. Winnie trails guiltily behind him. "Just a little slow to start this morning. And in case you were wondering, it's hard to sleep with a sixty-pound dog on your chest."

"She loves you," I say.

He looks at me with a tired but barely restrained smirk. "Her love is about as suffocating as yours."

I smile brightly at him from the other side of the island. "You say the nicest things."

Mom pulls out a chair. "Josh, honey, sit down. I brought breakfast and Hazel was making coffee." To me she adds, "Are you finished giving him concussions or shall we prepare for a third?"

I move to object but Josh speaks before I can. "I'm fine, really," he insists, but sits anyway. "Just glad I showered last night before I went to bed. Who knew the river smelled so bad?"

I reach around to set a plate in front of him, and press a careful kiss to the bruise-free side of his head. "I think it was less the river and more the fish-soaked blanket they wrapped you in after pulling you out."

....

Having learned a lesson about letting our inner circles cross, for date three we cast a much bigger net—so to speak.

The Sunday after our disastrous outing with Kota and

Kenzie, I meet Molly on the bus to the farmer's market, where I buy a paycheck's worth of produce to cook a fancy thank-you dinner for Josh for letting me stay with him the past two months. Although Molly is a random stranger, she is also *gorgeous*, and a sales rep for a local organic cosmetics company. I'll admit to having a slight ulterior motive here: Molly is friendly and was as charming as one can be during a single sixteen-minute bus ride across the city—so yes, I do think Josh will like her. But Molly's winged liner is also *perfect*, and even if things don't work out between her and Josh—hey, I can at least pick up a few makeup tips at dinner, right?

According to Josh, my date—Mark—is a former client of his, and Josh has nothing but great things to say about him. Apparently Mark is tall and good-looking and a genuinely great guy. They haven't seen each other for a while, but Josh is sure we are going to hit it off.

Turns out, Josh is right about all of it: my date is tall, good-looking, and we definitely hit it off, but there is one tiny surprise . . .

Mark is early in transition into Margaret, and thought she was being set up with Josh's *male* roommate.

Turns out, Josh called her from his car and the reception was a little spotty along the way. Margaret made sure to clarify that Josh had heard her explain that things were a little . . . *different* these days, but with Josh's Bluetooth cutting in and out and clueless to the details he was missing, he assured her with a "Yeah, definitely. I'll text you with the time and place," and ended the call.

It might not go entirely according to plan, but we *do* have a great night and my winged liner has never looked better.

....

My apartment is ready a couple of weeks before school begins, during the very last humid gasp of summer.

As happy as I'm sure Josh is to get me and Winnie out of his clean living space, I think he might almost miss us.

A little.

I say this because by the last day I think even Josh was surprised by how normal it was starting to feel to live together. Loud? Yes. Chaotic? Absolutely. But also: comfortable. Dare I say *easy*?

On a typical day, Josh would drag himself out of bed, Winnie trailing sleepily behind him, to find the cup of coffee I'd poured for him on the counter. I would cook some variation of burnt breakfast food, and we would talk as we ate, text all day, and then come home, eat dinner together, and fall asleep watching TV. It was as close to being in a normal relationship as I've ever been. I think it's been good for Josh, too: the name Tabby hasn't been brought up in weeks.

I've always loved my apartment *and* living alone, but as I walk through the freshly painted door and stop on the new wood floors to survey what they've done, it's impossible not to notice how empty it feels.

Winnie seems to have reached a similar conclusion. Sniffing a path through the doorway she does a quick circle of the front room before stepping outside again, emitting a heavy sigh, and then flopping down on the mat.

"I know what you mean," I tell her, making my way inside and dropping my bags on the newly delivered couch. Other than this, there isn't much furniture. A lot of it was ruined when the pipe broke, and most of what could be salvaged was old and not really worth saving anyway. Like every twenty-something I know, I ordered this new one at IKEA, but it seems a million miles away from the soft, worn-in leather in Josh's living room.

Winnie is reluctant to admit that this is where we'll be staying. Even after I coax her inside she insists on camping out near the door. Stubborn. I unpack a few things and get the rest of the animals situated, put new sheets on the new mattress and inspect the updated bathroom fixtures and kitchen cabinets. With nothing more than pet food in the house and no real desire to rectify that tonight, I order dinner and work on untangling the box of cords and hooking up the TV again.

I'm at the stage in the technology setup process where I'm whimpering and facedown on the living room floor when my phone chimes from the corner I threw it into not long ago.

It was weird not to trip on your shoes when I got home.

I knew you'd miss me.

Maybe a little.

I mean, who's gonna use all the hot water every morning?

Lose my number.

I'm kidding.

The house feels sort of empty.

Fondness squeezes at my heart but I push it away before I begin typing out a reply.

Winnie's being a sad sack and won't move away from the door.

> I think she misses you.

Winnie. Right.

> You know how clingy
> she can get.

How's the apartment, btw?

I think about that one as I look around the bright, clean living room. Empty walls, a stack of boxes that need to be unpacked, a disgruntled labradoodle. I suppose it could be worse.

> Pretty good. A little bare
> but we'll get it there.

I was going to stop by but thought you'd want to get settled.

Send me a pic.

I snap a few photos, including one where half my face takes up most of the screen, and another where a mass of tangled cords lies next to a sad, dark TV.

Because Josh is a caretaker, my phone rings almost immediately.

"Hazel's House of Hedonism."

"Do you want me to come help?" he asks, and there's a feeling inside my chest. Victory, yes, because I was hoping he'd come over, but something else, too. Like warm rain, a warmer blanket. I really want to see him. And I mean, so does Winnie. Look at her. "I could hook up the TV while you work on other stuff."

As a strong, independent woman, I should tell him no, that I'll take care of it myself—which I would, eventually—but *RuPaul's Drag Race* is on tonight and saying no would be both inefficient and inconvenient.

"I ordered dinner," I say instead. More than enough for two, now that I think of it. "Winnie will be happy to see you. Maybe she'll even stop sulking."

"Let me shower and I'll be over in twenty."

"Deal. I'll probably still be in this same spot when you get here so let yourself in."

"Got it. Oh, and Haze?"

I smile into my phone. "Hmm?"

"Tell Winnie I miss her, too."

TEN

JOSH

After I help her move things into her new classroom, I barely see Hazel for days—which, given that she only moved out about a week ago, is oddly disorienting. I went from being in a long-term relationship to being single, and having my life turned upside down with a roommate of sorts, in a matter of days. You'd think I'd be glad to have my own space again and not have to worry about what someone is doing—or lighting on fire. You'd think I'd be ready to find some kind of new normal. And yet, you'd be wrong.

Who knew normal could be so boring?

Just like I've seen my sister do half a dozen times before, Hazel dives into this intense teacher zone, and I can't exactly criticize her for being so focused. From what I can surmise in observing her bouncy bliss stapling borders to her bulletin boards, the beginning of the school year is better than Christmas and birthdays combined.

"I fucking love being a teacher," she says over the phone just after the pre-first-day Back to School Night. I'm not sure I've ever heard quite the same enthusiasm from Em after one of these things, but Hazel is Hazel. She loves big. "I am a hot mess ninety percent of the time, but man, third graders are my jam."

"I'm not surprised," I tell her. "Like eight-year-olds, you also struggle when reaching for things on high shelves and remembering to use the bathroom before long car rides."

"Nice, Jimin."

A tiny unknown organ in me aches at the way we're having such a familiar conversation over the phone, rather than across the couch.

The next day—Hazel's first day teaching at Riverview—I am greeted by a constant high-pitched hum of noise as I walk through the doors. It sounds a bit like a swarm of bees, emanating down the hall from the cafeteria. Hazel's classroom is number 12, so after waving at frazzled first-day-of-school Dave through the glass window of the principal's office, and peeking in on my sister as she wrangles a chaotic blur of fifth graders, I head across the hall to the door covered in hot sauce packets and the words *Taco 'bout a Great Class!*

Through the little window, I can see her standing at the front of the room, watching while the class works independently, and am already laughing. This is Hazel—of course she's wearing something like this. Her blue dress is cinched in at the waist by a belt decorated with red apples and brightly colored textbooks. I'm getting definite Ms. Frizzle vibes, a look I wouldn't have guessed I'd be into, but one glance at Hazel's long, delicate neck and the smooth gloss of her ponytail and . . . well, here we are.

She spots me through the glass, grinning widely before walking over—even though I'm waving at her to indicate I can wait until the class is in the cafeteria for lunch. Her eyes are scotch and flirtation. Her lips are a wild cherry red. Something inside me shivers.

"Welcome to the fiesta!" Wooden pencil earrings swing with the happy little shake of her head.

I hand her an apple and a cellophane-wrapped bunch of sunflowers. "I thought I'd catch you at lunch—I wanted to wish you a happy first day."

She takes the flowers and hugs them to her chest. "You already did that when you texted me this morning!"

"Well, I'm glad I decided to be thorough or I'd have missed all of this." I motion from her toes to the top of her head, where, incidentally, there's a ceramic bookworm pinned in her hair.

She does a little spin. "You like? It's my traditional first-day-of-school costume."

"And to think my sister is just wearing a new cardigan. How's it been so far?"

"Pretty good! No emotional meltdowns and only one tetherball incident at recess. The students are writing down their goals for the year. Do you want to come in and meet them?"

I'm in the middle of telling her no when she reaches for my jacket and yanks me inside.

"Class." Twenty-eight sets of eyes look up from their papers and focus squarely on me. "I want you to meet my best friend, Josh."

There is a combined verse of *ooooh* and one lone rebel who calls out, "So he's your *boy*friend?" followed by a chorus of giggles.

Hazel gives a very practiced tilt of her head and the room quickly quiets down. "Josh is a guest in our classroom, so we should be on our best behavior anyway, but he's also Mrs. Goldrich's brother. Let's all welcome our new friend to our classroom."

"Welcome, friend," they say in unison, and without the lingering boyfriend scandal to hold their attention, they quickly lose interest and return to their projects.

"Well done, Ms. Bradford. That was impressive," I tell her. "You are awesome at bossing small humans around. If only Winnie listened so well."

"The only way Winnie listens to me is if I put a bagel on my head," she says, and turns to set the flowers on her desk. "And thank you again for these. You're second only to a unicorn as far as best friends go, Josh Im."

"I wanted to see you in your element, and it gave me a good excuse to stop by with a development on the Josh and Hazel double-dating bonanza."

"Ooooh!" She claps her hands, watching as I pull out my phone.

"My friend Dax is a veterinarian and breeds Shetland ponies or something in Beaverton. Really good-looking, too." I open my Facebook app and find his name.

"You have a veterinarian friend with ponies and you're just now telling me about him? An imaginary talking badger has taken back second place in the best friend hierarchy."

"I completely forgot," I say, and click through to his profile, zooming in on the image so she can see. "We went to high school together and he popped up in my feed this morning."

Hazel leans in for a closer look. "Would he be bringing a pony on the date?"

"I can certainly request it."

She takes my phone and scrolls through his other photos. "He's not unfortunate-looking and the prospect of future pony rides does sweeten the pot."

"Should I call him?" I ask, studying her.

She hands me back my phone. "I've been thinking of asking the lifeguard at my pool," she says in lieu of an answer, her lips pursed as she considers. "She seems really cool *and* can save your life if you fall in the river again."

"I didn't *fall* in the river, I was more or less pushed."

"By gravity."

I ignore this. "Maybe we could set something up for Friday?"

"I'll stop by the pool on my way home and let you know."

The volume in the class behind us is rising, and I know that's my cue to let her go. "Sweet, I'll get a hold of Dax and we can coordinate."

It's only once I'm back at my car that I register the reason I was thinking of a double date again: I want to hang with Hazel.

....

When I get home Friday night, Hazel has clearly let herself in. I can hear the TV as soon as I step in from the garage, yelling, "Honey, I'm home."

Winnie skitters around the corner when she hears me, almost knocking me over as I slip off my shoes. I've missed this girl but she is a terrible guard dog.

Hazel sits up when I walk into the living room and grins at me over the back of the couch. "*Hola, señor.*"

"Sorry I'm late." Our dates with Dax and Michelle are tonight, and I have just enough time to shower and change if we're going to make it in time for our dinner reservation. "Appointments went long and I got caught up on some insurance stuff."

"My apartment was boring so I decided to just head over. Good thing, too, because your mom was just here." She holds up a steaming bowl and a pair of chopsticks. "And she brought food!"

I fold myself over the back of the couch to see what she's eating, and my stomach growls. "You know we'll be at dinner in, like, an hour."

"I dare you to face your mother's cooking and refuse it." Hazel lifts a strip of beef and green onion to my mouth, and I groan as I chew. I really should be getting ready, but instead I adjust her grip on the chopsticks, steal another bite, and round the couch to sit at her side.

"When did she leave?"

Hazel tears herself away from her food long enough to answer. "About twenty minutes ago? She was here for a while, though. She showed me some embarrassing baby pictures and we talked about how you work too much and have too many pairs of black tennis shoes." She giggles through another bite. "I really like her."

This catches my attention and I look over at her. I can count on one hand the number of times Umma and Tabby were together without me, and Tabby made sure to complain about each one as much as possible afterward. She never cared about getting to know either of my parents. She definitely never *liked* them.

"I guess it's convenient that she likes you, too."

"Of course she does," Hazel says, handing me the bowl and laughing when I immediately dig in. "I threw fruit at her the first time we met, and am the only one who ate that stinky fermented fish she made the other night. According to your sister I'm at least half-Korean now."

"It's called *hongeo* and even I won't eat it." I take another bite and then offer one to Hazel. It's been a long day, and a night out is sounding less appealing with every minute. "Umma likes you because you're bizarre, charming, and have her worrying a little less that I'll die miserable and alone."

"Miserable and alone." She scoffs. "Have you seen yourself? We just need to step up the search."

Applause from the TV catches my attention, and it's only now that I notice what she's been watching.

"Why are you watching the Olympics from . . . London?"

"I love highlight shows." When I lift a skeptical brow she sighs, shoulders slumping back against the couch. "I couldn't find the remote."

"Have you actually looked? You're probably sitting on it again." I move to stand but she stops me with a hand to my stomach.

"You can't change it now, I'm invested!"

"Haze, we have to go."

"Then record this for me."

"You realize you can Google to see how this ended, right?"

She gives me a grumpy Muppet face. "Where is the fun in that? Googling Olympic results is a joy killer."

"Or, I don't know, a time saver." I get up from the couch. "Let's get rolling. I'll clean up real quick."

....

I get an uneasy feeling about setting up Dax with Hazel the very moment she and I step foot in the restaurant and he sees her. Granted, I'm not an expert on the variety of human expressions, but his mild nostril flare and frown when his eyes drag over her—her trademark high bun, her cow-print tank top and frayed jean skirt with green cowboy boots—can't be a good sign.

We shake hands, introducing ourselves, and follow the hostess to our booth smack in the middle of the busy restaurant. Hazel smoothes her skirt over her thighs and turns to Dax, grinning. Inside my chest, my heart melts with the effort she gives every single person, even those who look at her like she's beneath them.

"So," she says, "where're you from, Dax?"

"Michigan, originally." He leans in, clasping his hands. "And you've lived in Oregon your whole life?"

Michelle is pretty enough, and being a lifeguard, she's obviously fit. But even if it feels like we might have a lot in common, I can't pay as close attention to her as I'd like given that what I'm overhearing from across the table turns more Spanish Inquisition than Getting to Know You.

Dax wants to know about Hazel's extended family, her job, her home. He asks her whether she plans to buy a house versus rent. He seems concerned that she doesn't know what kind of retirement plan the school district offers.

While Michelle and I make idle small talk, I overhear

Hazel answering his questions happily, even throwing in little anecdotes, about her mom ("She has the most beautiful singing voice, but really only in the shower"), her apartment ("It flooded like an ocean a couple months ago . . . maybe that's why all my dreams are about being on a boat?"), and her job ("Two days ago I came home smelling like tree sap, and I have no idea why. Third graders, man."). But, for all of her efforts to be amiable, Dax continually answers her return questions with single words—even monosyllables.

When Hazel gets up to make a call, Dax meets my eyes and gives me an exasperated look I think is supposed to communicate *Wow, this one is crazy*, but I pretend I don't understand.

"What?" I say, hearing the aggressive edge to my voice.

He laughs. "Nothing. Just . . ."

"Just *what?*"

I can feel Michelle looking at me, and the awkward tension rises like fog.

"She's, ah, a bit eccentric for my ta—" Dax snaps his mouth shut just as Hazel returns to the table.

She plops down onto her chair and explains, "Sorry. That was my mom. She got new boots, and I think she was going to keep spamming me with pictures until I called her and agreed that they're awesome." Stabbing her fork into her dinner, she adds, "For the record, they're rad. They're turquoise with shell beads around the top, and I bet they make her look like a fairy unicorn goddess when she's gardening. Even though they're, you know, cowboy boots."

Dax bites his lip, frowning down at the table. Although Hazel is handling him with her trademark breezy cheer, when he gets up to go to the restroom a few minutes later, she catches my eye and pantomimes drinking down a bottle of alcohol.

"Oof," she mumbles.

"He seems a little . . . intense," Michelle says quietly, wincing over at Hazel.

Hazel grins, popping a chip into her mouth. "A smidge. I thought he bred ponies? How can he be so grouchy when he breeds *ponies*?"

"Sorry." I reach across the table, squeezing her hand. "We can shuffle him into the Never Again pile."

Dax returns and immediately looks over at Hazel's plate, where only a small bit of beans and the last bite of her enchiladas remain. "You finished all that?"

She stares at him for a long, steady beat. Inside my chest, my heart feels like a chunk of hot coal. I watch as she pushes a grin across her face. "Hell yeah, I did. My dinner was fucking *awesome*."

Dax lifts his glass, and if it's possible to take a judgmental sip of water, he pulls it off. He sets the glass down carefully before looking up. "Is it fair of me to say now that I don't think this is a good fit?"

He hasn't said this only to Hazel, he's said it to me, to the entire table, and a hush falls over the four of us.

"Are you for real?" Michelle can't seem to hold it in anymore, and she throws her napkin on her half-eaten burrito. "I'm sure Hazel felt the same way the minute you asked her about her fucking 401(k)." She turns and levels her glare at me. "Josh? You seem like a nice guy. But can I give you some advice? You're on the wrong date tonight."

Standing, she waves limply at Hazel before leaving.

Dax lifts his napkin, tapping it to his mouth. "Good idea, Josh, wrong ballpark." He stands, too, reaching for his wallet and pulling out a twenty. Smiling over at me like nothing is wrong, he says, "Let's grab lunch this week?"

I meet Hazel's eyes. It's at this moment that I realize I know her as well as almost anyone alive does, except maybe Aileen. She's wearing a carefully practiced look of amused indifference, but inside she's scratching his eyeballs out.

He's hovering, waiting for me to reply.

Happily, I say, "Go fuck yourself, Dax."

....

"I feel like I got in a fistfight tonight," Hazel says, following me into my house. She collapses on the couch. "Dax is going to exhaust some decent woman someday."

"He used to be cool." I drop my keys in the bowl near the

door and toe off my shoes. "Or maybe he's always been a dick and I just never hung out with him around women."

"Lots of guys are great with other guys, and legit assholes with women."

I stop on my way to the kitchen, bending to plant a kiss on her forehead. "Sorry, Haze."

She waves a tired hand and points at the television, indicating that she wants me to turn it on. I reach under her couch cushion and pull out the remote, handing it to her.

Straightening, I continue to the kitchen, and I am immediately reminded that my mom was here earlier. My stomach rumbles to life; I'd essentially pushed my tilapia Veracruz around my plate—too preoccupied with Dax and Hazel to eat very much.

Is that what Michelle meant on her way out? That I should have been on the date with Hazel?

A rush of heat hits my cheeks, as if I've said it out loud and Hazel has heard me. On the counter the rice cooker is holding a batch of rice on the warm setting, and in the fridge I find shelves full of Tupperware and old butter containers, all labeled with whatever's inside and the dates they need to be used by. There are even a few with Hazel's name, filled with what I'm assuming is my mom's kimchi fried rice—Hazel's favorite.

As if she can read my mind, she calls out from the living room, "Don't eat my fried rice!"

I look at her around the refrigerator door. "Then why did you eat my bulgogi earlier?"

She gives me a dramatic *you're dumb* face. "Because it didn't have your name on it?"

I reach for one of the containers, dump it into two bowls, and pop them into the microwave, grabbing a couple of beers when the food is done, and carry it all into the living room.

Hazel is watching Olympic gymnastics where she left off earlier, and on the screen a group of young athletes anxiously pace the sidelines as they wait their turn on the vault. I already know the results—having seen the scores when it aired six years ago—but can't help but wince anyway when the third girl loses her balance and lands hard on her foot.

I peek at the screen through my fingers. "Isn't there anything else on?"

Hazel moves to the edge of the couch and turns to face me. "You're into the fitness, how can you not be into this?"

" 'Into the fitness'?"

"You know what I mean."

I use my chopsticks to point to the TV. "Because look at it. It wrecks your body."

Hazel glances back to the screen. "You mean, like, broken bones and stuff?"

"That, sure. But I'm also talking long term. These kids start so young, and that kind of exertion and training is hard on growing bodies. Stress fractures can occur later in life because low body fat can lead to delayed puberty and weaker bones. Even stunted growth. Not to mention the sheer force the body is being subjected to. Little wrists and ankles aren't made for that sort of impact."

She frowns. "I never thought about it like that. They all look so fit. Like little muscle machines."

"They are fit. That's part of the problem. They train non-stop and that kind of strenuous lifestyle is almost impossible to maintain. Why do you think most gymnasts retire in their twenties?"

"But then they get a whole new career. I should have done gymnastics. I bet I could do it now."

"You're what? Twenty-eight?"

She startles. "Twenty-seven."

I laugh at the shadow of insult on her face. "Okay, twenty-seven. I bet you used to do cartwheels all the time."

"Are you kidding? Constantly."

"But you probably couldn't do them as well now. Our center of gravity changes and even if we're still fit and strong, we become less flexible as we get older."

She lobs a frown in my direction. "Are you calling me old?"

I place my bowl on the coffee table in front of us before I'm wearing its contents. "Old*er*, not old."

Hazel sets her bowl next to mine and stands, reaching for my hand. "Come with me."

"What?" She lifts a brow in warning but doesn't elaborate.

I take the offered hand and let her help pull me up. "Okay . . . Where are we going?"

"Outside to be young again."

"Right. Of course. You hear that, Winnie? We're going outside to be young."

Winnie trots happily along behind us, because clearly the only thing she's heard is *outside*.

Hazel leads us through the kitchen and out the back door, and the screen falls closed at our backs. The sun is long gone but the motion-detector lights flicker on, casting shadows of the trees from one end of the yard to the other. The air is heavy and damp, thick with pine and the sweet scent of decaying mulch in the flower beds. It's a little on the chilly side, and feels like it might rain. Even in the night air, Hazel bounds down the stairs and out onto the grass.

Satisfied that she's found the right spot, she bends at the waist, gathering her long hair again and twisting it back into another gravity-defying bun. Winnie stops at my side, head tilted as we both watch, eager to see what Hazel has in store for us.

Straightening, she motions for me to join her.

I cross the yard. "What are you—" I start, but my words are cut off by a gust of air forced from my lungs as I'm tugged down into the dewy grass. Hazel kneels at my side and proceeds to tug off my socks, one at a time.

I look down to my bare feet and then to my dress pants and button-down shirt. "What . . . are we doing?"

She considers me for a moment but is not deterred, chewing on her lip as she moves to unbutton the top two buttons of my shirt.

"Can I ask you a personal question?" she says then, pulling my arm toward her to begin rolling up my sleeve.

"Of course."

"Do you ever miss Tabby?"

This takes me by surprise and I look up at her. She's so close, hovering just above me. I spot a tiny freckle I've never seen before on the underside of her chin.

"What makes you ask that?"

She shrugs. "You were right. Dating is rough. I think I forgot. Or maybe I've never done it like this before."

Hazel looks down, meeting my eyes briefly before she turns her attention back to where she's rolling up my other sleeve. Her touch is soft and focused; it makes me feel hyperaware, bringing the heat back to my face as I think again about what Michelle said. For the length of an inhale, I picture leaning forward, feeling the press of her mouth to mine. I swallow, not sure where the thought came from, or what to do with it.

"I can see why you were so reluctant to dive back in there," she says quietly. "I don't know. Just wondering whether you missed being in a relationship with her."

"I used to think I was a good boyfriend. Looking back, I think maybe not."

She catches my eyes again, a protective gleam there.

"I've talked to Emily. You were a great boyfriend. Tabby was a dick."

"I don't know . . . maybe that was sort of convenient for me? I was beginning to realize how much we'd grown apart but it was easier to keep things the way they were than be the one making the decision."

"That makes sense."

"I think what I liked was being someone's person."

Hazel's fingers come to rest on my wrist, and I blink up again to catch her reaction. She doesn't meet my eyes but a flush of color deepens along the tops of her cheeks. "You're my person," she says. "Thanks for sticking up for me tonight."

She gives these vulnerable words so freely it makes fondness clench at something in my chest. Taking her hand, I bring it to my mouth and press a quick kiss to the backs of her knuckles.

"I like being your person."

The corner of her mouth turns up, and she sits back on her heels. "And Winnie's, apparently. Who knew she was so easy for a pretty face."

I grin. "What can I say?"

Hazel groans, rolling her eyes skyward before she moves to her feet. "All right, lover boy. Let's do some cartwheels so I can laugh at you and wipe that smug look off your face."

"I'm not the one insisting I can still do this. I'm fine being an old man."

I follow, watching her legs as she makes her way across

the lawn. The sky is a bruise behind her, blue and purple in the dusky light pollution from downtown. I'm momentarily distracted by the way her skin looks under the beams of the backyard lights.

Hazel takes a moment to shake out her hands and roll her head a few times in each direction. "Honestly. How hard can this be?" She moves into as deep a lunge as she can in her denim skirt. "Like riding a bike, right?"

I motion back toward the house. "Should I get the first aid kit or . . . ?"

Straightening, she stretches her arms over her head, but not before shooting a glare in my direction. She waits one, two, three seconds, and goes for it—body tumbling forward, feet in the air, and flowy tank top going right up over her face and flashing me a prolonged shot of her neon yellow bra.

When she's right side up again, her bun has slipped to the side of her head but her expression is one of pure joy.

"Oh my God. That . . . was so FUN!" She bats the hair away from her face and tucks the front of her tank into her skirt. "And uh . . . sorry for the peep show."

I bite back a laugh. "It wasn't a hardship." I tilt my head. "You going again?"

She does, and if possible, her smile is even bigger than the first time.

"Why did I ever stop doing this?" she says, clearly dizzy but continuing on to do a line of cartwheels down the grass.

Once vertical, she points to me. "Your turn."

"*Me?*"

"Yeah!"

Wrapping her fingers around my wrists, she tugs me to stand in front of her.

"I can't. I'm taller than you."

She blinks a few times, confused. "So?"

"It's further to fall?"

"Come on. We'll do it together."

"Hazel."

"*Josh.*"

I glance around the yard, suddenly nervous. "The neighbors will see me."

Unswayed, she moves to my side and gets into position. "Come on, it's dark. Arms up. One . . . two . . . three!"

The world turns upside down and when it rights itself again, Hazel and I are a tangle of arms and legs in the grass, and I'm laughing so hard it hurts.

"Ow," I say, rubbing my stomach and everything else I managed to pull on the way down.

"But was I right?" She's breathless, hair wild and face flushed and how has nobody seen how crazy and fucking amazing she is?

I decide right there to make sure somebody does.

"Yeah, Haze. You were."

ELEVEN

HAZEL

I wouldn't exactly say we were scraping the bottom of the barrel by date seven, but Josh did feel the need to fake diarrhea, and I readily rushed him out to the car, apologizing profusely to our confused dates over my shoulder.

I'd set him up with a girl I met in line at the grocery store. A word to the wise: that's a bad idea, okay? She seemed so cool when we were talking about our shared love for the store's juice bar, but it turned out that juicing was pretty much the only thing Elsa wanted to talk about other than her private asides to Josh about how willing she was to suck his dick in the bathroom.

Josh set me up with a partner at the Fidelity branch that manages his money. (The fact that Josh has enough money to "manage" still boggles my mind. I'm thrilled when I have enough left over at the end of the month to order a pizza.) This partner, Tony, wasn't terrible to look at, but he spent the

first twenty minutes talking about what he could and couldn't
eat from the menu, and the next twenty minutes mansplain-
ing the rules of football to me and Elsa. Elsa didn't seem
to notice; according to Josh, she was reaching for his crotch
under the table every few seconds. He said it was like batting
away piranhas in the Amazon.

I probably would have suffered through it because my
chicken parm was delicious, but Josh couldn't take it and ran
to the men's room, with Elsa in close pursuit. Only his cry of
"My stomach! I need a toilet!" kept her from following him in.

He texted me from the bathroom, a manic SOS, and five
minutes later we're in his car with the music cranked and
the bliss of sheer, unadulterated relief coursing through our
bloodstreams.

"That was the worst so far," he tells me, turning right onto
Alder. "I still feel her fist around my balls."

"I'd apologize and wish that never happened, but then I
wouldn't have had the pleasure of hearing you use the phrase
'fist around my balls.' "

He glares at me briefly.

"Don't even say it's not funny, Josh. It's *incredibly* funny."

I see him check the time on the dashboard, and follow
his attention. It's barely eight on a Friday night. I don't feel
like going back to my apartment, and I know that if Josh goes
back to his he'll just get in his sweats and watch TV. According to Emily, there has been a dramatic resurgence in Josh's
sweatpants-wearing since I moved out.

"I'm still hungry," I tell him. Getting him to stay out won't be easy, and if theatrics are what it takes, I'm game. I rub at my stomach and do my best to look emaciated. "I left my delicious dinner to help protect your virtue."

It begins to drizzle outside, and Josh surprises me by turning down the music. I know him well enough to anticipate that this next part is a peace offering. For some crazy reason Josh will bend over backward to make me happy. "We could stay out for a bit."

I smile in the dark car. "You're reading my mind, Jiminnie."

He glances at me, and then flicks his turn indicator. "You up for some drinks with your food?"

"When am I not?"

....

I've only seen Josh tipsy on one occasion, at Emily's house over a couple bottles of soju. He got pink and giggly and just a little bit loud (well, loud for Josh) before falling asleep against my shoulder and waking up like nothing ever happened. Outside of that he isn't much of a drinker, and when he does drink, he's adorably slow. He nurses a single gin and tonic while I manage to quaff down three, an entire hamburger, and a basket of chips and salsa.

He holds his glass, long fingers brushing away the drops of condensation. "Why are we so bad at this?"

"Speak for yourself." I hold up my empty glass. "I'm awesome."

"I mean the dating thing." He runs his hand through the front of his hair. "People either have zero interest or want to bang in the restaurant."

The bartender takes the empty basket and replaces it with a new one full of fresh chips. I tell myself I really don't need any more, but who am I kidding. I reach for a handful, saying, "That sounds pretty normal to me. It's nothing, or sex."

He shakes his head, sipping from the drink that must be mostly melted ice by now. "I swear your dating experience is the oddest."

I look over at him. He's so ridiculously hot, it amazes me that all women don't react to him the way Elsa did. But he's also so innocent in some ways. "No, Josh, listen. Haven't you ever just wanted to rip someone's clothes off?"

"Of course."

"So you agree, don't you, that you've had an instant attraction to every person you ended up sleeping with?"

"Well, sure," he concedes, "but most of the time I'm not trying to finger her under the table the first time we go to dinner."

Heat flashes across my face and I clear my throat. The image that just burned a trail of fire through my brain—Josh reaching over, pressing his open mouth to my neck and sliding his hand down my pants—was . . . unexpected. "Maybe you're just hard to resist."

He gives a skeptical look down at his glass. I watch him carefully use his straw to take another sip. When he doesn't reply I ask, "How many women have you been with?"

He pauses, staring at the ceiling as he counts. I watch as the bartender pours seven drinks in the time it takes Josh to finish tallying. I may have to readjust my mental image of his sex life. Go Josh.

After another moment of silence he turns to me and says, "Five."

I drop my chip. "It took you four minutes to count to five? They must not have been very memorable."

"I was just messing with you." He picks up my chip and grins at me, showing me all of his perfect white teeth. "They were all pretty long term, though. You may have noticed I'm not great at the casual thing." He takes another gulp, a bigger one this time, draining it with a long swallow. "Your turn."

"Me?" I honestly have no idea how many guys I've been with, so I pull a lowball number out of the air. "Maybe twenty."

His eyes go wide and he coughs as he swallows. "Twenty?"

"Actually probably more? Let's say thirty."

Josh shakes his head and laughs. "Wow, okay."

This response is not an improvement.

"Don't do that." I point a finger at him. "Don't act like I've crossed some magical threshold of appropriate numbers for a woman. If I was a dude and said that, you'd reply, 'In *high school*, right?' and then high-five me and call me *brah*."

I drain my drink, too, and he watches, looking both amused and chastened.

"Fair enough." He stares at me, eyes moving over my features as if gauging them somehow. "Sorry." Lifting his hand, he offers a conciliatory high five. "Right on, *brah*."

I laugh, smacking his hand, and he reaches for his glass, swirling the liquid inside. "What's your longest relationship?"

Humming, I think back. "Six months, I guess?"

"Seriously?"

I turn and stare at him. "You need to stop being a judgmental ass. I already told you relationships are hard for me. I think most guys are sort of boring, and every guy I like ends up deciding I'm too wild or weird after a couple weeks. I can only keep what's hidden below the tip of this crazy iceberg for so long."

Something softens in his expression then, like he's flipping a flash card from shocked to tender. "For the record, I've seen what's below the tip and it's pretty great. Odd, but great." He narrows his eyes at my delighted expression. "I know there's a 'just the tip' joke in there but I need another drink first." He lifts his hand, waving the bartender over to bring us another round.

But this time, instead of ordering a gin and tonic for himself, he orders a Talisker, neat. And this drink he finishes in less than fifteen minutes, soon ordering another.

As we drink, and talk, and drink some more, Josh's face grows flushed and warm, and eventually his words come more easily: His first love was a girl named Claire, in high school. She was Korean American, just like Josh, and their families knew each other. They went to the same church, and lost their virginity to each other after dating for a year. She immediately told her parents, who told his parents, who were furious and made them break up.

"And?"

"And they grounded me for the rest of the year."

"That seems a little harsh. I probably would have thrown a fit and eventually snuck out to meet her."

"Your mom is great, so I don't mean this as disrespectful to her, but it's different in Korean families. I'm the oldest son and that's a big responsibility."

"So that was the end of it?"

"We don't disobey our parents."

"Ever?"

He shakes his head, sipping.

I lean forward on my elbow, my three . . . four? gin and tonics making me feel all fond and warm. "Did you love her?"

Josh is amused by this, and leans on the table, mimicking my position. "I loved her in the way we love in high school, sort of intensely, idealistically, and without knowing each other all that well."

In some ways it seems crazy that we've been hanging out all this time—even living together for a while—and I don't know any of this about him.

I sigh. "My first love was a guy named Tyler. Freshman year in college."

"Let me guess, he was a fratty white dude."

This makes me giggle because Tyler *was* pretty fratty. Backwards Yankees cap, square superhero jaw, baseball player, insisted he drank PBR because of some subtle flavor that most people missed. "Yeah, but there was depth there, too."

Josh snorts into his glass.

"There was! He was nice on the inside. He was my six months," I say, wistful. "I thought we'd be this wacky combination couple of eccentric woman and jock dude, but then he told me one night I was embarrassing him and I was like, fuck you, I'm out."

"Good for you."

"Will you think I'm lame if I say that I still liked him?"

He looks at me over the top of his glass. "You're looking at the guy whose girlfriend was banging someone else for over a year."

I suck in a breath through my teeth. "Right. I mean . . . Tyler would come around when he was drunk and lonely and I'd let him in, wondering whether I made the right decision, and we'd have sex again. Then at the next party, he'd be like"—I put on my stoner voice—" 'Dude. Hazel, you're so *weird.*' "

"I had one of those." He finishes his second scotch. His cheeks are so adorably pink and I give them a mental pinch. "The ex who comes over when they're lonely. Mine was Sarah. Except we were together for a year and a half and she cried when we broke up, telling me she wanted to marry me some-day, just not *yet*. She wanted to see other people to be sure."

I groan. "Gross." Though in the interest of full transparency, I'll admit it comes out a little more like *Grosssssthss*.

"She would come over drunk and seduce me, and the next day I'd hate myself."

"It's hard to say no when there's a naked woman in your bed."

His face flushes redder. "Very true."

"Did it bother your parents that Tabby wasn't Korean?"

Josh takes his third scotch from the bartender with two hands, thanking her quietly. "I think it bothered them more that she never took the time to get to know them, and she never tried to connect with Em, either. As I'm sure you've noticed, my parents are pretty mellow. They aren't going to push themselves on anyone, but it matters to them that they know what's going on and that the person I'm with becomes a part of our family. Tabby was never interested in that. It's funny that I'm only now realizing why they never pushed for us to get married. It was awkward, a little, when Emily told us Dave proposed, and I wasn't even with anyone. I think we all assumed I would get married first simply because I'm older. But they knew she wasn't right for me, even if I didn't yet."

I think of my mom, and how she knows almost every detail of my life. I can't really imagine it any other way. "That makes sense."

He swallows and nods at me. His eyes are growing a little unfocused. "Yeah, you get it. Tabby never did."

"Well, I think we can agree Tabby is an asshole. Which is why she never got her own personalized fried rice."

Josh clinks my glass.

"The first time your mom came over and you were still at work," I say, "she spent fifteen minutes cutting paper napkins in half. She told me they were too expensive to use only once." I remember the matter-of-fact way she explained what she was doing and it made me look back on every paper napkin I've wasted in my life. "I mean, if I did that, you'd chalk it up to me being odd, but she does it and it totally makes sense, right?"

"She's pretty great at finding ways to save and reuse."

The room is a little swishy around the edges and I lean against his shoulder, starting to feel sleepy. Against the side of my head, he's so solid, but above that sensation is the vibrant heat of him. "You're a furnace."

Josh nods, and I feel the side of his face brush against my hair. "I run pretty hot."

"You sure do."

He laughs, shaking a little against me. His voice comes out slurred: "You ready to head out?"

We turn to the window, and only now do we realize the rain is coming down in thick sheets, and neither of us is in a state to get behind the wheel.

"Cab?" Josh asks.

"My place is two blocks from here. We can run it. You can sleep on the couch with Winnie."

....

We're soaked, freezing, and hammered, sprinting up the five flights to my apartment in a drunken attempt to get warm. Josh stops just inside the door, dripping on the small rug there, cupping his shoulders and shivering. He still takes the time to slip off his shoes.

Winnie gives him a courtesy sniff before deciding it is too late for this nonsense and walking away again. I'm sure she assumes he'll just follow her into bed.

"Give me your clothes." I motion him forward. "Come on." I am breathless from the run, and high from my cocktails. The floor undulates beneath my feet.

He giggles. "If I give you my clothes, then I'll have no clothes on."

He seems to have grown even drunker on the run home. Drunk Josh is my favorite.

"Okay." I put my fingertip to my nose. "I have an idea. Go to the bathroom. Get undressed and get in the shower. I'll sneak in, take your clothes without peeking, put them in the dryer, and bring you a blanket. Boom."

He tiptoes down the hall, laughing when his shoulder collides with the doorway to the bathroom, offering it a quiet "Sorry."

The door closes and the shower starts, and I'm suddenly distracted by the wet slap of Josh's clothes on the floor and stark awareness that he's *naked* in there. With a clarity I'm surprised my booze-soaked brain can muster, my thoughts bend to the memory of him talking about fingering someone under the table.

Settle down, Drunk Hazel. Josh has been naked in places near you before. I used to live at his house and he was naked all the time. Josh naked isn't interesting, right?

STOP SAYING NAKED.

I shake my head, and it makes the world tilt and then slowly right itself. Winnie appears again and licks my hand. I reach to pet her, missing her head the first time.

The shower curtain screeches open and then closed again as he climbs in, and his low groan of happiness reaches me all the way out in the living room.

The sound does weird things to me. Weird, warm, slithery things, making me suddenly very aware of the bits of my body below my waist that have been ignored for so very long.

But as soon as I'm aware of those bits, the bladder pushes its way front and center, practically punching me from the inside. *LOTS OF LIQUID*, it screams. *I AM FULL OF GIN AND TONIC*. I squeeze my legs closed, hopping around a little and cursing that I only have one bathroom and didn't think to go before we left the restaurant. I need to get his wet clothes anyway . . . Maybe I can just sneak in and pee really quick and he'd never know I was doing anything other than taking his stuff for the dryer?

I also curse my lack of home maintenance as the door-knob creaks under my hand, and I hear the drunken slur of my voice when I warn him: "Josh, I'm coming in for your clothes."

"Okay!" He is the happiest drunk I've ever known. It smells like my body wash in here, and he must notice, too, because he laughs again. "I'm going to smell like cake!"

With as much ninja stealth as I can muster, I unzip my jeans, pull them down with my underwear, and sit on the toilet, but the relief is so amazing that I let out a groan of my own before I can slap a hand over my mouth. I look in horror over at the shower curtain when it quietly squeaks open. Josh stares back at me, his jaw slack.

I yell the obvious: "I'm on the toilet!"

He laughs, his dark eyes shining with inebriation and the joy of a hot shower after a cold run through the rain. "What are you doing there?"

I frantically start shooing him back behind the curtain. "I'm peeing! Go away!"

He looks down the length of my body to my feet and back up again before diving back behind the curtain. His laugh echoes off the tiles.

I want to flush myself down this toilet. "I can't believe you saw me peeing!"

"I saw your *butt*." Clearly he wants to torture me.

"You did not!"

"And your thighs." He speaks all garbled, as if he's got water running over his face. "You have nice thighs, though, Hazie."

I stand with a growl, flush with mild vengeance, wash my hands, and kick off my wet jeans, nearly falling over in the process. Bending, I pick up his wet clothing with mine and leave the bathroom to put everything in the dryer.

The faucet squeaks as Josh turns off the shower, and just as I'm leaving my bedroom in my dalmatian pajama shorts and tank, he emerges with a towel around his waist. "You said you were going to bring me a blanket."

I pull up short, and my brain becomes a cup overturned: his words spill out onto the floor.

Josh's bare torso is a study in lines and shadow. "I . . . what?" Even I can feel the depth of my drunken leer as my eyes find his happy trail.

"Blanket," he prompts.

It's relatively dark in the hall, which you'd think would be helpful. Somehow it's just making it better. Or worse. I don't even know anymore. "Yeah," I mumble, "I . . . blankets."

Silence falls over us for a few breaths. "You're staring, Haze."

I look up and honestly, with his jaw and sensual dark eyes and smooth, straight nose, his face is just as appealing as his bare chest. Everything about him is perfect. "Can't you be flawed in some way?"

"Huh?"

"It feels really unfair that I get to see wildlife framed in its natural element"—I gesture to his body—"and you saw me on the *toilet*."

I think he's smiling at me but I continue to stare at his chest.

"I just. Your"—I motion to his chest and the man nipples I like a lot—"and the"—I wave vaguely to his stomach and the soft line of dark hair there. "It's nice." I'm mortified all over again imagining myself curled furtively over the porcelain, groaning in relief. "*Toilet*. So unfair, Josh."

I don't anticipate what he's doing when his hand comes up to the place where the towel is tucked in around his waist until he tugs it. The blue cotton falls soundlessly to the floor, and my heart vaults up into my throat.

Josh

is

naked.

In front of me it seems like Josh has miles and miles of golden skin. I don't even remember how to blink; he has muscles TA Josh once taught me the names of but now I just know as the Tight Curve of His Bicep, That Appealing Ridge Below His Collarbone, the Edible Eight Pack, and That Lickable Shadow Above His Hipbone.

I also notice he isn't making any move to cover himself. Instead, he's watching me with a cocky half smile, like he knows he's been hiding this bit of artwork under clothes all this time and agrees I'm pretty lucky to be seeing it bare. Drunk giggly Josh is my favorite, but drunk confident Josh is my new religion.

My gaze drops lower and I realize I've half expected him to bend down and pick up the towel and ask for a blanket again. But in the time since I first peeked and then did a leisurely perusal of his torso, Josh has gotten . . . hard.

And, with my eyes focused on that hard part of him . . .

he goes the rest of the way.

Just watching me looking at him got him hard. I don't even know what to do with that information. I'm afraid to blink, afraid all of this will disappear in the split second my lids close. When I look at his face, I see his mouth is open slightly. He has a question in his eyes, but he's also looking at me in a way I imagine is similar to how I'm looking at him.

I can't look away.

What is breathing? Why do I need to do it again?

In a rush it feels like all the elements in my body pool low, between my legs. I take a step forward, and—because I have zero impulse control when I'm sober, let alone drunk—slide my hands up and over the warm skin of his chest. His groan is barely audible. It's not a sound I've ever heard him make before, but it fits him—restrained and quiet, an understated gust of relief.

In contrast, I let out a colorful string of expletives when my fingers dip into the hollows of his collarbones. Josh is so smooth and yummy. I want to dust him with sugar and lick him clean.

Apparently I've said it out loud, because he whispers, "You could. If you wanted."

What?

Josh Im is giving me permission. I'm touching the unattainable.

Holy shit, what are we doing?

"This is a bad idea," I tell him.

He nods, but his hands come up anyway, thumbs sliding beneath the elastic of my shorts, stroking my bare hipbones. He gently works my shorts down until they're a puddle of dalmatian polka dots at my feet.

I let my fingers go where they want, and apparently they want to slide down the ridges of his stomach and wrap around where he is so warm and hard and perfect. He lets out a little grunt, and his eyes fall closed.

"We'll only do it once," I promise him.

His voice comes out tight, and I have to let go of him when he slides my tank up and off, throwing it behind him onto the floor. "Once."

"We both just need to burn off some steam."

His hand finds my breast, thumb gliding back and forth over the sensitive peak, before he presses, hard. "Exactly."

"Because you don't want to date me," I remind him in a shaky voice.

"You don't want to date me, either." But as soon as he says this, his hands come to my face and his mouth comes over mine and it's intense, just the way I always dreamed it might be, to kiss someone I love so deeply already and who's seen me exactly as I am. He still tastes a little like scotch, his mouth is soft and firm, and he kisses me so good, like this is exactly what he needed tonight.

Tilting his head, he comes at me again, and deeper, tasting my sounds.

I can't get enough. I feel like a worshipper wrapped around a golden god.

Josh's hands have undressed me with a fantastic combination of impatience and skill, and his tongue slides over mine, his sounds of pleasure and need echoing in my mouth and brain. I'm reminded how not sober we are when we collapse gracelessly onto the floor; it's clear we're doing this here, right now, and won't even bother to move out of the hallway. My last bit of clothing is pulled free and then Josh climbs between my legs, reaching down to feel, eyes closed as he holds his breath and slides in deep.

But I can't close my eyes. I can't stop looking at him no matter how much his form swims over me—even in the dark, even drunk, I can see clearly enough: the solid mass of muscle and bone, the perfect angles of his shoulders, his jaw, the way his mouth is open and soft, letting out these quiet, deep grunts with each shift forward, each drag back.

He leans down, sucking a nipple into his mouth and then

tugging with his teeth. I pull in a sharp breath at the twist of pleasure and pain, and feel more than see the way he smiles against my skin.

In the morning, I'm sure I'll try to remember every little bit of it, because it feels frantic and wild here on the floor, with my hands on that perfect ass and my legs wrapped around him, pulling him in, silently telling him, *Deeper*. I'll want to confirm internally that I really did have drunk sex with my best friend.

In the morning, I'll tell myself it's okay that I scream into his ear when my orgasm hits me with the momentum of a train. I'll tell myself it's fine that I bite his shoulder when I surprise us both and melt beneath him again. But right now, I only want to think about how warm he is, how good he feels moving inside me. I want to focus on how his hair slips between my fingers and how he babbles about *soft* and *skin*, how the words *fucking* and *wet* sound both filthy and reverent in my ear. I focus on how he kisses my neck and grows rigid all over when he tells me he thinks he's coming.

So hard, Haze. Oh, God, I'm coming so hard.

I know I'm drunk, and I know it's Josh Im—the blueprint for Perfect, who should never want Hazel Bradford—but when it's done, and he goes still over me, breathing heavily into my neck, I choose to melt into that sublime blur of pleasure, the way I used to think it might feel to live in a cloud.

TWELVE

HAZEL

I must have fallen asleep beneath Josh on the new hardwood floors of my hallway, because I don't remember getting into bed. The only reminder that last night happened is the fact that I'm naked, sore, and a little sticky. Josh is gone.

But Josh being Josh, there's a little note on my pillow that says, simply,

I'll call you later this morning
—J.

My stomach takes an anxious leap. On the one hand, last night was pretty great—I think?—so I don't imagine he'll be mad that we both got laid. On the other hand, sex always changes things, and the last thing I want is for anything to change between us. I might have enjoyed the sex more than

I'll admit to him, but I'm Crazy Hazie and he's Awesome Josh (hangover prevents me from finding something that rhymes with Josh) and nothing—I mean *nothing*—scares me more than the idea of us dating and him deciding that I'm too wild, too weird, too chaotic. Too much.

Rolling over, I attempt to avoid all of this by falling back asleep, but my cotton mouth rears its head and I'm aware I'll need to hit the ibuprofen sooner rather than later. As soon as I stand, I feel the sickening lurch of my bad drinking decisions waking up. And my phone rings.

It's 7:17, and Josh is calling.

I drop back down to the bed. "Hazel's Den of Sin," I answer in a dry rasp.

"Hey, Haze."

My throat tightens at the deep vibration of his voice, at the memory of his words last night:

You feel as soft as you look.

Ah, fuck. You're wet. It's good. It's so good . . .

Oh, God, I'm coming so hard.

"Hey . . . you."

Josh clears his throat, and I'm realizing we've seen each other naked. Maybe he's thinking the same thing, because all he can manage is "So."

I laugh, and it sounds like a screech. "So."

"I hope . . . you're okay?"

"Yeah." I look down at my bare legs. There's a bruise on my knee, and my tailbone is a little sore from the unrelenting reality of being fucked against the wood floor, but other than that, I'm intact. "I'm good."

"And *we're* okay?"

Nodding, I rush to reassure him. "I'm your best friend, Hazel. Of course. We agreed just once. We're perfect."

I understand the relief in his slow exhale. "Good. Good." He pauses and I hear him inhale like he's going to speak, but then the quiet stretches into five, ten, fifteen throbbing seconds. I like to think I'm more confident than the average person, but his silence makes tiny bubbles of insecurity rise to the surface. I know it wasn't the best idea, but I don't want him to like, *regret* it, either.

Regret *me*.

"The thing is," he begins, "we didn't use a condom."

Well, that explains why I'm so sticky. My stomach tilts. "Oh. No, it's okay. I'm covered."

"You're on the pill?"

This feels so weird. This isn't exactly how I imagined this conversation going. Then again, when did I actually imagine having this conversation with Josh? "Yeah. The pill."

"So, I guess I also need to ask whether you've been tested recently?"

Oh.

"I don't mean—" he starts, and I can practically hear him wincing.

"Yeah," I cut in, "no, it makes sense. I haven't been with anyone else in over a year. But I've been tested since then."

Defensiveness crawls hotly up my neck. "What about you? I mean, after the whole Tabby and Darby thing . . ."

"Sorry," he says immediately. "Of course. I should have said that first. I'm good."

A hush falls over the line and I feel oddly melancholy. I'm not sure why. Josh and I are going to be fine. We're bullet-proof. Last night was fun, and look—he's calling me at 7:17 the morning after. He didn't avoid me for days following our drunken hookup. Everything is fine.

"Haze," he says quietly, "I'm sorry I left."

"No, I totally get it. I'm sure it was weird to wake up naked and on top of me in the hall."

"I didn't actually fall asleep. I carried you to bed."

And now I have the image of me, a bag of drunken bones, snoring asleep immediately after sex and needing to be hauled naked and sweaty and *sticky* into bed. Awesome. "Well, I'm sure that was a great reminder of my undatability."

He doesn't say anything to this.

In fact, his silence feels brutal.

For once I'm able to stop myself from saying the words I shouldn't, words that appear at the front of my mind as if projected across a screen: *Am I delusional or did it feel a little like making love?* Even I can tell that would tip us into the weird(er) zone, and who am I to know what making love feels like anyway? The longest relationship I've had was six stupid months.

Finally, he speaks. "My ass is pretty sore."

An unexpected cackle tears out of me. "I think I remember grabbing it a lot. Your ass is pretty great. You probably
have claw marks in your cheeks."

"Your boobs are pretty great, too."

"Emily told you that ages ago. See, you should listen to
your sister."

He pauses, and I suspect we're both thinking of how
Emily would react to this information. It could go either way,
and adds more turbulence to my uneasy stomach.

"It's probably a good thing I don't remember every detail,"
he says quietly.

This is undoubtedly the better opinion to have, but I'm
actually wishing it all eventually comes back to me. It will
likely never happen again, and I want to be able to remember
it forever.

"Yeah, probably," I say.

THIRTEEN

JOSH

My head is a mess.

I slide my phone onto my nightstand and collapse back on the bed. Hazel sounds fine today. Which is good.

I should be glad that she's the same Hazel she was when she woke up yesterday.

But I'm not the same Josh.

FOURTEEN

HAZEL

I haven't seen Josh in three days, but we've been texting on and off like before, about nothing in particular. Today, I told him how Winnie barked and it sounded like she said "Gimme!" He replied that his chicken salad sandwich had too much mayo. I told him I found a perfect new bikini to wear on our Diarrhea Cruise next spring. He told me not to mention diarrhea after he just ate too much mayo.

All in all, I'd say things are as close to normal as they're going to get.

The question is whether we're still doing the whole double-dating thing after we did the whole drunk-sex thing. For obvious reasons, it's different now, but I tell myself it doesn't necessarily have to be. Neither of us is really in it for a love connection, but doing the dating game together has been super fun and a good distraction from work, and bills, and having to be a grown-up all the time. I don't always trust my judgment when it comes to dudes, but Josh would never intentionally set me up with trash (dates six and seven shall be struck from the record). I also like being around him, and when the dates are lame, we have each other.

Apparently I'm not the only one who needs a status check. When we meet at Emily and Dave's for dinner, the first thing they ask is how the dating game is going. Josh's immediate reaction is to look at me to answer because, ha! That's a great question!

"Well," I say, taking a deep breath and floundering a little. I try to stall for time by slipping off my shoes and placing them with laser-like precision next to Josh's by the door, but in my head, the image of him moving purposefully over me seems to block out any hope of coherent thought. I intend to tell them only that most of the dates have been flops and see what they suggest about moving on, but in true Hazel form, my mouth decides to take over and what comes out is "Josh and I ended up having sex with each other after we bolted from date seven."

Silence fills the small entryway like fog and I turn to Josh to save me. His eyes are wide, like he's watching a plane go down and is silently praying it will pull back up at the last minute. We both know it won't.

"So, that happened!" I do a spastic little dance. "It was *really* fun."

I squeeze my eyes closed because *Oh, God, why did I say that?*

Josh clears his throat.

"We agreed it's just a one-time thing. We *agreed*," I repeat, holding up my hand in a gesture that's meant to invoke understanding, or something.

Josh doesn't come to my rescue, so I'm left free to make this more awkward for everyone. Which I do. "But I mean, for two people where one has been inside of the other, we're good, right? We're fine. I think we're ready to dive back into making plans for the next date?"

I nod, looking for consensus around me. Emily stares at us, wide-eyed. "You guys . . . *what?*"

Sometime during my breathless ramble Dave has bent at the waist, unable to contain his laughter.

Emily turns to stare at her brother, some sort of silent sibling communication happening. As always, Josh is mildly expressionless, and with a tiny swallow he seems to refocus, and nods at me with a slow-growing smile. "Yeah, we're good. Nothing's changed, thank God."

Emily says something to Josh in Korean and he replies to her, quietly. This is not the moment to be thinking of how hot he sounds.

I meet Dave's eyes, because neither of us has a clue what they've just said but we can't pretend to think it isn't about the sex his brother-in-law had with his wife's best friend.

Awkward!

Dave claps his hands, and the moment snaps loose. Josh puts his hand to my lower back, silently telling me to lead the way into the dining room, where Dave has put his latest culinary masterpiece out on the table.

Josh takes the seat to my left, and Emily and Dave sit across from us. I watch as Dave pours wine into his wife's glass, and my eyes widen as he fills it nearly to the brim. Josh and I stare on as she lifts it and takes down half before breathing again.

I glance at Josh, who glances at me at the same time. We share a *This is going well!* look, and his transitions into a *Well, what did you expect?* look. I can't argue.

Dave hands me the bread. Josh takes some chicken onto his plate.

The silence is homicidal.

Emily finishes her wine and Dave pours her more. For such a small thing, Emily can really pack it away.

"Winnie has worms," I tell the table, and spread some butter on my bread. "Took her to the vet earlier. I was so worried I was going to have to treat it with some ointment in her butt, but—nope—just a pill."

I take a sip of wine and grin at them. Josh puts his fork down and cups his forehead. But in a few beats they all break into laughter, and Emily looks over at me with my favorite kind of fondness.

"She doesn't really have worms. I was just kidding."

I am nothing if not a decent icebreaker.

After this, conversation eventually flows. Dave vents about the rain gutters he has to clean again this weekend.

Emily tells us about a kid in her class who didn't make it to the bathroom in time and pooped his pants, and how that poor kid is going to be known as Pooper Peter until he's eighty. I talk about the project we're working on where students choose various careers to write a small report about, and how one of my boys informed the class that his dad (a plastic surgeon) touched boobs for a living. Josh tells us about his new patient, a seventy-year-old woman seeing him pre–hip replacement who has propositioned him no fewer than ten times in the past week.

Even given how the evening started, dinner is fine, mostly.

And as soon as I have the thought—in the car, as Josh drives me home—I turn to him and say it: "Dinner was mostly fine. *Mostly.*"

If he gets the *Aliens* joke, I can't tell. He stares straight forward and gives me a tiny half smile aimed at the windshield.

I sigh, and poke my finger into the dimple in his right cheek. "Do we need to talk about it?"

He swallows, tightening his hands on the steering wheel. "Talk about what?"

I nod, dropping my hand and saying a quiet "Okay" out the passenger-side window. I can play that game, too. *Sex? What sex?*

"You mean about us having sex?" he says. "Or the fact that you told my sister and brother-in-law, aka your best friend and your boss?"

Ugh. Stomach flip-flops. Angst. I peek at him again. "It just came out, I'm sorry."

He shakes his head. "I don't actually care that they know."

"I just blurted it. I'm broken."

"They'd probably see it on our faces anyway," he reassures me. And although we talked about it over the phone, it's so good to talk about it here, too. Face-to-face. Nothing between us. Hazel and Josh.

"Sometimes your lack of filter kills me," he says. "It's not even like you lack a filter; you lack a funnel."

"But seriously." I turn in my seat to face him, pulling my leg under me. "I understand what it was, and there's no reason it has to change anything. In some ways, it makes sense. You're my best friend, and attractive. Of course I drunkenly mauled you."

His smile slips a little. "Is that how you remember it?"

"I mean, you participated," I concede, "but I practically begged you to show me your goods."

This makes him laugh and I can tell he fought it for a few seconds. "Because I saw you peeing. You're unreal."

I sink down into my seat. "I'll never get over that."

"You vomited hot dog on television," he says, sparing me a tiny glance at a red light, "but me seeing you pee is the mortification that's going to stick with you forever?"

"I'm also still mortified about the hot dog thing." I shudder at the visceral memory that winds through me. "I'm thrilled you remember that."

He reaches over, taking my hand. "We're good, Haze. I promise."

With a little squeeze, he lets go, and my hand feels oddly cold.

....

Mom reaches down, not even trying to be subtle when she fishes a tiny brown cookie out of her apron pocket and hands it to Winnie. Lord, the woman doesn't even have a dog of her own and she's stashing dog treats in her gardening apron. "Okay, kid." She rests her hands on her hips. "Out with it."

I stand up, brushing dirt off my butt and adjusting my gloves. "Out with what?"

Her eyes narrow and she cups my chin, leaving a smudge of dirt there as she tilts my face to the sun. "You're off today."

I hold my breath, feeling my face begin to heat in her hand. Her eyes relax, expression softening. "Out with it, honey."

"The other night, Josh and I . . ." I shrug.

She bites her lips before saying, "I *knew* it."

"Oh, come on. You did not know it. *I* didn't even know it."

"Mother's intuition."

"I think that's a myth."

She cackles like I'm a moron. "Was it at least fun?"

"I think so? It was mostly drunk, but what I remember was pretty great, yeah."

Mom hums, and pulls a small weed up where she sees it by her shoe.

I groan. I thought telling her would make me feel better, but I still feel all twisty inside. "And things are already different. We decided they wouldn't be, but—"

"You 'decided'? Oh, kids." She laughs as she picks up the small spade and a pack of cabbage starts, and tilts her chin for me to follow her to the next flower bed. "Honey, that's not something you can decide. Sex changes things."

We squat by the freshly turned dirt, and I ease a cluster of roots from the package, handing it to her once she's dug a small hole. "But I don't want things to change," I say.

Mom rests a dirty hand on her knee where she's squatted and turns to look at me. "Really? You want it to be like this between you and Josh forever? Setting each other up on bad dates? Coming home to just Winnie?"

"And Vodka, Janis, and Daniel Craig."

She ignores my humor defense mechanism and digs another hole, holding out her hand for another cube of dirt and airy roots.

"I don't know how to explain it," I add quietly, handing it over.

"Try."

"Josh has always been this person who I admired. I mean, he's beautiful, we all know that. But he also has that impossible kind of smart, and poise, and is emotionally-controlled. I've never been able to manage that type of calm, but he comes by it so naturally." I stab the ground with the point of a small shovel. "And as a friend? He's just . . . lovely. Loyal, and aware, and kind, and thoughtful. I sort of worship him." Mom laughs, and I hand her another clump of roots. "I know I'm like Pig-Pen in Charlie Brown, and I have chaos around me, but it's like he doesn't even care. He doesn't need me to change or pretend to be someone else. He's my person. He's my best friend."

Mom straightens, surveying her work. "I don't know, honey, that seems sort of wonderful to me."

A dark streak of anxiety spirals through me. "It is. It was. But then we had sex. The thing is, I know on some instinctive level that I'm not right for Josh. I'm messy and silly and flighty. I forget to pay bills and sing made-up songs to my dog in public before realizing what I'm doing. I spent an entire summer arguing with the city council about not being able to have chickens in my apartment, and remember that time I bought all those balloons because they were a nickel each and then I couldn't even fit into my car? I know without a doubt that *that* isn't the kind of woman he needs."

A little bit of fire flickers through her eyes. "How can you say that?"

I shrug. "I know him. He loves me as a friend. Maybe like a sister."

"He had *sex* with you," Mom reminds me, and I feel the memory like a pulse in my chest. "In most places, that's not a sisterly thing. Hazel, honey, are you in love with him?"

Her question slams into me and I have no idea why. We've been headed there this entire conversation. I press my hands to my stomach, taking stock of what's there and trying to translate the ache into words. "I'm not, you know, because I think there's a fail-safe somewhere inside here. I don't think I'd come back from that."

Mom nods, her eyes softening. "Is it strange that I've never had one of those? I've never really had a love that could consume me. I want to know that kind of fire."

"I'm not even sure *I* want that. If I set my heart on someone and they move on, I think it would wreck me."

Mom reaches up, running a muddy thumb along my jaw. "I get it, honey. I just want you to have the world. And if your world is Josh, then I want you to be brave and go after it."

"Because you're my mama."

She nods. "Someday you'll understand."

FIFTEEN

JOSH

As usual, it takes Emily a solid ten minutes of silent menu perusal before she decides what she wants. We've been eating at this restaurant for years. I always get the same thing, so I spend her menu inspection time sorting the sugars, straightening the salt and pepper, staring out the window trying not to think about Hazel.

Hazel beneath me, the warmth of her hands moving down my back, the bite of her nails. Her teeth on my shoulder and the sharp cry she made the second time she came.

The *second* time. When she came, and came, and came.

I'm definitely not thinking about the quiet way she mumbled she loved me when I carefully lowered her semiconscious naked body onto her bed.

Emily slides the menu on the table, snapping my focus away from the window and back to the approaching waiter. She smiles up at him, giving her order before I give mine, and handing over our menus. We've yet to say a word to each other, and it feels like the tense beginning of a chess match, or the hush before the first serve at Wimbledon.

My sister and I unroll our napkins in unison, tucking them onto our laps, and then we inhale, eyes meeting. When she looks at me, she doesn't have to say what she's thinking. But this is Emily, so of course she does.

"Dude."

I nod. "I know."

"Josh." With her elbows planted on the table, she leans in closer. "Like . . . seriously."

I shake my head, and thank the waiter when he returns to set my coffee in front of me. "I know, Em."

"What is this?" she asks, spreading her hands as if Hazel and I are naked right here at the table.

I lift a shoulder. Honestly, I have no idea. It just happened. But looking back, it feels like we'd been headed there since the first time we saw each other at the barbecue. Even on our dates, she's always been the center of my attention, the person I'm really *with*.

"Is it a thing?"

Emily's foot bounces under the table and I reach out with my own, stilling it. "To who?" I ask. "Her or me?"

"Either! Or both."

I pour a splash of cream into my mug. "I don't know what it is, okay? My head is a mess."

"I know you, Josh," she practically growls. "I know you.

You're the most serially monogamous guy I've ever met. You don't *just have sex* with someone. I don't care how drunk you are."

What can I say to this? It's the same thing she said under her breath at her house before dinner. She isn't wrong. I've never had casual sex. I've honestly never understood the impulse; sex is so supremely intimate. I give away a nonrefundable piece of myself, every time.

When I don't answer, she taps her index finger on the table as if to further emphasize her point. "You're not that guy. You've never even tried to be that guy."

"Emily." I put the cream down gently, feeling the tension from my fingertips all the way up my arm. "I know this about myself. Look at me, I'm not being blasé. It's messing with my head, okay?"

"Oppa," she asks, sliding into Korean, "do you love her?"

I don't answer. I can't, because it feels like the idea of saying it breaks something inside me open, exposing this precious organ. I've been avoiding the word since I stepped back from her bed, found my clothes in the dryer, and left her apartment. I gave love away so easily to Tabby, and compared to what I feel for Hazel? Those emotions now seem pathetically dilute, and still—I was bruised. That word—*love*—feels like a wrecking ball. I get the mental image of cracking open a walnut and staring at the pieces of flesh in my palm, knowing it can't ever go back together.

"Josh?"

It seems hard to find enough air to form words. Hazel's mouth and her shoulders, the soft pink tips of her breasts, her bursting laugh, and the quiet way she told me to stay inside her before she fell asleep beneath me on the floor—it all swims in my head. "I don't know."

My sister leans back in her chair like she's been pushed. " 'I don't know' means yes."

"I think I might." I look at Emily. "I think I might be in love with her."

Our food is delivered and we thank the waiter with mumbled words. I watch Emily lift her fork and poke at her salad. Suddenly, I can't even imagine eating.

What if it's not just a confused infatuation after good sex? What if it's what my brain and heart seem to believe, and I really do love Hazel? What if she's it for me, and I'm not it for her?

I push my plate an inch or two farther away.

"Josh, you guys are *so* different."

It's honestly the last thing I need to hear right now. "Come on. I know that."

"She's never going to be chill. Hazel has no chill."

Despite my mood, this makes me laugh. "Em. Anyone who's spent more than five minutes with her knows that." I'm hit with a mental image of Hazel's purple palm while she was cooking me pancakes. I wonder whether I'll ever learn where the stain came from.

And as if she's said something unkind, Emily adds in a whisper, "But she's the best. Hazel has the biggest heart."

A beast inside me has tightened a fist around my own heart when she says this. Hazel is without a doubt the best person I've ever known.

"I thought you wanted to set us up, Em. After the barbecue?"

"I did," she says. "But you're so close now. It worries me."

"Me too."

"You can't hurt her."

I meet my sister's eyes and see the heat there. It's a moment before I can speak past the emotion clogging my throat. "I wouldn't—I won't."

"I'm serious." She points her fork at me. "You have to be sure. You have to be positive. Hazel's like this rogue star that just sort of floats around. She has a lot of friends—because how can you not love her?—but only a few she's close to. You're *really* important to her. She would honestly break if she lost you, Josh."

I look up at her, skeptical. Hazel is made of brick and fire and iron. "Come on, Em."

"You don't think I'm serious?"

"Hazel isn't fragile. She's a brute."

"Where you're concerned she is. She idolizes you." She pulls her cheek up in a sarcastic smile. "God knows why."

I sigh, blinking down at the swirling white in the brown coffee.

"But if you changed your mind about something like that," Emily says, "I think that's the one thing that could dim her light. We both know Hazel is a butterfly. I think you have the power to take the dust from her wings."

SIXTEEN

HAZEL

A month of normal hang-out time is what Josh and I seem to need in order to stop having to make a joke about the Drunk Sex all the time to show how OKAY WITH IT we are. Every weekend for the subsequent four weeks, we do very friend-appropriate things, like catch a couple of plays, peruse local art galleries, have dinner with Emily and Dave where we assure them we haven't slept together again, and avoid bars and drinking (and nudity) whenever possible. Josh even starts bringing me lunch every Wednesday at school so we can Just Hang Out.

In the end, maybe it's good that I have intimate knowledge of his penis so that I can confidently recommend him to my friends for the dating?

We are definitely—very *vocally*—Totally Ready to Try the Double-Dating Thing Again, so I pick up his date, Sasha, at the yoga studio where she teaches, because she says it will be easier for her to shower and get ready there than go all the way home on the bus. Things I have learned about Sasha since asking her to come on this blind double date:

1. She has never owned a car, nor does she ever plan to.
2. Her clothes are all made from hemp, vegan leather, or recycled soda bottles.
3. She hasn't cut her hair in four years because she doesn't feel it's given her permission.

Although she seems like a conscientious and lovely person, I'm no longer feeling very confident that she's a good match for Josh, per se. To be perfectly honest, it might be time to admit I'm not a very good matchmaker—we've had a lot of duds.

We're having dinner at one of John Gorham's restaurants, Tasty n Sons. Toro Bravo is probably my favorite restaurant in all of Portland, but I've never been to this one of his, and I have purposefully not eaten anything since breakfast so that I can stuff my gob and require Josh to roll me home in a wheelbarrow, date or no date.

When I pick her up, Sasha looks fantastic. She's wearing black jeans and a cute red T-shirt that shows off great boobs. Good job, hemp! Her hair is up in some sort of Rapunzel braid that looks like it weighs about seventy pounds. When we walk into the crowded restaurant, heads turn. I'm pretty sure if Josh and the guy he's bringing—someone named Jones—didn't show up, Sasha and I could have a pretty hot ladies' night out.

But a hand goes up in the back and waves us over; of course Josh is already here.

"Oh my God, is that him?" Sasha leans to the side, staring toward the table where Josh has now stood. I start to agree that yes, I am the most generous yoga student in her class and she should totally give me a discount, but then the person beside him stands, too, and oh.

My head goes blank for

one,

    two,

        three,

            four breaths.

I already *know* "Jones."

He isn't Jones Something. He's Tyler Jones.

I rarely have moments that throw me, but this one is a doozy. Tyler was my six months. Six months together followed by years of him studiously manipulating me into thinking we might happen again someday so that I'd sleep with him again, and again.

Josh knows about Tyler, but not the extent of the head games he played, and without a doubt Josh has no idea that my ex Tyler is the gym buddy he calls Jones.

And damn it, Ty looks good. He's still got that soft floppy blond skater hair that falls over his left eye. His knee-buckling smile hasn't changed with time, the scar on his chin is still the best way to make a great face better, and he's still insanely tall for no good reason. Tonight he has on a well-worn flannel and some perfectly beat-up button-fly jeans that cover up what I know to be a magical dong. I bet under the table I'd see his requisite black Chuck Taylors and in his back pocket he's tucked his Yankees cap. It's like walking backward into my life from six years ago.

The expectant smile is wiped clean off Tyler's face when he sees me and moves around the table. He pushes his way through the crowd, coming at me like a predator, and I'm the prey with no survival skills—just rooted in place. Sasha has made her way to Josh and I assume they're doing the introductions without us because all I can really see is Tyler marching closer, heads turning because—let's face it—he's a hot man on a mission. Before I've decided whether I'm going to stay, or turn and run, his arms are around my waist and I'm off the floor with his face pressed into my neck as he says my name over, and over, and over.

Hazel, Hazel, Hazel.

Oh my God.

Holy shit, what are you doing here?

How are you?

I had no idea it would be you!

Holy shit. Holy shit. Holy shit.

Josh's eyes meet my wide gaze over Tyler's shoulder, and I can see him trying to work this out. Without context it must look like one hell of a blind date greeting. His brows pinch down in question, and I mouth a simple *Tyler*.

I can make out the swear word from here. *Tyler* Jones? his lips say next, and I nod.

Sasha puts her hand on his arm to redirect his attention back to her, but I can tell he's only ten percent there. Every few seconds he looks up at me, and I'm watching him as if he can somehow guide me on what to do here.

"I can't believe it's you," Tyler says, putting my feet back on the floor, cupping my jaw, and bending so we're face-to-face.

I bite my lip, pulling back a little because I have the distinct impression he's about to kiss me. "It was . . . a surprise for me, too."

"Really?" His mouth takes on a cockily skeptical curve. "I thought Josh told you who you were meeting."

"Yeah, but . . . I never knew you as 'Jones.' "

Only now does it occur to him that I wasn't trying to surprise him with this "blind" date, and that I had no idea that he would be here. God, it's so typical of Tyler to think this has somehow all been orchestrated for him.

He ducks down again, catching my eyes. "I hope it's a good surprise?"

This throws me a little, this display of hesitance.

"I'm still deciding," I tell him. "The last time I saw you, you were sneaking out of my bedroom without saying goodbye. You left for Europe the next day with the person I later realized was your girlfriend."

His eyes hold on to mine, and he's nodding the entire time I'm speaking, like my words are gifts bestowed by a benevolent goddess. "I was a shit. I was a complete *shit* to you, Hazel, and it's haunted me every day." Tyler lets out a shaking exhale, and he seems genuinely thrown. "Holy crap, I can't believe you're here."

He jerks me again into his chest, and my expression of surprise is smashed against his sternum.

My fingers are shaking when his giant hand engulfs them and he tugs, leading me back to the table where Josh and Sasha are seated and ordering drinks. I come up right as Josh is saying, "Aaaand the woman walking up just now will have a double Bulleit and ginger." He meets my eyes, and adds, "In a short glass."

Josh knows I need to toss one back right now. It must be written all over my face.

"Josh, dude!" Tyler smacks the table and the salt and pepper shakers clatter together. "You didn't tell me Hazel is Hazel *Bradford*! Did you know she's the love of my *life*?"

Josh's jaw drops to the floor, and I too want to guffaw heartily at Tyler's declaration. How many Hazels has he met in his life? I also want to let out a banshee scream loud enough to break every window in the establishment.

"We were together for two and a half years, man," Tyler says, and as I start to challenge this calculation, he sees Sasha and apologizes for being rude (Tyler? Apologizing for social snubs?), reaching to shake her hand with the one that isn't still wrapped around mine. "Sorry, sorry. I'm Tyler."

"Sasha," she says, dazed, like we are as fascinating as early-days reality television.

"I'm totally freaking out right now." Tyler looks back at me and wipes his free hand across his forehead as if he's sweating from the shock of it all. "Josh and I work out together sometimes. I had no idea he was fixing me up with my ex. I've been thinking about this woman every day for the past four years."

I'm not even sure how to absorb these superlatives, so I just give him a tight smile and sit down across from Josh, who's staring at me with such singular intensity I worry he's burning a red dot into my forehead.

The delivery of our drinks, and the time Tyler takes to order one for himself, gives me a few seconds of oxygen, and head space.

1. Tyler looks fantastic.
2. He seems genuinely apologetic, if not a little over the top.
3. My brain is goo. This is the Tyler Jones Effect. He's charming, and beautiful, and has always been my kryptonite.

So much for growth.

I remember the first time he broke up with me, how it felt to hear him say that I was fun, but not long-term material.

I remember the first time he left my bed after coming over for sex, and told me it was always so good that way between us, and thanks for a fun night.

We probably had sex twenty more times after that, and every time I felt like shit afterward. It got to the point where it wasn't even that I wanted Tyler Jones so much as I just wanted to not have this weak spot in my heart. Every time I thought, *This time, I'm going to say no! This time, I'm going to ask him to get out after I've come but before he has!*

This time, this time, this time.

I reenter the conversation as Tyler is telling the story of the time we went skiing and I made it down the mountain alive after somehow losing my poles and careening face-first over a thick sheet of ice. It's not a story I particularly relish him starting off with, but at least it's one where my undergarments are intact and my skirt isn't over my head.

Yet.

"Yeah, Hazel has a pretty hard skull," Josh jokes quietly, and I'm the only one to burst out in a nervous, too-loud cackle. He looks at me, grinning at my awkward hysteria too close to the surface. Josh reaches across the table and brushes his fingertips across the back of my hand in what is either an *I'm right here, you're okay* gesture or a *Be cool* one.

Tyler is full of *Hazel Bradford is the wildest ever!* stories, and regales a riveted Sasha and Josh with The Time I Looked into Adopting a Tiger, The Time Senior Hazel Went Streaking Through Freshman Orientation, and most mortifyingly, The Time We Decided We Should Have Sex in the Bathrooms at Every Major Museum in Portland.

Josh gives me a pruney face because we were just at the Portland Art Museum two days ago. "Gross," he whispers, and wipes his hands on the thighs of his jeans.

I admit Tyler's a good storyteller, and I come off sounding like the Olivia Pope of Fun in most of them. I can tell Sasha and Josh are genuinely entertained. But as he goes on and on with all this shared history, I'm weighed down by the drooping awareness that I gave Tyler so much of my heart and my time, and received so little in return.

It is astonishing to me that, in all the time we were together and the years we've been apart, *this* is what he remembers. If I had to share my Tyler Jones stories, there would be a couple of great ones, including The Night He First Brandished the Magic Dong™ and The Time He Showed Me Why Women Love Oral Sex, but otherwise, they'd mostly be That Time Tyler Said He Loved Me to Get in My Pants, and That Other Time Tyler Said He Loved Me to Get in My Mouth.

A glance at Josh tells me that, as his gym buddy rambles on and on about our escapades and sexcapades, the bloom is coming off the rose. I understand immediately; if you asked me which is the more meaningful relationship in my life, I'd say Josh without hesitation. But for sure Josh can see as clearly as I can the imprint that Tyler has left on me. I'd have a spoiled-milk expression, too, if Tabby were here talking about all the shenanigans she and Josh shared.

His jaw ticks, and when Tyler stops to actually *breathe*, Josh cuts in to engage Sasha on her interests, her job, her life.

Tyler takes this opportunity to turn, and reach for my hand again, bringing it to his mouth. "Hazel?"

"Yeah?"

"I'm sorry."

Something squeezes my lungs until the air is all gone. "For what?"

He nods, eyes closed, and his lips move up and down my knuckles with the movement. Over Tyler's bowed head, Josh catches my eye and we both quickly look away.

"I'm sorry for ending things, and making you feel that you weren't worth my time long term." So Tyler *does* remember. "I'm sorry I couldn't let you move on afterward. I'm sorry I used you as an escape whenever things got hard in other areas of my life. And I'm sorry I disappeared without a word."

When he looks at me, I give him a little smile. It's nice to hear all this. I can't pretend it isn't. But I'm obviously still in shock because I don't really have words in response, even all the wrong ones.

The waiter deposits a Diet Coke in front of him and with that, things click into place.

"You're in recovery," I blurt.

He nods. "Yeah. Yeah. I am. I'm so much happier." He lets

go of my hand to lift his glass and take a sip. "I wish I could do a lot of things over again."

I'm thrilled for him, because it's obviously a good decision, but I'm so windblown by Tyler's appearance that I can't even enjoy the food. One sip in and my drink tastes rotten. My meal is overflavored and feels like a fluorescent bulb in my mouth.

Tyler and Sasha—and to a lesser extent Josh—seem to do just fine with minimal input from me, but I can't pretend I'm not relieved when the check comes, and the two dudes whip out their wallets. I don't even put up a fight.

"Haze," Josh says quietly, "you want to box that up and take it home?"

I look at my plate. I've had maybe two bites. "Okay. Sure."

Josh grabs my bag of food as we stand, and puts a brotherly arm around my shoulders before Tyler can pull me aside. "That was a fun night," Josh says quietly, looking down at me.

"It was great." I can hear the question in my words, like *Wait, was it fun? I was on Planet Freak-Out for most of it and didn't notice.*

"Let me give you my number." Tyler slips my phone from where it's loosely held in my hand, and opens a new text box, texting himself This is Hazel's number, followed by a little smiley face.

I want to snatch his phone and see how many of those texts he has with different girls' names. But then I feel like an asshole for thinking it, because he bends down and puts a chaste kiss on my cheek.

"You're a bigger person than I am," Tyler says, and it's awkward because Josh still has his arm around my shoulders so Tyler's practically kissing Josh's hand, but Tyler doesn't seem to mind baring his soul in public anymore. "It was really good to see you."

Josh walks Sasha out; he says he's going to drive her home, and something in my chest forms a fist and punches both of them for that. Tyler hops in a Jeep Cherokee, and waves as he drives off. My car starts on the second try, and I drive home in a haze, pulling up outside my building without paying attention to anything along the way.

Because Josh is at Sasha's.

The thought sticks in my head like a tack in a corkboard: *Pay attention to this. Josh is at Sasha's. Obsess about this later. Just . . . not yet.*

I pull off my clothes and drop them on the floor right next to the laundry hamper in an act of rebellion that, most likely, Josh won't even see. I scrub off my minimal makeup and throw the wipe in the trash with a violence that Tyler doesn't get to appreciate. I get into my bed in my BAD BITCH T-shirt and DRAGON PUSSY underwear, and turn on the TV on my dresser with every intention of watching *Steel Magnolias*.

Five minutes in, I burst into tears.

"Hey. Hey."

I gasp, clutching my boob as if it's my heart, and look up at my bedroom doorway.

Josh is there.

Josh is *here*? I didn't even hear him come in, and he's moving over and sitting on the side of my bed while I melt down at the sight of Sally Field running around the house in curlers.

"I used the key you gave me. I hope that's okay?"

I can only nod.

"Hey," he says gently. "What's wrong? What happened after I left?"

"Nothing." I wipe away the evidence on my cheeks. "I just feel emotional." I stretch across him to my bedside drawer, where not only are there several vibrators but there is chocolate. He watches me push past a messy pile of sex toys for sugar without saying a single thing, and also doesn't say anything when I shove an entire Twix into my mouth, then start talking around it. "Seeing Tyler was a lot. I thought you were going home with Sasha and I wanted to talk to you."

I bury my face in his shirt and inhale like I'm huffing him. He smells like Tide and the echoing tang of vinegar from his parents' house, and I imagine opening my mouth and eating his shirt, swallowing it with the chocolate bar.

Then I realize that the blanket has slid off my body and he can see the back of my Dragon Pussy underpants. He pulls his attention to my face, eyes wide and unfocused.

"This night could be better," I tell him, tucking my shirt over my butt.

"I had no idea Jones and Tyler were the same guy." He runs an apologetic hand through my crazy hair. "I would never have set you guys up." A pause. "I mean, obviously."

"I know." I watch him read my Bad Bitch T-shirt a couple of times before he laughs.

"Strangely enough," he says quietly, "I adore you in this mood."

I ignore the silvery, giddy monster that wiggles through me when he says this. "It threw me because he was being so nice, and I swear that for like two years all I wanted to hear were the things he was saying tonight." I start crying again. Holy bejeezus I am a mess. "Tyler was the guy who broke my heart and has made me so wary of getting emotionally involved again and then he was there. He looked the same, but remembered all the ways he was shitty and apologized for them." I let out a wail and use Josh's shirt as a handkerchief. "And then you went home with Sasha and I wanted to talk to you."

"You said that already, Haze."

"Well, I really, really mean it."

He holds me for a few minutes. Who knows, maybe it's an hour. I lose track of time and space; if someone decided to invent a comfort machine, it should be shaped just like Josh Im. His right hand rubs slow circles on my back, and his left hand is anchored in the hair at the back of my head, and he's saying quiet things like

I'm sorry.

I could tell how shocked you were.

Shh, I know. Come here, Haze. It's okay.

Finally, I pull back and apologize in a sob-thick voice for covering his shirt in my melodramatic tears and snot. "You should totally go home and watch some TV and forget this ever happened. I don't know why I'm such a mess."

"I don't know . . . I feel like I should stay." He cups my face the same way Tyler did earlier, but instead of feeling mildly intimidating, it feels wonderful, even though he's close enough to stare straight into my pores and I know I'm not a pretty crier. "I don't like leaving when you're sad." His brows pinch together. "Actually, I've never seen you sad."

"I'm okay."

"I can stay."

I go for lighthearted—for playful—but unfortunately my singsong words come out like bricks: "You can stay, but, I mean, I'm not going to have sex with you again."

Insert record-screech sound here.

Josh rolls his eyes and lets go of my face. "Yup. Okay. I'm headed home."

"Wait." I swallow down the desperate edge to my voice. "I was kidding." I try to salvage the joke: "I would totally have sex with you again."

His expression goes dark and he slumps slightly in exasperation. His voice is rough and quiet. "Come on, Haze. I just want to make sure you're okay."

"I know," I say. "I'm sorry. I'm a mess." I wipe my face and try to look as collected as possible. "I really would love the company."

He's already kicked off his shoes at the front door, so all he has to do is step out of his jeans and he's only in boxers and his T-shirt. His boxers have little jalapeño peppers all over them, and he draws my eyes away from the shape of his cock—*Friend* cock! Not for you!—by pulling back my sheets and climbing into bed beside me.

"Scoot over." He takes the remote, and I rest my head on his broad shoulder, knowing as soon as I get a whiff of the warm tangy spice of him that I'm probably ten minutes away from sleep.

"But none of this *Steel Magnolias* junk," he whispers. "Let's watch the first *Alien* movie."

SEVENTEEN

JOSH

I wake up on the brink of orgasm. I'm still dressed but my chest is sweaty, my blood rushing hot and frantic, and as soon as I come into awareness, I can feel the electric storm building at the base of my spine.

What roused me was the sound of Hazel crying out in my ear. An ancient part of me must have understood the pitch of her noises and heeded it before I was even fully awake, because I'm still rocking my hips when I register that (1) I'm awake and (2) she's gone limp beside me.

Everything falls still as we pant, breathless. Her leg is around my hip, her hands are fists in my hair, and her mouth is only inches from mine.

"Whoa." I swallow, lifting my head to glance over my shoulder at her dark bedroom around us. The only light comes from the television. The Apple TV is cycling through the screensavers—a revolving series of flowers and wildlife.

The clock on her nightstand tells me it's 3:21 a.m.; the movie must have ended hours ago. I'm only barely oriented, and I look down at her, mouth soft and lips parted, her eyes open now and lit in the dark.

So here we are: somehow, in our sleep, we started to move together through our clothes, and I think Hazel just . . .

"Oh my God." She swallows. "I thought I was dreaming."

"Me too."

"I woke up as I was coming."

So she *did* come. Holy shit. My stomach tenses with need. "That's about when I woke up."

"I'm sorry, Josh. I didn't mean—"

"No, stop, it was both of us."

She must be able to feel the hard line of me, pressed against the heat of her, because she whispers, "Are you okay?"

Every muscle in my body is flexed. Hazel's hands are still in my hair and she scratches her nails gently against my scalp, shifting her hips up just slightly, rocking into me as if she needs to clarify her meaning.

I'm rigid; I can feel the ache, the pulsing tension in my navel that will slowly morph into a leaden, throbbing discomfort. Tomorrow I'll worry about the fallout. For now, "I . . . need to come."

With a whispered, "Yeah?" she lifts her head just enough to press her mouth to mine. It's soft and warm, and her hips rise from the bed, urging, circling up into me.

"I don't mind . . . doing it myself," I stammer between kisses, "if that's better . . ."

"That's a nice image, but . . ." Hazel hooks her thumb in my boxers and slides them down over my ass, to my thighs.

Before I climb over her, I have a moment of pause—*What are we doing, and what does this mean?*—but it evaporates like steam in cold air. We have to untangle slightly to get her underwear off, and I want to feel her, skin to skin. I pull off her shirt, and then mine.

The relief of it—of her bare skin against me, of her legs sliding up and around my hips—is nearly obliterating. I can sense how close my orgasm is, just beneath the surface.

She reaches down, holding me, playing with me against her, and I have to pull my mind somewhere else—I imagine running, scrubbing the shower, chopping carrots—so I don't come from the heat and friction of her against the head of my cock.

"I know I shouldn't talk because I'll ruin it but holy shit, Josh. This feels so good."

I grit my teeth, tighten the muscles of my abdomen, and force my hips to stay exactly where they are: far enough away that she's in control, but close enough that she can do whatever she wants.

"I think I could come again. Like this."

Holy shit.

"Like . . ." Her voice unravels into a gravelly little sigh and she arches her neck, the words becoming harder to find. "How does something so simple—" She slides the tip of me along her wet skin, back and forth, up and down, in between. I have no idea how I'm even still breathing. "How does this"—a little gasp—"feel so good?"

I'm shaking my head because I have no idea—or maybe my brain is just trying to convince the rest of me to slow down—but I'm distracted by the feel of Hazel's knees sliding up to rest against my ribs.

She kisses my lips, pulling the bottom one into her mouth. "Do you think it feels good?"

I suck in a breath, light-headed. "I think you feel better than anything."

"Did you know there are, like, seven thousand nerves in the head of the penis?" she gasps. "More than any other part of your body?"

My arms shake with the effort of holding back. "That seems about right."

She laughs but the sound breaks apart and floats away as she moves underneath me, hips tilted up as she positions me just where she wants. Everything stops and her eyes meet mine in the odd light emanating from the TV. "Is this okay?"

I let out a single breath, a short laugh at the absurdity of this, kissing her chin. "Are you kidding?"

"We'll just do it *twice*, then."

I'd normally smile at this except my brain can't process anything but the unbelievable heat of her, the knowledge that I'm about to get exactly what I want. My open mouth rests on hers as I push in, and it means I feel the way her breath shakes.

"Josh."

She's right, holy shit it's so good. "I know."

"Is this the worst idea ever?"

"I don't know. Right now it feels like the best idea ever." I cup her backside, lifting her hips to me, working myself in and out of her, deeper on each pass.

I feel a flash of guilt, like this sex should be for the sake of taking care of business only—an accident that happened in our sleep—and I shouldn't be enjoying it so much. But how can I not? Hazel is gorgeous beneath me: her hair is a tumble of curls on the pillow, her mouth is full and wet, her breasts move with me every time I push deep into her.

And I get the sense that she's relishing it, too. She touches me like she's memorizing my shape, with fingertips and palms, thumbs tracing the lines of my back. Her hands slide down to my ass, back up to my shoulders, my neck, and into my hair. When I push up onto my hands to see what I'm feeling, her hands make a circuit of my front: my shoulders, collarbones, chest, stomach, and down to where I'm moving in and out of her.

Her fingers come away wet and before I can think about it I pull them up and into my mouth before bending to kiss her. It's such a rare filthy thought but I want her to feel what we're doing with every one of her senses. If she wants to memorize it, I want to tattoo it into her thoughts.

Look at this, I think. *We're making something right now.*

God, there's a different awareness this time that makes me feel both more relaxed and more inhibited. For one, we've done this already, so there's the familiarity of her body under mine and knowing—even barely—what she likes. But I'm sober, and so every movement is intentional, every touch is conscious.

I also realize, when I hear her sounds and feel the hungry wandering of her hands, that for me at least, this isn't just infatuation or a flash of desire, it's deeper. I think this is love, I think she's it for me, but I can't quite reach that emotional place with her noises pressed right into my ear; I know I'll be hearing them for days.

"Josh."

"Yeah?"

She goes quiet, almost like she's suddenly shy.

My mouth presses to her jaw, my hand finds her breast as I narrow my movements to the tiniest circles. "Tell me."

Instead of answering, she cups my face and brings my mouth over to hers. Her kiss is so searching, so desperate that I have to wonder whether she's asking me something with the touch.

Is this real?

"I feel it, too," I tell her. Whatever this is. "I'm right there with you."

Hazel slides her tongue over mine, spreading her legs

wide and pulling me deeper, until she's crying out into my mouth, telling me

Yes

I'm coming

I feel every bit of air leave me as I follow her down the spiral—a relieved gust drains me. The pleasure is unreal: metal and liquid and light, pulling a long groan from my throat that comes out strangled.

Her hands grip my backside, holding me deep as I shake.

Other than our gasping breaths, quiet surrounds us.

"Did you come again?" I whisper. I need to know she did. If the answer is no, I'm not done here.

She nods, her forehead damp against the side of my face. "Did *you*?"

I cough out an incredulous sound, and she giggles, but when I begin to pull back, she grips me with her arms around my shoulder and her legs around my thighs, keeping me inside her.

"Don't." She presses her mouth to my neck. "I'm not ready for this to be over yet."

I know exactly what she means.

....

Hazel is already up when I wake, naked in her bed. I hear dishes clattering in the kitchen, and a flash of relief ripples through me that she hasn't taken off on a run, needing to process this somewhere else.

I cup my forehead and try to figure out what to do. I love Hazel; with the clarity of the morning sun beaming in the window, I know I do. But in the long run, am I what she needs? I don't want to root her down if she's not ready, and if she wants someone boisterous and gregarious like Tyler, who am I to say she shouldn't have that?

I wonder, too, where her head is after what we did last night. Hazel has done this before—casual sex, hookups. But I remember the moments last night when it felt nearly desperate between us, like she didn't want to let me go. I know that could also be the weight of our friendship, and her fear of losing it. It could have been a comfort screw and nothing more.

I have no idea what to think.

It's calculated, but I pull on my boxers and jeans, leaving my shirt off. I figure, if she makes some crack about my body, or comes over to touch me—that's good, right? If she wants to figure out what's going on between us, I'm totally down for that.

In the kitchen, she's pulling spoons out of a drawer and glances up when I come in. She's wearing her favorite dalmatian pajamas—tiny shorts and an even tinier tank, which makes them my favorite, too.

Her chest and neck flush when she sees me, but I notice that her eyes stay firmly on my face. "Hey."

I rub a casual hand over my stomach. "Hey."

She quickly turns back to the silverware drawer, closing it with her hip.

"What are you making?" I ask.

Pointing to a box of Shredded Wheat on the counter, she says, "Just cereal. I figured you'd want some, too." Then she lifts her chin to the coffeepot.

"No blue pancakes? No banana waffles?"

Hazel laughs down at the counter. "I'd probably burn them."

I pause on my way to grab a mug. "When did that ever stop you before?"

I'm treated to a flash of a real smile before she tucks it away and turns to pull the milk from the fridge.

And seriously, what the hell? Where is my Crazy Hazie?

A sinking feeling spreads from my stomach up through my chest. Did last night break something good between us?

"Haze."

She looks up at me as she pours some cereal into her bowl. "Yeah?"

"You okay?"

I don't think I've ever seen her blush before. "Yeah, why?"

"You're being . . . normal."

She doesn't seem to get it.

I put my mug down and hold out my hand, curling my fingers. "Come here."

She comes over to me across the kitchen. Her hair is a

wild mess, tumbling down her back. The words are so close to the surface: *I know this is confusing, but can we try to figure it out?*

But she isn't looking at me, and I can't tell if the tightness in her eyes is fear or a need to put some distance between us. Am I missing something?

Unfortunately, she's going to have to do that with words, not expressions and mumbled phrases. I put my hands on her hips and it's an invitation to touch me. Instead she curls her hands into fists and tucks them against her chest.

"Is this about Tyler?"

She blinks with incomprehension and then shakes her head.

"Then did last night freak you out?" I ask.

She hesitates, but then shakes her head again. But she was pretty emotional last night, and it's hard for me to know how to read that: if the most insecure part of me is right, and she wants to give this thing with Tyler a shot, I have to let her.

Right?

"Okay, so what is it? Why aren't you wearing a chicken costume and frying me homemade doughnuts in the sink?"

"I guess it's a little about last night." She gnaws on her lower lip before admitting, "I . . . worry about what would happen . . ." She screws her mouth to the side, plucking words carefully, but lets the last bit out in a rush: "If we were to pretend we're compatible."

Ummmm. It *felt* pretty compatible. I squeeze her hips

gently. "I don't think we're *pretending* anything. We've slept together twice, and that's okay, right? It doesn't have to mean anything we don't want it to mean. You're okay?"

"I am. Are you?"

I laugh a little. "Of course I am. You're my best friend, Haze."

Her eyes meet mine and they're wide with surprise.

"What?" I ask.

"You've never said that before."

"Yes, I have."

"No, you haven't."

I start to think back but it's honestly immaterial. "Well, it's true. I'm okay. You're okay. Most importantly, we're okay?"

She nods, and finally meets my eyes.

"Now come on. Make me some bad pancakes."

She slumps with a dopey grin, shuffling back toward the stove. "I mean, if you insist."

Something unwinds in me at the same time something else tightens. On the one hand, *Hazel* is back. On the other hand, I feel like we just agreed to maintain the status quo, when I think I want us to evolve.

We made love last night. She has to know that.

She pulls out a mixing bowl. "Did you have fun last night?"

I stare at her. "Um. I thought we already established that, yes, I had fun."

Laughing, she amends, "I mean before we got back here."

"Oh. I guess—Sasha is nice. Tyler seemed okay. Mostly I was worried about you." I study her for a reaction to this. She does a quick scrunch of her nose as if stifling a sneeze. "Feeling better about it this morning?"

She's only just gotten the flour out and already she has a streak of white on her cheek. "Yeah. I don't really know why it hit me so hard. It's good to see him. He seems like he's in a good place." Hazel nods a few times, as if she's convincing herself.

"I thought you told me you were only together for six months. He said two and a half years."

"He strung me along for two of those years. We weren't really together; he was just nailing me on the side." She meets my eyes and crosses hers goofily. "Yeah, I know. I'm an idiot."

"*Guys* are idiots when they're that age. I'm sure he said all the right things to make you think he was coming back every time. He's several years older now. He seemed pretty remorseful."

She makes a weird little grimace and then looks away. I wonder if she's thinking the same thing I am: *Why the hell am I defending him?*

Hazel moves to the fridge for eggs. Her phone vibrates on the counter.

"Who is it?" she asks over her shoulder.

I look down and my stomach drops.

When I don't answer, she leans over to catch my eyes. "Josh. What's wrong?"

"Oh. Nothing." I show her the screen. "But Tyler texted you."

"Seriously?" She shuts the fridge door. "Already? What'd he say?" Is that anticipation in her voice?

I don't want to read it. Literally the last thing in the world I want to read is this text.

But that might be a lie, because I also really, really want to read this text.

"You honestly want me to read this aloud?"

"Yeah, come on, we have no secrets."

With a heavy sigh, I unlock her phone with the thumbprint she had me program months ago, and read the text.

" 'Hey, Hazel. I've had more time to process the shock of last night.' " I pause, looking up at her. "You sure?"

She cracks an egg into the bowl and nods.

" 'You looked beautiful. I've never used the word radiant, but it kept looping through my head every time you smiled at me.' " I rub my finger below my lower lip. He's right; she did. She looks even more radiant now—I like to think *I* did that. " 'You're different, but still the same untamed wild thing I loved. It nearly hurt to see you because I know I fucked up.' "

Damn it.

"I really think you should read this yourself," I say.

She looks at me, pleading.

I lift my coffee, washing down the fire that bubbles up from my stomach. " 'I said it last night, and I'll say it again today: I walked away from something good, and I would do anything to undo it. Will you give me one more chance?' "

I put her phone down and run a hand down my face. "That's it."

It's a few seconds before she speaks, and in that time I watch her whip the eggs into a frothy peak.

"That wasn't bad, was it?" she asks.

I want to punch the wall. "What are you gonna say?"

She drops the whisk and drags the back of her hand—and another smear of flour—across her forehead. "Josh. He's my ex—*the* Ex—and he's back, trying to fix things. You're *here*. You're shirtless. We had sex again last night, and was it good? Yes, hell yes. But am I right for you? Are we anything? Or are we just friends who bang? What would you say, if you were me? Tell me what to *do*."

I let out a long, controlled breath.

If she felt what I felt, it wouldn't be a question. If Hazel is at all torn about the question of Josh versus Tyler, then it's pretty clear she needs to figure it out before she and I can move forward—if she even wants to. The kitchen clock ticks while we maintain eye contact, and I calculate the odds of this going to complete shit.

She's my best friend, I'm hers.

We've had sex twice.

Amazing sex.

I might be in love with her.

"Josh."

She may, or may not, be in love with me.

Either way, she's not settled yet.

"*Josh.*" Her voice is so thin, it's like blown glass.

I rap my knuckles on her countertop. "If this is where your head is, then I think it's worth giving Tyler another chance."

EIGHTEEN

HAZEL

I realize it's melodramatic, but when Josh leaves that morning, I stare at the closed door for a full fifteen minutes.

I used to wonder what it felt like to stand in the middle of a cyclone, a tornado, at the epicenter of an earthquake. Once or twice, when Tyler had bruised my feelings without any awareness of it, I would think, *These emotions are tiny. Imagine standing right there when the entire Earth rumbles.* I wonder whether what's happening inside me is simply a smaller version of a tropical storm: everything is being blown around and upended.

Being near Josh feels like landing after a yearlong flight—arms flapping, energy depleted. The feelings I have for him have become so enormous, they're nearly debilitating. They terrify me, and make it clear that whatever I felt for Tyler six years ago was like a drop in a bucket; last night with Josh was a tidal wave.

But I honestly don't know if I want a tidal wave. Mom says she wishes she had one; I'm not so sure we're tidal wave kind of women.

Tyler wants another chance, and Josh thinks I should give it to him. That seems to be what everyone else would do—what *normal* people would do. My gut isn't totally on board, but without any experience in this degree of emotional combustion, my internal barometer feels unbalanced. I just don't know what the right answer is.

So I straighten my shoulders, kiss Winnie for good luck, pray to Daniel Craig for wisdom, and reply to Tyler's text.

> I think we have a lot to talk about.
> Come over for dinner on Friday.

....

Tyler shows up at my doorstep holding a piece of paper and two bottles of red wine. It would be easier for all involved if we went out to dinner, but if he really wants to redeem himself, he can eat my cooking and endure the car wreck that takes place while I do it. If that doesn't test a person's constitution, nothing will.

As soon as he steps into my apartment, he seems to crowd

everything out of the space, looking around, nodding as if it's what he expected before turning to me with a smile and the offered gifts.

I stare at the bottles of wine he's put in my hands, admittedly confused. "Is this all for me?"

"We can share it."

Pausing, I'm not sure if my question qualifies as Horrible Things That Slip Out of Hazel's Mouth, but I go for it. "So, you're *not* in recovery?"

With an easy laugh, he nods. "I don't drink in bars anymore. I just drink at home. It's cool."

". . . Oh."

"Nice place, *wow*." Tyler nods, impressed, and I have to follow his attention around the space to figure out what he's seeing. Although I cleaned, my apartment just isn't that much to look at, not really.

But he is being nice. There's something to be said for that, after all.

A tiny voice reminds me that Josh didn't bother to blow smoke up my butt and tell me what a lovely place I had. He never lies, or fakes enthusiasm. He just accepts me.

Why am I comparing Tyler to Josh Im right now?

Probably the same reason I've been thinking about Josh Im for the past week.

Winnie comes up, gives Tyler a cursory sniff, and proceeds to look at me like I'm a trollop and a traitor. Unimpressed, she returns to where she was curled up by the window. Vodka squawks once and then tucks his head under a wing. The fish doesn't even spare him a glance. The only thing I get from my animal family is a resounding *meh*, and although Tyler looks awesome in black jeans, his Chucks, and a tight black T-shirt, I can't help but think my animals are comparing him to Josh Im, too.

With a deep breath, I push all that aside. I've decided I'll give him another chance, and comparing him to the blueprint for Perfect isn't any way to do that.

So, here we are.

I've attempted lasagna for our dinner, but when Tyler follows me into the kitchen to open the wine, I see the room through his eyes: it looks like a massacre happened in here.

"Wow. What're we having?"

"Road kill?" I say, grinning.

He laughs, and surprises me by bending to kiss my forehead. "Should I get you some wine?"

My stomach does a weird tilt. I don't feel like drinking with Tyler; I don't want to get loose and comfortable and fall back into old patterns. But I don't want to be rude, either. "Sure."

The cork squeaks in the bottle as he opens it. "The entire way over," he says, "I was remembering that time we went to see *The Crying Game* at the old dollar theater and you got into a shoving match with the dude behind us who used the word *faggot*."

It takes me a few seconds to remember this one, but then it comes back with startling clarity. The redneck who ruined the end for those of us who hadn't seen it years earlier.

"Oh. Yeah, he was lame."

"God, those were good old days."

I nod, disagreeing internally as I watch him pour two enormous glasses of Shiraz. He hands me the hulking dose and raises his glass in a toast. "To old loves and new beginnings."

I let out a deflated "Cheers," lifting my glass and letting the liquid touch my lips. The toast feels so cheesy and overbaked, I half wish Josh were here to give me a knowing eye roll over the rim of his own wineglass. Josh is a wonder when he's serving his parents a drink; I love to watch the way he pours with both hands, the way he reverently accepts a drink in return just the same way.

The wine tastes a little off to me, so I put it down under the guise of needing to check the lasagna, and start the salad.

Dinner comes out pretty well. The cheese is bubbly and nicely browned, the salad came from a bag so it was impossible to mess it up, and the garlic bread required nothing more than to be pulled out of the freezer and dropped in the oven for twenty minutes. The Barefoot Contessa I am not, but I didn't burn anything and for that I am giving myself a mighty mental high five.

My brain whirs continually while Tyler talks about his job, his apartment, and the friends he's still in touch with from college. Am I really doing this? Having a date, at my apartment, with Tyler Douchebag Jones? Is this what it's come to?

I have honestly never spent as much time thinking about my love life as I have in the past few days. I'm not an idiot. I know that my feelings for Josh Im go beyond the friend zone—hello, we had orbit-bending sex only one week ago— but whenever I imagine trying to *date* him, I get this panicky feeling in my chest and have to stick my head out the window or unbutton my shirt. The thought of dating him and having him ever say that I'm weird or embarrassing makes everything inside me duck for cover. Sex I can do. But baring my emotional soul to Josh and watching his proverbial lip curl in distaste? *Gah.*

I think about Mom, and the way she reacted to Dad when he said those four words to her—*you're so fucking embarrassing*—and how it didn't seem to faze her at all. I used to think it was because she was so strong and was able to hide her pain, but now I know that it's because his opinion didn't matter. She didn't love him.

And whether I love Josh as a friend or more, I *do* love him. Deeply.

". . . so I took it to another shop," Tyler is saying loudly, as if he knows I've spaced out and is turning up the volume to get my attention back where he wants it, "and the guy there agreed with me. Fucking timing belt. Who misdiagnoses a *timing belt*?"

"Right?" I say, giving what I hope is the appropriate degree of disbelief on his behalf. I add an indignant scowl at my plate, pushing the lasagna around a little. It looked so good coming out of the oven, but right now nothing has ever seemed so unappetizing. I wonder whether it'd be cool with Tyler if I just busted out some Cap'n Crunch for my dinner instead.

"So anyway," he says, "that's why I had no flowers."

I look up. "Huh?"

"To bring you," he says, leaning in and cupping a hand around my forearm. "I gave you a drawing of flowers? At the door?"

He did? "Right, right. It was so pretty, though."

He ducks, smiles humbly. "Well, I wanted to bring actual flowers, and wine. Do the romantic thing."

The romantic thing. To Tyler, that used to be a six-pack of PBR and the promise of some good ol' fuckin' later. I wonder if it's still true, and he's just upped his seduction tangibles a little. I push back from the table and out of his reach. "That's so nice. You know I've never needed flowers."

"No one *needs* flowers." Grabbing his plate, he follows me into the kitchen, rolling up his sleeves like he intends to do the dishes. "But everyone likes them."

Apparently, I'm right. Tyler turns on the water, filling the sink. I notice that he doesn't get the water particularly hot before plugging the drain and filling it, and I mentally cover

Josh's eyes so he doesn't have to watch such blatant disregard for proper cleaning technique.

"So tell me something about yourself," Tyler says, reaching for my plate. He frowns at it before scraping the entirety of my lasagna helping into the trash. "Something that's happened in the past few years." He's been here over an hour and this is the first question that's been directed to me.

I lean against the counter, watching him.

He might be somewhat clueless, but he sure is pretty from behind. And from the front, too.

And he's here, trying. Washing dishes, making conversation. My stomach feels like a houseboat on a rolling river and if I could just calm the hell down, I might actually enjoy his company.

"Well, you know I'm a teacher."

"Yup. Fourth grade?"

"Third." I reach for my wine, sniff it, and decide against it again. "This is my first year at Riverview. Let's see . . . what else. My mom lives in Portland now."

"Moved from Eugene, right?"

Okay. Maybe not so clueless after all. "Yeah." A tiny flicker of light ignites in my chest. He remembers things about me. Things completely unrelated to my cup size or erogenous zones. "My closest friend here is a woman named Emily—"

"Josh's sister? I think he mentioned her at dinner."

I allow myself a mental knee-slapping laugh. Josh probably mentioned a lot of things that I missed entirely during my mental meltdown. "Yeah, good memory. And she's married to our principal, this sequoia of a man named Dave, who—I swear to you—makes the best barbecue this side of the Mississippi."

"That sounds awesome."

"I mean, I'll admit that I've never been east of the Mississippi, nor have I sampled barbecue at all that many places, but Dave makes good food."

Tyler laughs at this. "Maybe we can have dinner over there sometime."

And just like that, just when I'd been starting to relax, something tenses inside me again. The idea of sitting next to Tyler at Emily and Dave's dinner table feels dirty. I imagine Josh across from us, sitting beside Sasha, and then I imagine throwing a sauce-slathered rib at him. In my head, it lands with a dark splat on his pristine work shirt and he glares at me.

I mumble a belated "Sure" before making a cabinet dive for the Cap'n Crunch.

Shoving a hand into the box, I continue, "You know, I've got animal family in town as well. You've met Winnie the Poodle, Vodka, Janis Hoplin, and Daniel Craig."

Tyler looks at me over his shoulder and I answer the question in his eyes, "Sorry. My fish. Daniel Craig." Another question lingers there, and I answer that one, too: "Daniel Craig is a fitting homage. My fish has got a great tail."

I catch the amused smirk just before he turns back to the sink.

Maybe it *is* different this time. Maybe Tyler really has grown up, and maybe that makes it okay that I never will.

....

When the doorbell rings, Tyler is halfway through the second bottle of wine. The single glass he poured me earlier sits mostly untouched on the kitchen counter.

He turns toward the sound. "Did you call me a cab?" he jokes, voice low and slow. "I thought I'd stay here tonight."

The awkward laugh that comes out of me sounds like a cyborg malfunctioning, and I stand to answer. Up until now, we've been having a genuinely good time—I mean, not *I'm gonna get some* good time, but it's been nice. Yes, there's a lot of Glory Days reminiscing on his part, but I'm surprised to find that Tyler remembers things pretty accurately, and with not a lot of reimagined glossing.

I'm also surprised to find Josh and Sasha standing at the door. She's got all her hair in a bun that looks like it could house a family of eagles, and is holding another bottle of wine. In Josh's fist there's a small bouquet of sunflowers.

"Hey!" Sasha smooches my cheek before pushing past me into the apartment. She sees Tyler there. "What a coincidence! Double date, take two!"

I look up at Josh, who is busy studying Tyler's long frame

sprawled familiarly on one end of my couch. Although we text almost constantly, I haven't seen him all week, not since he left my apartment after we . . .

My chest seems to fill with helium.

"Hey," I say. Josh blinks, refocusing his attention on me. "What's going on, date crasher?"

He gives a little shrug. "Guess I forgot he was coming over tonight."

Winnie barrels down the hall at the sound of his voice, running to the door.

"And you thought I'd make a swell third wheel to your hot date?"

"I thought you might want company?" he offers instead, reaching down to scratch behind Winnie's ears.

Even though the idea of this makes me feel all glowy, I wonder if I reject this explanation whether he'll keep cycling through them until he lands on something that lets him past the doorway.

I give it a whirl. "Try again."

"We had extra wine and wanted to share."

"No."

"I haven't had dinner, and smelled the delicious lasagna."

I am a terrible cook and Josh knows it. "That's the worst one yet, Jimin."

He shoves the flowers at me. "You like sunflowers."

My heart beams, and I step back, letting him in. He stops

just inside to toe off his shoes, and says under his breath, "Unless you'd prefer to keep things . . . *private* tonight."

Tires screech to a halt in my head when he says this—so tight, almost probing. Does Josh really think I would have sex with him a week ago and then bang Tyler tonight? I mean, I haven't even changed my sheets yet.

Which I probably shouldn't tell Josh. He would be horrified.

"We're having a nice time," I say, "but I'm happy to see you." It seems like the best way to wipe the protective worry off his face, and also let him know that it's pretty awesome that he's come by because no way am I letting Tyler Jones *inside* inside tonight.

But a cloud passes over Josh's face just before half of his mouth smiles. "Well . . . good."

I hear a cork pop in the kitchen, and the *glug-glug-glug* of a hearty glass of wine being poured. "Haze," Sasha calls, and Josh and I exchange a brief look at her unauthorized use of my nickname, "do you want some wine?"

"I've got some on the counter, I'm good."

"She's been nursing that same glass for three hours," Tyler grouses. "You may as well pour her a new one."

"On a Friday? That doesn't sound like her." Josh moves past me to take off his coat and hang it on the wall, with a lovesick labradoodle right on his heels. Even Vodka is sitting up straighter. "Usually by this point in the night, she's two bottles in and designing a saddle for Winnie out of cereal boxes."

From the couch, Tyler lets out a bro-y, "*Right?*"

I pinch Josh's bicep in bratty retaliation, and then give it an appreciative stroke because he seems extra buff under my hand. To cover the shiver that runs through me, I let out a playful, "Ooh. You're all flexed and beefy tonight."

He slaps my hand away. "Pervert."

"Did you do pre-date push-ups?"

"No."

"This muscle tone is all just from jerking off, then? Wow."

He flicks my ear, hard, and our eyes snag for

one

I need to come.

two

I need to come.

three seconds

He gives a dark half smile. "I hit the gym a lot this week."

Holy shit. The entire duration of our banging flashes through my eyes when he says this, his voice all low and growly.

We were sober last Friday.

We had intentional sex.

Oh my God, *I know Josh Im's sex sounds.*

Josh's eyes go to my neck, my cheeks, and his eyes widen a little so I know the heat I'm feeling beneath my skin is visible to him. "Haze . . ."

"What are you two talking about?" We startle into awareness as Sasha sashays into the living room with a veritable fishbowl of wine cupped in her hand and takes half of it down in a few long swallows. Both Josh and Tyler watch this with interest.

"Nothing," Josh and I mumble in unison.

Sasha indelicately wipes the back of her hand across her mouth in a move that earns her about seventy Fun Points and then lets out a long *Ahhhhhhhh* afterward, earning her another twenty.

"Thirsty?" Tyler asks. His tone surprises me; for the first time tonight, it's bordering on dickish. I wouldn't blame him for being a little irked at the date crashers if he thought he stood a shot at getting laid.

But Sasha doesn't even seem to realize he's spoken. "Josh took me to the cutest little play earlier."

Something inside pinches my left lung, and I rub my rib to ease it. "Yeah? Which one?"

"It was an all-female production of *King Lear.*"

Tyler feigns snoring, but I look over at Josh, trying madly to stifle my genuine hurt. "You saw it without me?"

A panicky shine comes into his eyes. "I wasn't sure you— Zach had two extra—and Sasha was free—"

"It's fine." I quickly tuck my little pout away because I can tell from the look on his face that he feels sincerely guilty.

He settles in a chair across from Tyler, mouths *Sorry* to me again, and gives a covert, wide-eyed glance at Sasha as she rounds the couch, as if to say to me, *I didn't know what else to possibly do with her!*

At least, that's how I'm choosing to interpret it.

"What about you guys?" Sasha plops down next to the mostly prone Tyler, jostling the glass of wine balanced on his chest. He lifts it to avert a spill, and uses the opportunity to pull a few long swigs into his mouth. I take a seat on the arm of the couch.

"Craze made dinner," he says, and then burps into his fist. Josh and I exchange a brief confused-by-this-nickname glance, and his eyes narrow a fraction of a second before Tyler reaches up and slides his burp hand into the hair at the back of my head, massaging. "Lasagna. We're just chilling at home, catching up."

At this, Josh's left eyebrow arches significantly and I cut in quickly, rolling over Tyler's awkward use of *home* with a bursting "I also made garlic bread and a bag of salad!"

Knowing exactly what I'm trying to distract him from, Josh turns his full attention to me. I see it in his face: *So this is a thing then, huh? You and Tyler? Hangin' at 'home'? Ripping bags of salad open for your man?*

I return the glare, trying to convey my thoughts right back to him. *Did I misunderstand you the other day? Didn't you want me to explore this with Tyler? Or was that a way to get me to stop inviting you into my vagina? It's just dinner, anyway!*

Will you be driving him to his AA meeting later, as well?

Maybe!

He's still staring at me, but his expression has morphed from that perplexing possessiveness into amusement, as if he is enjoying my obvious mental bender. I scowl at him, and he laughs.

"So, hey," Sasha says, draining her glass and standing, presumably to get another. "I have these tickets to Harvest Fest. Four, actually."

Tyler bolts up, eyes wide. They are very bloodshot. "Seriously? We should totally all go."

Josh stills with his bottle of water against his lips. "What's Harvest Fest?"

"An all-day concert at Tom McCall Park," Sasha says and adds more slowly, as if this hasn't yet been enough to clear it up for Josh, "A *music* festival."

Tyler looks at each of us, surprised that he doesn't have immediate consensus. "Dude. *Metallica* will be there."

Sasha gives a smug nod. "Yup. We could totally all go together."

I mentally stab a fork through my eye.

Tyler wipes an incredulous hand over his mouth before exhaling a reverent "Limp *Bizkit*, dude."

Across the room, Josh lets out a tiny whimper of pain.

I scratch an eyebrow. "Are we going to be the youngest people there?"

Josh guffaws at this, but I give him a skeptical eye roll. He doesn't get to play cool kid here. This is a man whose car radio seems glued to *KQAC, All Classical Portland*.

"Oh, there's way more than that," Sasha says from the kitchen, raising her voice against the *glug-glug-glug* of the wine bottle. Her words and the glugging are followed by the cacophonous crash of the empty bottle into the recycling bin. Two glasses. She took down a bottle of wine in two glasses. I can't decide if this is impressive or concerning. "Three Days Grace, Simple Plan . . ."

Josh and I exchange pained looks again.

"My Chemical Romance," Tyler says, having looked it up on his phone. "Three Days Grace—"

Sasha waves a hand, swallowing a sip of wine. "I said that one already."

"I'm just reading the list." Tyler turns back to his phone. "Um, oh! Julian Casablancas will be there. And Jack White." He looks up at me and I admit, the last two have fluffed my interest somewhat. "Outdoors. Lots of happy people." He pauses, and smirks at me. "Hippies everywhere, dancing with their eyes closed."

My interest is officially piqued. From across the room, I can see Josh's shoulders slump in resignation.

"We're in," I tell them.

NINETEEN

JOSH

*D*ave has the exact response I expect when I mention that we're headed to Harvest Fest on Sunday: "What's Harvest Fest?"

"See?" I slap my hand down on the table and look at Hazel, who seems primarily interested in arranging the long grains of her wild rice into even rows. "Even Dave doesn't know what this is, and he knows music stuff." I look over at him, explaining, "It's some all-day concert with a bunch of bands from the nineties and early two thousands."

"Oh, okay." He takes a bite of his dinner, chews, and swallows. "Actually, now that you mention it, I did know about it. I just didn't . . . care."

I smirk at Hazel, whose response is to turn and try to engage me in a staring contest. I cup my hand over her eyes and look away.

"Who's going?" Dave asks.

"Hazel, me, Sasha, and Tyler."

"Tyler again, huh?" Emily asks, and her tone makes me go limp all over. I drop my hand from Hazel's face.

She blinks across the table at my sister. "Yeah. He's probably more excited about it than any of us."

A strand of her hair catches on her lip, and I reach to free it, but she beats me to it. I find myself pulling my hand back, awkwardly and abruptly. Emily catches my eye across the table, and I offer her a little *whatever* shrug before looking away and reaching for the enormous platter of meat Dave has grilled for us.

My pulse is like gunfire. Quite frankly, I don't think Hazel is all that into Tyler, but the fact that she's giving him this much of a chance makes me think she's not all that into me, either. I just hope we've put an end to this friends-who-sleep-together thing early enough that I won't be the guy pining after her for the rest of our lives.

"Tyler and Sasha, episode three." Dave looks directly at me. "So, it sounds like you guys are done with the blind date experiment for a while?"

With effort, I avoid looking over at Hazel. "Oh, for sure we are," I say.

In my peripheral vision, I can see her poking at her plate. She's not eating a ton, and hasn't touched the margarita in front of her. Aside from basically anything my mom makes her, Dave's carne asada is her favorite food in the world. Usually she eats it as though she's restraining herself from shoving it into her mouth by the fistful. "You feeling okay?"

Startling a little, she looks up. "Yeah. I'm good. I was just thinking about what Dave said. I'm sort of sad to think we're not going to be doing any more double blind dates."

"Really?" I rear back in playful shock. "You actually enjoyed that string of disasters?"

Hazel shrugs, and her enormous brown eyes meet mine. "I like hanging out with you."

Emily kicks me, hard, under the table, and Dave's foot reaches diagonally across and steps on mine. I kick at them both, and Emily lets out a little yelp.

"We can still hang out, goober."

"I know." She picks up her margarita, licks some salt off the rim, and then puts it down again. "But it was like we were having *adventures*."

"*Terrible* adventures," Emily reminds her.

"Terrible adventures that *never* ended in sex," Dave adds with triumphant emphasis, and the table falls into a nuclear-winter-level silence. "Well," he amends, "except for that one time."

Hazel peeks at me and I have to take a long swig of my water to keep from coughing.

Emily plants her elbows on the table, leaning in. "Was there *another* time?"

My smile straightens at her judgmental tone. "Can I remind you that my sex life isn't your business?"

"If I remember correctly, *I* wasn't the one bringing it up at the *front door* a few weeks back."

"That was me," Hazel agrees, "and only because I am constitutionally incapable of keeping my mouth shut."

Dave looks like he wants to take a good swing at that one, but wisely keeps it restrained to a gleeful gleam in his eyes when he looks at me.

"You guys really slept together again?" Emily asks.

I look over at her, replying quietly, in Korean. "Ten seconds later, and it still isn't your business, Yujin."

She purses her lips but lets it go.

....

When we climb out of Tyler's Jeep in the parking lot on Sunday, it seems as if everyone around us is still recovering from whatever debauchery they took part in the night before. There are a lot of man buns, plaid shirts tied around waists, beards, and artfully distressed jeans.

It's also barely ten in the morning, and everyone I see milling about on the lawn has a beer in their hand. On the distant stage, a pair of roadies strum a few echoing chords before switching guitars for the sound check, and the scattered crowd rustles nearby, beginning to press forward. Sasha packed a picnic of what I imagine is something like bulgur and tofu wrapped in grape leaves, or hemp tortillas stuffed with tempeh, but she looks really happy carrying the basket over her arm so I'll eat some to be a good sport and then get a giant hot dog with Hazel from one of the vendors. Sasha's also left her hair down . . . I've never seen it all, and it completely freaks me out. It's *really* long—as in several inches past her butt long—and with her window down for most of the drive, her hair ended up crawling all over me. When I closed my eyes to try not to freak out about it, it wasn't any better; it was like being pushed in a wheelchair through a room of cobwebs. I can now definitively check the *no* box regarding hair fetish.

This is just as well, because there is zero chemistry between us, and it doesn't seem to bother her, either. We haven't kissed, we haven't really even flirted. I'm not really sure why we went out on Friday. It was almost like . . . well, Hazel was having Tyler over for dinner, I may as well take Sasha out, too. The fact that I took her to see *King Lear* when I knew that Hazel wanted to see it was actually unintentional—I'd just spaced about it—but in hindsight I wonder whether my subconscious was stabbing little holes in the Hazel kite.

Beside me, Hazel is carrying a small pile of blankets in her arms. Her perfect-kind-of-long hair is still wet, and twisted up in two side buns high on her head. She smells like some kind of flower I'm sure grows in my mother's garden every spring, and the scent has me feeling both nostalgic and queasily lovesick.

We reach a stretch of grass, and it looked so much nicer at a distance. Up close, it's patchy and muddy. Sasha heads out to locate the bathrooms, and Hazel gamely spreads the blankets over the threadbare ground, gestures for me to take a seat, and then promptly kicks off her shoes and jogs a little in place.

"I forgot how much I love these things!"

"Outdoor events with day-drunk, aging Gen Xers?" I ask.

She smacks my shoulder and then turns, bouncing, throwing her arms up in a distractingly catlike stretch. I glance at Tyler as he watches Hazel sway to nothing but voices and the crowd shifting around us. His attention goes from her to the groups in our immediate proximity, some of whom are watching her with curious looks. And then he looks back to her, eyes tight.

"Come sit by me, Craze."

Irritation shoves the words out of me: "I'm not sure that's a great nickname, *Ty*."

Tyler—I've known him at the gym for a few years now. He's always seemed like a good guy, usually smiling, helps spot anyone who needs it. But right now, he's looking at me like he sees every seductive thought I have about the woman dancing before us and he's figuring out how he can pull my brain out through my nostrils.

"Well, it's my nickname for her, *Josh*."

"Always?"

He shrugs. "Starting now."

I can't help but push. "What did you call her in college?"

Tyler smirks. " 'Babe.' "

Well, I guess I can understand why he'd want to go for something more original this time around.

"Because that's what she *was*," he says, looking me up and down a little now, appraising what he must realize is the competition. How did he not see it before? Hazel and I are together all the time. "She was my babe."

With impeccable timing, Hazel turns and plops down cross-legged in front of us. "Who was your babe?"

Tyler scratches his jaw, fidgeting. "You."

Her frown is immediate. "I was your *babe*?"

I lean back on my hands, grinning at them both.

"I was just telling Josh, that's what I called you in college," he clarifies.

"You did?"

God, this is so deliciously awkward. He glances at me, huffing a little. "Yeah. Remember?"

She screws up her nose, and then looks at me, gauging my reaction. The realization that she always looks to me, for solidarity, for my opinion, for reassurance, lights a fuse in me, and it's honestly all I can do to keep from leaning forward and kissing her in front of him.

The roadies clear the stage closest to us, and cheers rise like a wave across the park. My phone buzzes at my hip with a text from Sasha. "Sasha says she found some friends down in the pit and is going to hang there if anyone wants to join her."

"Who's opening?" Hazel asks Tyler.

He blinks blankly at her for a beat, and then smiles patiently. "*Metallica.*"

"They're opening? I thought they were headlining."

Tyler's wince makes me want to giggle. "No, they're getting it started."

"I don't think I can handle that much body slamming at ten in the morning," she says, with a genuine smile back.

With a look to me, and then a look to her, he pushes up and lopes off to meet Sasha down near the stage.

....

As soon as he's gone, we both flop back on the grass and stare up at the churning clouds overhead.

"It might rain," I say.

"That cloud looks like a turtle."

I follow where she's pointing. "It looks like a bowl of popcorn to me."

She responds to this with a simple "I feel like you and Tyler don't like each other anymore."

Rolling my head to the side to look at her, I say, "What makes you think that?"

"There was some testosterone-y thing happening just now."

"About him calling you 'babe'?" I look back at the sky. "I don't know, I think 'babe' is the world's lamest nickname."

That might be hyperbole; I just really don't like Tyler today.

"You never called anyone 'babe'? Not even Tabby?"

"Not even Tabby."

She makes a little thoughtful noise next to me and then falls quiet.

"Did you have fun on your date the other night?" I ask.

I can hear her grin when she says, "You mean, before you showed up?"

"Yeah."

"It was okay. I wasn't feeling great, and he really loves to reminisce about Ye Olden Days, but it seems like he's trying so hard, I don't really want to dog him."

When I don't reply, she adds, "I think you're right that it's worth giving him another chance."

The air around me goes still. "When did I tell you to give him another chance?"

Her neck flushes and she looks at me, brow furrowed. "The morning after . . . the last time we . . . You said to give him another chance."

Pushing up onto an elbow, I stare down at her. "I said if it's where your head is, then it's worth giving him another chance. It was about *you*, and what you need to explore, not about him and what he deserves or what *I* think you should do."

She absorbs this for a few quiet breaths before turning away. "The weird thing about our dating game was that it's left me feeling like I need to come out of this with someone at the end."

I stare down at her, at the few strands of hair that have come free of the buns, and the way I can tell she didn't bother putting on makeup this morning and she still looks stunning.

"I think we both know that's bull."

She nods. "I know. But it's a feeling."

"And even if it were true, it doesn't have to be Tyler," I remind her.

She turns back to me again, and her gaze drags across my mouth. "No. It doesn't have to be Tyler."

TWENTY

HAZEL

We're quiet during the first few songs of the Metallica set. In fact, we're so quiet, I wonder whether Josh has fallen asleep beside me. I've been people-watching, but neither of us has been paying any particular attention to the actual show. When I peek at him, I see that he's awake, and just staring thoughtfully up at the sky.

"Don't ask me what I'm thinking," he says, grinning over at me when he sees me looking at him.

"I wasn't going to!"

"You totally were."

He's right. I was. I lie down on my side and prop my head on my hand to study him. This is the perfect light for photographs: muted but bright, with vibrant green all around us. I'm tempted to pull my phone out of my bag and take a picture of his profile. I love the smooth, straight line of his nose, the powerful curve of his cheekbones, the geometry of his jawline.

"You're staring."

I love your face, I think. I tap his temple with my index finger. "I just like knowing what's going on in that brain of yours."

He shrugs, and adjusts his hands where they're crossed over his stomach. "I was wondering what Sasha packed in the lunch basket."

"Are you hungry?" I ask.

"I will be eventually, and was thinking I might want to figure out where the hot dogs are instead."

Laughing, I push up and crawl over him to peek. "She's got apples, celery with peanut butter, and what looks like some sort of wheat berry salad. No sandwiches or like . . . food."

He doesn't respond to this at all, and given that he's craving a hot dog, I'm pretty sure he'll find no satisfaction in this basket. I look down at him from where I'm propped on all fours, and realize that he's staring directly down my shirt.

"Are you looking at my boobs?"

His eyes move from my chest to my face, and instead of wisecracking or making a joke about how he forgot to bring tape and staples to keep my shirt on later when I'm drinking beer, he just closes his eyes and sighs.

It looks like defeat, or frustration, or something similar to the uncomfortable yearning that's pressing tight against my breastbone. It feels like there's a pile of bricks on my chest. I want to bend down and just put my mouth on his.

With a tiny whimper, I imagine the relief of that, of kissing him outside, of how he might slide his hands to my face, cupping me and holding me there. For some reason, I don't think he'd turn away. I stare down at Josh, with his eyes closed, and imagine straddling him, feeling him tense beneath me, teasing him where we can't do anything about it.

Those are boyfriend things. These are girlfriend feelings.

I'm Josh's girlfriend, whether he wants me or not.

I curl back up next to him. "Josh."

Slowly, so slowly, he opens his eyes and turns his head to see me. "Yeah?"

Voices rise and I look up to see Sasha and Tyler stomping toward our blankets, grinning, sweaty, breathless. They tumble down beside us, chests heaving.

The quiet intimacy between Josh and me dissolves into a mist.

"Holy shit," Tyler says. "That was epic."

A tiny ripple of guilt works its way through me. I wasn't paying any attention to the band, even though I knew how excited Tyler was to see them. I feel like I'm doing everything just a tiny bit wrong today.

I sit up and lean over to squeeze his hand, impulsively. "I'm so glad you had a good time down there."

Josh pushes to stand. "I'm going to get a beer. Anyone else want something? Tyler? Beer?"

"I don't drink," Tyler reminds him.

Josh barks out a laughing "Okay" before turning.

Sasha follows him, and he doesn't even look at me before he's marching down the small hill toward the bank of vendor booths to the right of the stage.

"Can I ask you something?" Tyler says, sitting up.

Unease swirls in my belly. "Sure."

"Did you and Josh ever . . . ?"

"Ever what?"

"Date?"

"Each other?"

He nods, and I shift, reasoning that it's not exactly a lie. "No. We never dated each other."

"It sometimes seems like there's more going on with you two."

And honestly, the only way to avoid this conversation is to stand when System of a Down comes on, and pretend I am very, very excited to hear all of their songs that I'm not even sure I know. I close my eyes, and for just fifteen minutes, I try to push out all of these emotions.

I dance away the feeling that I'm trying to talk myself into being attracted to Tyler.

I dance away the feeling that I'm in love with Josh, and am prolonging his rejection because I know it will slaughter me.

I dance away the feeling that I'm putting way too much of my energy into this, when I should be just enjoying my day, and the air, and the music.

I spin, and spin, and it's so fucking *fun*, I haven't had this kind of fun in forever, just dancing like a maniac. The air is cold on my bare arms when I toss away my sweater and I'm aware that most people on the lawn are sitting, but if they knew how good it felt to let it all out and dance like this—arms out, hips rocking, the grass cold and wet underfoot—they would be up here doing the exact same—

"*Hazel.*"

I turn and look at Tyler behind me on the grass. "Come dance!"

I reach out for him but he laughs uncomfortably, and then looks to the side, to the family on a blanket near us, who are watching us with smiles.

"Just—come sit here." He pats the blanket next to him.

"I'm dancing!"

Tyler leans in. "You're . . . being sort of embarrassing."

It falls flatly, with a clang, like a penny into an empty bucket.

So this is what it feels like.

My smile doesn't even break, and I laugh out an incredulous, "*What?*"

He stands, coming closer. "You're like the only person dancing up here. Just come sit and talk to me."

Finally, my feet stop moving. "Please tell me you're not that guy right now."

"What guy?"

"The guy you've always been, who wants me to be quirky

but not weird, who wants me to dance only when other people are dancing, who likes telling all the stories about me but doesn't remember how much he bitched about each of those moments when it happened."

His expression falls. "I'm not trying to do that. You're just—"

A fire is lit beneath my breastbone. "Just having fun?"

Grimacing, he shrugs. "Do you have to be so *out there* all the time? Can't we just hang?"

"We are hanging!"

He looks around. "It's just that some people were looking, and I didn't want you to be embarrassed."

"*I'm* not embarrassed."

"Hazel doesn't get embarrassed," Josh says from behind me with a laugh. But his smile falls when I turn to him, and he sees the expression on my face. "Whoa, what did I miss?"

"Hazel was *dancing*," Tyler says, leaning into the word like he knows Josh will Get It.

Josh, however, does not Get It. "And?"

"And . . . come on." He looks to Sasha now, but she is similarly unswayed.

She piles her eighty feet of hair on her head and rests her hands there. "You were dancing in the pit like fifteen minutes ago."

"But it's the *pit*," Tyler reasons, losing steam.

"Fuck off, Tyler," I say, and then I notice it: the baseball hat on Josh's head. The sight of it temporarily wipes clear my irritation. It's a bright orange-yellow—I mean, a nearly blinding color—with giant black block letters across the entire front: CHEESY.

And I don't know why, but it just makes me burst out laughing.

"Where did you get this?"

Josh breaks his stern attention from Tyler to pull the hat off his head and put it on mine. "I saw it and I thought it would make you laugh." Josh's eyes soften, and he gives me such an adoring smile, it's nearly painful. "You look ridiculous in that. I hope you wear it all day."

....

"So, back up. Josh gave you a hat and that's when you decided you're in love with him?"

I drop an avocado into my shopping basket and growl at Emily. It's a school holiday and I seem to be fighting some kind of stomach bug, so I talked her into joining me for a little morning grocery shopping. Maybe a little *too* early, judging by her expression. "Are you paying attention?"

"I think so, but my brain is also still spiraling from the first words out of your mouth a half hour ago."

She has a fair point. The first thing I said when she climbed into Giuseppe the Saturn was "I'm in love with your brother, and I need you to tell me whether I've got a chance."

Emily went silent for about ten openmouthed seconds before demanding that I start at the beginning.

But what is the beginning?

Is the beginning when I first saw Josh at a party ten years ago and there was something about him that just . . . sang to me? Or is the beginning when he came over and we made clay and we discovered that Tabby was cheating on him?

Or is the beginning the drunken night on my floor, or the sober, sleepy, tender night in my bed?

It's only been six months since we started hanging out, but already it feels like he's this redwood in the forest of my life, and so *starting at the beginning* is bewildering.

I started with the night he brought Tyler to Tasty n Sons. She knew a lot of this already—how thrown I'd been, how conflicted. Of course, now I know I was conflicted because *I'm in motherfucking love with Josh Im*, but at the time it seemed so much more convoluted. And I detailed everything—from my sobfest, to Josh appearing out of thin air, to the night sex, and the morning after, when it felt like my head was filled with cotton balls and Josh told me to give Tyler another chance.

I growl again. "Tyler had just told me how embarrassing I was being, and then Josh walked up with this stupid hat"—I point to it, still perched on my head—"and told me I looked ridiculous and to never take it off. Don't you get it?"

Emily stops near a display of bananas. "Yeah. I get it."

"And? Is Josh going to crush my heart like a grape beneath a boot?"

"You mean," she says carefully, "is Josh in love with you, too?"

I nod. My heart is climbing up from my chest into my throat. I don't think I could get another word out with the question put so plainly in the space between us.

"I know Josh has feelings." She shifts her basket to her other arm. "I know he was trying to figure out what they meant, and where you were with it." Emily winces. "I don't want to give you false hope and tell you that I think he feels the same, because he's been really careful to not be too . . . descriptive of his feelings when he talks to me."

I groan.

"Why don't you ask him?"

"Because I'm a coward?" I say, which I thought was pretty well established already. When she doesn't bite I try again. "Because asking might ruin this."

"Hazie, you know I hate to burst your bubble, but I don't think things are ever going to be the way they were before anyway. You guys have already had sex. *Twice*. *Most* friends don't have sex, period." Frowning, she turns and starts walking again. "Which reminds me, I need to grab some tampons."

The color of the produce in a bin across the aisle goes all wavy at the edges, and the crack near my feet doesn't register until Emily is there, bending to put things back in my basket, looking up at me from where she's kneeling. "Hazel."

"Oh my God." My heart is a fist, punching punching

punching, and a lurching, upside down feeling takes hold of my stomach.

She stands, holding my basket, and I can't focus on her face because my heart is pounding in my eyeballs.

"Are you okay?"

"No." I squeeze my eyes closed, trying to clear the film of panic from the surface. Opening them, I meet Emily's gaze. "I haven't had a period in like . . . two months."

TWENTY-ONE

JOSH

*E*mily and Dave are gone when I drop by with a giant container of kimchi and a twenty-pound bag of rice from Umma. If Hazel thinks I'm a neat freak, I've got nothing on my sister. The immaculate house looks like something out of a magazine spread—decorated simply with a collection of midcentury vintage furniture I know Emily has spent the last ten years carefully cultivating, fresh flowers in vases, and original art and funky light sconces decorating the walls.

But the pristine shine to the counters in the kitchen makes it very easy to spot the note she's left for me.

> J—
> *I'm out. Dave should be home soon. If Umma gave you rice, don't leave it. I don't need any.*
> E.

I smirk, stowing the rice in the pantry anyway, beside four other bags the same size. My rice situation is equally absurd—no way am I taking this back home. When I open the fridge to find room for the kimchi, I have to take out the container of leftover carne asada from Friday night.

A plate of leftovers and a beer later, they're still not home.

Emily is often on my case for not having enough guy friends . . . is this what she means? That I'm sitting at my sister's house, eating leftovers from her fridge and frowning at my watch when they stay out past six on a weeknight?

I call Hazel, but it goes straight to voicemail.

I call Emily—same. Does *everyone* have a life but me?

I know my restlessness is compounded because I'm sitting in my sister's house, and there are signs of her happy marriage everywhere. Photos of her and Dave in Maui in a frame on a side table. A painting Dave did for her when they first met is mounted on a wall in the hallway. Their shoes are neatly lined up side by side on a rack just inside from the garage.

My house is clean, my furniture is nice, but the space is like an echo chamber lately. It's so quiet. I never expected to think this, but I miss having Winnie there, watching her odd twilight mania around five every night when she sprinted through the house excitedly for ten minutes before flopping at my feet.

I miss tripping over shoes every time I walk in the door.

I miss Hazel. I'd buy a lifetime supply of fire extinguishers and eat bad pancakes every day to have her around again.

It could be different than it was before. *We're* different now. She's not just a new friend, she's my best friend. The woman I love. We could have lingering talks over coffee or on a shared pillow, long into the night. She could bring her entire farm of animals, and I would be fine, I think. We could make a home of it.

The thought gives me such an intense pain in my chest that I stand, moving to the sink to wash my dish, and then pace circles around the house. Impulsively, I pull my phone out of my pocket, texting Dave.

> Up for a beer?

> Bailey's taproom in 20?

I send him a thumbs-up and duck into the bathroom before I leave. On the wall, Emily has a framed painting of Umma and Appa's hometown. Lush woods, a small creek beside a house. I wonder how Umma feels about this being stuck in the bathroom.

But when I glance down to flush, my eyes are drawn to the left, to the trash can just beside the sink. Inside it is a messy pile of white plastic sticks.

I think I know what these are.

And I think I know what the blue plus on every single one of them means.

....

It's not your place to say anything.

It's not your place to say anything.

I repeat the mantra my entire drive to Bailey's.

Dave might not know yet that his wife is pregnant. And if he does, and he doesn't mention it, then it's certainly not my place to bring it up.

Oh my God, my sister is pregnant. She's going to be a mom—I'm going to be someone's uncle. I'm almost breathless with how happy it makes me. But there's also something else: a sinking lead ball in my gut. I loathe admitting it, but it's jealousy.

Emily was the first to get married. As the older brother, I took it in stride, reminding myself that we aren't bound to tradition in the same way. My entire family welcomed Dave; the wedding was a blast.

But now she's pregnant, and I'm . . . what? In love with a woman who doesn't know what she wants? Who thinks she's not right for me? I'm not even settled, let alone on my way to starting a family. And my parents aren't getting any younger. I'm flexible about a number of traditions, but I'm unwilling to shrug off the responsibility that parents move in with the eldest son when they're older. Umma wouldn't say anything, but I know it wouldn't be her choice to have me still a bachelor when that happens.

I park outside and lean forward, pressing my forehead to the steering wheel. I'd wanted to meet Dave for a beer to unwind and hang. Now it's loaded with *this*—and we can't even talk about it.

He's already inside and at the bar with a beer in front of him, looking up at the television mounted on the wall. *SportsCenter* is recapping the biggest Oregon football rivalry from Saturday—the U of O Ducks versus the OSU Beavers, and I know without having to look that the Ducks won handily.

"Hey." Dave puts his beer down and claps me on the shoulder when I sit.

"You got here fast."

"The traffic gods were on my side," he says, "and I was intensely motivated by the prospect of beer."

"Bad day?"

"Teachers are out today so I was meeting with a parent." He takes a drink. "It's the job, and I seriously love hanging with the kids all day. It's the rest I could do without. I think your sister went shopping or something."

I nod, and try not to do that thing Em accuses me of where I smile when I'm hiding something. It doesn't help that I feel oddly jittery. Not only am I stressing over the whole being-in-love-with-Hazel situation, I'm still shocked by the sight of all those pregnancy tests. Isn't one sufficient? There had to be at least five in there.

I still can't believe it. I take a second to imagine it all: Emily pregnant, the baby, and who it might resemble. Umma and Appa happily losing their minds as grandparents.

"You seem pensive," Dave says.

I nod, and take a few wasabi peanuts from a bowl between us. "Just digesting the food I ate at your place."

He laughs. "Is work okay?"

I thank the bartender when she deposits my beer in front of me. "Yeah, actually, work is great." And it is. We're talking about hiring another physical therapist to handle the workload. It would bring in more revenue and allow me to take a bit more time off from the practice. I love my job, but I frequently work ten- or eleven-hour days just to make sure I see everyone, and if Hazel and I . . .

I stop the thought before I can take it too far.

"I'm actually wondering whether I need to get a bigger place soon. I was home earlier, and Umma just looks so tiny."

"She does seem to be shrinking." Dave grins when he says this. "But," he says, and then frowns a little, "and I know this bucks tradition, so please ignore me if this comes off as insulting, but you know Em and I would be happy to have them come live with us."

The idea of it makes my heart drop. "Oh, that's okay."

"I mean," he continues, "we probably aren't even going

to have kids, and we have all that space. It seems sort of a waste."

I lift my beer, drinking about half of it in a few long swallows.

So Dave doesn't know that Em is pregnant. And he's not expecting a baby, maybe ever. A protective fire rises in my chest. Is that where Emily is? He thinks she's shopping, but is she really off somewhere freaking out?

I realize I've been silent for an impolite amount of time. "I know what you mean, and I honestly do appreciate that offer, but it's something I've been looking forward to." I try to explain this to Dave without sounding ungrateful *or* dropping the baby bomb. "It's an honor for me to take them."

He nods and opens his mouth to speak, but I need to change the subject quickly. "I think I need to do something about Hazel."

Beside me, Dave goes still. "Like what?"

I take a deep breath. "I'm in love with her. I don't think she's going to see Tyler anymore, so I wonder whether I should tell her."

Dave slowly lifts his beer to his lips, drinks, and swallows. "I mean, yeah, maybe you should talk to her."

This response isn't immediately encouraging. How much does Dave know about this? Why isn't he more shocked? Does he know more about Hazel's feelings than I do? Does Hazel talk to Emily, who then talks to Dave about it?

"Unless you think she's just undecided," I say, probing for

a reaction I can then dissect until I am insane. "I mean, we've had the opportunity to be together, and the last time I tried to approach it, she still seemed conflicted about the whole Tyler thing."

"I don't . . ." Dave starts, and then shakes his head.

I lean infinitesimally closer. "What?"

He seems to be picking his words carefully and I can't decide if he really doesn't know anything, or his eyes keep flicking up to the ceiling because he's really into the architecture. "I don't think she was ever conflicted about Tyler, per se."

I search for the hidden meaning tucked into that handful of words. "I . . . don't know what that means."

He turns to look at me. "Hazel is a wild one."

I'm immediately confused. "Yeah? So?"

This makes him laugh. "So, it's who she *is*. She's just . . . Hazel." He shrugs, and his smile is genuinely adoring. "There's no one like her."

Where is he going with this? "I agree . . ."

"But I get the sense that . . . sometimes Hazel . . . is very aware of how different she is from other women. She's not ever going to change, but she's aware that she's quirky, and a lot to take."

I look on, confused. We're on the same page. "No, I totally agree with you, but what does this have to do with me and Tyler?"

Dave takes another sip of his beer. "From what I can

tell, Hazel has worshipped you—sort of singularly—since college."

The fog clears, and I understand his meaning. "You mean, she's not sure she's right for me."

I've heard her say this before, too.

"That's sort of what I mean," Dave says, nodding side to side. "But I also mean your opinion matters more to her than anyone's. And so if things don't work with Tyler, well, that's to be expected. But if things don't work with you—well, it's obviously because of who she is."

"But I *love* who she is," I say simply.

I'm at the dead end of this alley. I'm in love, and there is absolutely no going back.

Dave finishes his beer and blinks down at the bar for a few beats. When he looks up, his eyes are red-rimmed. "Then you should probably tell her, man."

TWENTY-TWO

HAZEL

*F*or the past twenty-four hours, I've carried around the most precious piece of paper I've ever held. In the pocket of my jeans, it's sure to bend in a thousand places. My purse is a Mary Poppins rabbit hole, so if I put it there, I'm likely to never see it again. In my sweaty palm, I can feel the thin photo paper turning tacky and limp from the handling, but I simply cannot put it down.

I'm obsessing about this ultrasound photo. The moment I put it on the table, or nightstand, or counter, I want to pick it back up and look one more time at the white text on the black borders:

Bradford, Hazel

November 12

9w3d

And then my eyes drop to the object of greatest interest: my tiny sweet blob, a nebulous white figure in a sea of speckled black. Nine weeks and three days and it's already the love of my life.

I press my hand to my stomach, and my pulse lurches to a thundering stampede. The embryo in the photo looks like a gummy bear, curled into a delicate C. *My little monster*, I think. My sweet little monster, with a fluttering heartbeat, little buds for limbs, and who is half me, half Josh Im.

Not my preferred reaction, but nausea rolls up from my stomach. I have just enough time to set down my precious piece of paper and bolt into the bathroom before I'm losing the cracker and three sips of water I've had today. Guess it wasn't a bug after all.

After brushing my teeth—and almost throwing up again—I come back to the kitchen. I've got a text from Josh.

> Are you around tonight?

If I hadn't just tossed my cookies—or crackers, rather—I might have tossed them now. With a trembling hand, I type out a

> Yes.

I stare at the photo again, and my heart feels too full.

After getting a last-minute appointment with my doctor yesterday and doing a blood test, then an in-office ultrasound—where Emily held my clammy hand, and we both cried our faces off when the monster came into clear view—I gave myself twenty-four hours to digest the news, and swore Emily to absolute secrecy.

Her response? "I already texted Dave, and I'm sorry for that. But if you think I'm going to be the one to tell my brother that he knocked up our best friend, you're high."

Today, I called in for a sub at work, and have spent the entire day walking around my neighborhood, staring intermittently at the photo. I'm in love with him.

I'm in love with Josh.

And I'm pregnant.

Yesterday, when I got home I was sweaty and panicky and eventually threw up. Now when I look at the photo, I feel jubilant.

Well, jubilant through whatever weird and exhausting things are going on in my body right now. Dr. Sanders told me not to Google pregnancy—said it's a minefield of panic—and instead she gave me a few pamphlets and recommendations for books to read. But I'm sure every single person she's given that advice to has ignored it similarly. Alas, the internet tells me that it's normal to be tired in the first trimester.

So when Josh knocks on my door, I'm prone on the couch, one leg thrown over the back. All I can manage to do is moan out a zombified "It's open."

Josh steps in, kicking off his shoes. He greets Winnie as she races for him. And just the sight of him in my apartment is such a relief I have to swallow down a sob.

He's carrying flowers and wearing my favorite purple shirt. Pushing to sit up, I become aware that I wasn't expecting Fancy Josh. I'm Dumpy Hazel right now, wearing an old Lewis & Clark T-shirt and paint-splattered cutoffs, with my hair stuffed in a bun under my CHEESY hat.

For some reason—Some reason, ha! *Pregnancy*—I feel my throat go tight again. "Well, you look nice."

Frowning, Josh walks around the couch, sitting next to me, reaching under the hat's brim to put his free hand on my forehead. "You feel okay?"

Now *that* is a million-dollar question. "Yeah."

"You look . . ."

Pregnant? "Dumpy?"

He smiles. "I was going to say 'flushed.' "

If I'm going to tell him I'm carrying his child, it should be easy to start with the smaller admissions. But my words come out hoarse: "It's probably because I'm absurdly happy to see you."

His eyes dip to my lips, and in turn, my gaze shifts down his face, over his nose, to his jaw, cheekbones, and then back to his eyes.

"I'm happy to see you, too." Josh leans forward—he's a little breathless—and presses a kiss to my cheek. I've brushed my teeth but God I hope I don't still smell like barf. "I've been thinking about you all day."

He has? A crack of lightning bolts through my chest.

"Um. Same."

He laughs at this like I might be kidding, and stands, moving to the kitchen to find a vase for the flowers.

"In the oven," I tell him . . . which could mean so, *so* many things right now.

Sound falls away—no doubt Josh has frozen and is silently taking this in—but then the creak of the oven door breaks through the quiet, and I hear a soft "Huh."

"If I put them on top of the fridge," I explain, "Vodka lands on the rims and knocks them over."

He turns on the tap, and I hear water filling the vase. "Makes sense."

But does it? Does it make sense that I put my vases in the oven when it's not in use, so that my parrot doesn't knock them over? These are the things other people might question—but not Josh.

He has never, not once, asked me to be someone I'm not.

When he returns, his hands are free, and he resumes his spot next to me on the couch, pulling my legs into his lap. For the first time in our friendship, as his hands come over my legs, I am intensely conscious of how not-sexy I appear.

I blurt, "I didn't shave today."

His hand runs up my shin anyway. "I don't care."

"I showered, but then . . ." I point to my head, and the hat perched there. "Sort of let it go to seed."

"I don't care what you look like." His hands drift back

down, and strong thumbs dig into the arch of my foot. My eyes cross a little in pleasure.

This is new. This kind of touching, and the tentative awkward smiles. I know why I'm being a bumbling idiot—I'm pregnant and in love—but why is *he*?

"What's up with you?" I ask quietly. "Why are you massaging me and bringing me flowers and looking particularly *adorable*?"

Clearing his throat, he stares down at where his hands work on my feet. "Yeah, about that." He looks up at me. "Are you going out with Tyler again?"

I bark out a laugh. "Negatory."

He nods, and nods, and keeps nodding as his gaze slowly moves back to my legs, up to my hips, torso, chest, and face. "Well, then would you go out with *me* sometime?"

All my life I assumed I had one heart inside my chest. But the force slamming me from the inside can't be only a single organ. I knew he was sufficiently attracted to me to have sex—twice—but to want to go out with me?

"Like a date?"

"Like a date." His hand moves up my shin, over my knee, around to the inside of my thigh, where he strokes maddening circles with his thumb. "But only me and you this time."

And just like that, I'm liquid heat. My heart has vaulted into my throat. "Do you want to stay over tonight?"

Without hesitation, he answers, "Yes."

"I mean, like a naked sleepover."

He leans in until his breath mixes with mine, and he gently pulls off my baseball cap, tossing it to the floor. "I knew what you meant."

His fingers work my hair free from the bun, and he meets my eyes for just a breath before he leans the rest of the way and kisses the wide-eyed shock right off my face.

It's not our first kiss, but in a way it feels like it is. Yes, I know his mouth, but I've never known this emotion before, the careful press, the way his hands come up to my face so he can tilt me how he wants, so he can lean forward while I lean back until he's hovering over me on the couch, his dress pants smooth against the insides of my thighs.

"I need to tell you some things," I say against his lips.

"Me too."

"*Big* things," I emphasize.

He nods. "Let's say all our big things afterward, okay? There's no rush."

I have a pulse of anxiety—I really need to tell him—but the *I'm carrying your baby* talk is a fairly intense conversation and his body seems to agree with the lower half of mine that sex can come first, no problem. Besides, it's not like I can get more pregnant.

My clothes seem to dissolve away as soon as he touches them. I don't actually remember taking my shirt off. My shorts are dragged down my legs.

Our eyes meet and I'm sure he can see the mania in

mine because he smiles and then it turns into a laugh when my mouth falls open as he unbuttons his shirt—too slowly. I start from the bottom, meeting his hands in the middle, and together we push it off his shoulders. They're warm and hard under my hands when I try to tug him back down over me, but he resists, sliding his pants off and kicking them into a puddle on the floor.

"Josh?"

He bends, kissing my neck, humming. "Hazel?"

"Is this a 'Ha ha, we'll just do it *three* times' sort of thing?"

"Not for me," he says, and when his mouth finds my collarbone he scrapes his teeth across it. "For me it's a 'We'll do this again and again' sort of thing." He kisses me once, lightly on the mouth. "I want us to be together. Not just friends. Okay?"

Inside me, there is a fist curling around my heart, squeezing. "Yes."

"But I don't want to do it on the couch."

"Like, ever?"

He presses small kisses to my jaw, my neck, my ear. "Sure, over time we'll christen each piece of furniture, but right now—" He pulls back, lifting his chin toward the bedroom.

I imagine a cartoon dust cloud behind me as I practically sprint there. Josh, of course, takes a calmer approach, and strolls in a few seconds after I've launched myself onto the center of the mattress. My energy level has miraculously recovered.

"I don't want to feel like I'm *dragging* you here," he jokes.

But my smile is only a flash, because it all turns very intense as soon as he puts a knee on the mattress and climbs up my bed, between my legs.

Josh Im.

Josh Im is in my bed, about to get naked, and—from the looks of things—about to fuck me very, very thoroughly.

"I'm worried I might make a lot of noise tonight," I babble, breathless.

"That wouldn't be a bad thing." His hands reduce my focus down to just this: The feel of his fingers dragging my underwear down my legs. The way he stares at me. The warm slide of his palms up over my knees, spreading them as he kneels.

The knotted rope inside begins unfurling, loosening as I wonder whether this pregnancy isn't even a little bit bad. It might be the *best* thing. I imagine tomorrow morning, how he might shuffle out of my bed, still naked, hair standing straight up like a silken forest. I imagine kissing him, getting distracted and forgetting what I was supposed to be doing before I remember again.

The rest of the thought is cut off as his hands slide up and down my legs, tormenting me, pulling that heavy weight low in my belly, making me so hungry for him to touch me that I ache. I push up on an elbow, wanting to retaliate the teasing, and he laughs in a tight, incredulous breath when my fingers come over him, above his boxers. He is hot in my hand, pulsing steel.

"You're so hard." I am a master at stating the obvious.

He watches my hands as I coax the elastic down, but he doesn't do what I expect after he kicks the boxers off. He doesn't rise over me and settle between my legs. He ducks lower, kissing the inside of each knee, up my thigh and then down the other. His breath is hot when he comes up again— only inches away now from where my heartbeat has settled— and he stares up at my face from between my legs.

"This okay?"

"What? Yeah. Of course. *Yes.*" Frankly it's a struggle to not grab his hair and pull him down.

He smiles, but it's not a smile I've ever seen before. It's a dangerous smile; he's a movie villain, the seductive one, the one who robs you but fucks you real good first.

And then he ducks, and kisses me between my legs, and my body becomes a bomb.

He places tiny kisses—from lower, where I am wet and aching, up to the fuse that lights under the sweet press of his mouth. I can feel when it opens, feel the heat of his exhale across that most sensitive place when he moans. His tongue swipes away my sanity but misses the place where I need it—intentionally—sliding around and around, dipping inside me and then arcing high, teasing, narrowing in on his target. Slowly, seductively circling.

The tension in my body is so tight, and I ache so deeply it's nearly painful. I need his tongue *there*, and I want him inside me, and I feel like I want to climb out of my skin I'm so desperate to feel him.

"Please."

He pulls away just slightly and I whimper in torment when he kisses my thighs again, speaking into them. "Hmm?"

"Josh." My hand goes into his hair, pressing silent radio commands to the brain beneath: *Suck on me. Suck on me.*

"I could lose my mind down here."

My other hand dives into my own hair, pulling to keep me from screaming. I let out a tight "I mean, that would be okay."

His mouth presses warm against the very top of my thigh, and I feel my legs shaking against his hands as he whispers, "Isn't it nice when I take my time?"

"Oh. Oh my God, yes it is nice." I sound like I've just run a mile.

"You feel like silk in my mouth." My brain melts inside my cranium at his words and the heat of them across my skin, and Josh—the beast—sucks a small hickey into my inner thigh. I swear he's smiling when he says, "You're shaking."

"I know . . . because I want . . ." A sob seems to rise in my throat at the force of this *want*, and my heartbeat is everywhere, slamming up against my skin.

"You want?" He comes back over me then, mouth open, eyes closed, and the suction pulls any coherence out of me.

I've had oral sex before, but never like this. Never with such focus, such precision. His mouth fixes over me, gently sucking as he hums. He doesn't play or bite or lick around, doesn't roughly push his fingers in me. He remains just there, but it seems to be only a matter of seconds before I feel a shift inside me, a tide rolling in and a wave that builds. When he moans—a spontaneous, encouraging sound—I tip over, falling with my head pressed back into the pillow and my entire body curling in pleasure.

I'm nonverbal for a good thirty seconds afterward, lying on the bed in a pose that I really hope looks more Sated Goddess than Deflated Hobo, but I can't be bothered regardless. "That was the most mind-numbing sexual experience of my life."

He laughs into a kiss to my thigh. "Good."

"I don't want to know where you learned that particular technique."

Josh doesn't bother to argue, he just kisses his way up my navel to my breasts, where he stops and plays for a bit while my brain returns from orbit. My breasts are tender and wildly sensitive, but the gentle assault of his tongue and hands seems to make my body forget that I just came not two minutes ago. I tug at his shoulders, impatient.

"Up here."

"I like being *here*," he says from between my breasts, but he comes over me anyway, kneeling between my legs. He hesitates for a breath, then, "We could use condoms, too, if you want? I don't want you to feel it's all your responsibility."

It's an effort not to let a tiny, hysterical laugh burst free, followed by a *Well, now that you mention it . . .* "It's okay," I say instead.

"You sure?"

I swallow. *Tomorrow.* "Yeah."

He remains kneeling there, eyes roaming over my body, hands sweeping up and down my thighs. "I've wanted this for a while now." Pausing, he adds, "I mean, *this* kind of sex."

The gentle fist around my heart tightens. "Me too."

His voice is hoarse with frustration, maybe over all the time wasted. "Why didn't you tell me?"

"Why didn't *you*?"

"I thought you wanted Tyler."

"I thought you'd be well suited with . . . someone else."

His brows pull in. "Who?"

"Just someone less Hazel."

Josh frowns down at me. "Can we address that?"

"We can't do it after sex?" Because his hands haven't stopped their slow circuit up and down my thighs, up and down, and over my hips and I'm melting into the sheets.

"No. Are you listening?"

"Barely."

"You are perfect for me."

A star is born inside my rib cage. "I am?"

He nods, pinning me with his attention. "You are."

He stares at my face for another few breaths before resuming his visual perusal of my naked body. Hovering above me, he's a statue: broad shoulders, smooth bulky chest. Soft black hair low on his navel, and his cock—perfect, jutting straight up. It brings to mind steel rods, I-beams, precision engineering, and—

His words come out quiet: "You're staring."

"Because you're perfect there."

I love the way his smile comes out in his voice. " 'There'?"

"Everywhere, but . . . there, in particular." I point, and he catches my hand, lifting it over my head and trapping it on the pillow as he leans over me. His cock brushes the inside of my thigh. "I was thinking you're shaped like my favorite dildo."

"That's a compliment I haven't heard before."

I open my mouth to say more but he bends, kissing me once. "Haze, I love you, but I'm going to lose my mind if I don't get closer to you soon."

We both go still and his words bounce around the space between us.

He *loves* me?

I stare up at him, and the rolling bubble of thrill works its way up from my belly, through my chest, and into my throat. I bite my lip, but not even my teeth can trap this smile. It breaks free and he sees it, and his answering smile is at first relieved, but then it falls into earnest focus.

"I do, you know," he says.

Raw emotion paints his expression. I've honestly never seen anyone look at me this way . . . it's more than desire. It's *need*.

My hand comes up to cup the back of his neck, to pull him down just as he's falling over me and his mouth covers mine with a quiet moan. With a shift of his hips forward, he's pressing into me, and we both cry out as he slides in, deep.

It's not gentle or slow, not even to start. His hips rock into mine, and soon they're slapping as he grunts with every pass. Josh rises with a groan, hooking my legs over his arms and spreading me wide. His sounds are rhythmic and hoarse, and something about them—the grate and vibration of Josh's pleasure—makes my body even wilder. He grinds into me, fucking fast—

"*Jimin.*"

His rhythm falters, and his laugh comes out as a burst of air against my neck. "That was," he pants, "the first time you got my name right."

I'd be celebrating, but my orgasm is right there

right *here*

and my back arches away from the mattress as I start to come. Josh grunts out these soft, encouraging words as pleasure bursts through me, rippling on, and on, and on and finally I feel him go tight everywhere—inside me and under my hands and against my thighs. I hear the catch in his throat, his relieved "*Yes,*" and then he's shaking through a long groan, pressed so deep inside.

Carefully, he unhooks my legs and lowers his body so we're chest to sweaty chest. Josh kisses me through sharp, jagged pants. "I'd planned for that to be more lovemaking and less . . . desperate fucking."

A tiny thrill works its way through me at the rare curse word from his lips. "You will hear no complaints from me."

Carefully he pulls back, watching his body's retreat while I watch his face. I love his little frown, his tiny grunt as he slips from me.

His frown deepens and he reaches down, touching me. "Did I hurt you?"

"No?"

He looks up. "Okay. You sure?" He holds up his fingers. "You're bleeding."

....

Don't panic.

Don't panic.

I grabbed my phone on my sprint into the bathroom, and am now sitting on the toilet, madly Googling *bleeding in pregnancy*.

The results are reassuring. Apparently it's common. Apparently it happens in about one-third of all pregnancies. And especially early.

But it can also be a sign that something is wrong,
and it wasn't a little bit of blood,
it was all over my sheets,

and I can't breathe.

I dial my doctor's after-hours number, and speak as softly into the phone as I can.

Yes, nine weeks.

Yes, I saw the doctor yesterday.

No, there isn't any cramping.

After a few words of quiet reassurance, I'm told to do my best not to worry, to rest, and am scheduled to come into the office tomorrow morning.

I end the call just as Josh's voice comes through the closed door. "Haze?"

I look up and try to sound as calm as possible. "Hey. Yeah, I'm okay."

Oh my God, what do I do? He *loves* me. I mean, I don't think he'll be angry that I'm pregnant. Instinct and my intricate knowledge of Josh Im's brain tell me he's actually going to be really happy. He wants a family. But what if I lose it? I know this sort of thing happens all the time, so is it worth telling him and getting his hopes up that everything might be okay if I'm going to lose my monster? Oh God, I want to shred the walls just thinking it. What if I lose it what if I lose—

I close my eyes. Take a deep breath.

"Hazel." I hear his head thunk against the door. "I'm so sorry."

I take a deep breath, standing to splash some water on my face. "It wasn't you," I croak.

Silence. And then, "I mean, I'm pretty sure it *was* me and the hard sex we just had." He pauses. "Can I come in and, um . . . ?"

Oh crap, that's right. He's got blood on him. I open the door and he slips in, kissing me. "Are you hurt?"

"No, I'm totally fine!"

"Okay, good." With one more kiss, he leans past me to turn on the shower.

I stand and press my face to his back, between the bulk of his shoulders. "Sorry."

Josh turns, tilts my face up to look at him. "For what?"

"Bleeding on you. Sprinting out of bed."

His brows pull down. "I don't mind that. I just wanted to make sure you're okay."

Tell him.

Tell him.

Talk to Dr. Sanders first.

"I'm okay."

He bends, kissing me slowly, and then steps into the shower, pulling me in after him.

Steam fills the room as he lathers the soap in his hands, rubbing it first over my shoulders and breasts, and then gently between my legs and along my thighs before washing his own body.

Staring up at him as he washes his stomach, cock, and chest, I note the way the drops of water build on his eyelashes and then fall, like rain. "You said you love me."

He looks up, blinking away the water. His lashes are long, and clumped together. He is so beautiful.

Josh leans forward, kissing my nose. "I did."

I stretch, and his mouth is slippery against mine, his tongue tastes like water. His hand slides over my backside, slipping between, stroking, feeling, and then slides up my back, down between my breasts, like he's acquainting himself with every tiny curve.

Josh Im loves *me*.

"I love you too, you know."

His kiss turns into a smile. "Yeah?"

"I've probably loved you longer."

A trickster grin. "Probably."

I pinch his splendid ass for that and he growls, pressing into me.

"We don't have to make love again," he says quietly into my neck. "You just feel so good, all wet and soft."

After wanting him for so long, I can't quite wrap my brain around the fact that he's here, using words like *love*. Having Josh naked against me isn't for tonight only. This could be a very, very addicting problem because my desire for Josh is a clawing, impatient, frantic energy: I want him again and again and again.

I push the panic into a tiny room in my brain, and narrow that down to a closet and a shoe box and a tiny drop of throbbing light in the background. There's nothing I can do tonight. I just need to breathe.

His hand makes a slow journey over my breasts and down my navel, drawing little swirls and circles with the soap. I'm so full of emotion that I'm not surprised when a single tear slips down my cheek, lost in the spray from the shower. I take the soap and do the same for him, savoring every second of this until we're all clean and the water has started to run cold.

"Okay, Haze." He leans in to kiss me, eyes shining as he shifts away to turn off the taps. "Let's go to bed."

TWENTY-THREE

JOSH

*I*n Hazel's bed, I sleep like a rock. I don't think I even dream, or if I do, it's just a series of nebulous flashes of her body, and her laugh, and the unreal heat of her wrapped around me all night.

We wake up to the blast of her alarm, entangled, with the covers kicked to the floor. I'm naked, she's wearing only underwear, and although I come into consciousness slowly, trapped in a syrupy warmth I'm not quite ready to leave, Hazel sits up after only a few breaths into awareness and looks down at me, eyes blurry. Her eyes stay unfocused for a few seconds before she blinks, clearing them, and bends, kissing me in a soft peck. "You're still here."

In a wave of happiness, I wonder whether we'll move in together . . . and when.

Hazel pulls back and her attention is snagged over my

shoulder. She grimaces at the sheets in the hamper in the corner, the ones we pulled off the bed and replaced before falling onto the mattress in an exhausted heap. As if remembering, she stands, and moves quickly out of the room and to the bathroom, closing the door down the hall with a solid click.

Last night wasn't the first time I've encountered blood during sex, but maybe it was for her? I can hardly imagine that, but it seems to have shaken her more than I would have expected.

Rolling to sit, I perch at the side of the bed, blinking down at Winnie where she stares adoringly up from the floor. "Morning, sweetie." I rub her head and can tell the restraint it's taking her to not jump up here and join me, but thankfully she resists. Being naked in bed with Hazel is bliss. Being naked in bed with her dog would be awkward.

In the kitchen, and inside one of Hazel's Muppet canisters, I find just enough coffee beans to brew a pot. By the time she comes out—still dressed only in her underwear—I've got two cups poured, and reach for her sleep-rumpled form, pulling her between my legs.

"You left," she mumbles into my neck.

Her chest pressed against mine is distracting enough to make her words slow to process. So instead of replying with anything witty, I just suck on her neck and ask, "What time do you have to be at school?"

"Normally seven thirty, and I'd be so late that I'd probably put my clothes on backwards. But I'm going to stop by my doctor's before I head in. They know I'll be a little late today."

Her doctor? I'm not sure how to ask about what happened last night, so I go for vague. "You okay this morning?"

A tiny hesitation, then, "Are you kidding? I'm amazing."

She *is* amazing—creamy skin, the maddening freckle on her shoulder, the full swell of her breasts—and the thought that she's *mine*, and I'm hers, rolls around in my head. A burst of light cuts through me, a flash of joy, and I reach for her, gripping the back of her neck and pulling closer.

The minute our lips touch, my mind quiets but my body seems to take off, ramping toward that place where I can't think, can only feel. My fingers graze the exposed curve of her throat down to her collarbones. Her hands come to my waist immediately and I feel her push up onto her toes, closing any distance between us and stretching, eager for one kiss, and another.

It's chaste, but it's not simple. Nothing with Hazel ever is.

I tilt her head, kissing her bottom lip, her cheek, her jaw.

I glance over her shoulder to the illuminated clock dial on the front of the stove. It's 7:18. I take a breath, silencing the need to make up for lost time.

My mouth settles on hers and lingers. She smiles.

"Good morning, Josh Im."

I kiss her chaotic hair. "I'll say."

I let myself savor this, the simple joy of standing in the bright light of her kitchen, arms wrapped around each other, and knowing that I don't have to hold back now. But it's the way she's holding me—the way she clings with her face pressed to my neck—that gives me pause. She's not playfully gnawing on my shoulder, or threatening to suck giant hickeys into my skin. She's not asking if I want to go roller-skating to the bagel shop before work. She's just so *quiet*.

Of course, it's okay for Hazel to be quiet sometimes, but this feels different. It feels like a silence that's full of something—a worry, a question, maybe an uncertainty.

I search my brain for something to say. I want to ask her if she knows about Emily being pregnant. I want to ask her whether she'll stay at my house tonight, and every night after. I want to ask her to say the words one more time before she leaves for work, the quiet *I love you too, you know*.

She turns her luminous brown eyes up to my face. "What are you thinking?"

"I was wondering what *you're* thinking," I say with a grin.

"We have big things to discuss," she says quietly. "Remember?"

"Still? I thought the 'I love you' covered it. What else is there?"

She stretches, kissing me. "You love me?"

"I do."

"And you're free tonight?"

I run my hands down her body. "You don't want to talk now, while you get ready?"

She shakes her head and it drags her lips across mine,

back and forth. "Tonight." With a smile, she steps back and turns to walk to her bedroom.

There's a stack of mail on the counter, a Harry Potter coloring book, and a receipt under a pile of change. Three letters stand out to me.

e.p.t.

Nothing sinks in right away, but the letters are like a dissonant chime. Almost distractedly, I lean in, pushing aside a quarter to read the entire line.

e.p.t. first respo . . . 5 @ $8.99 ea

Pregnancy tests? Did Hazel buy the tests for Emily?

Confusion laces my thoughts together, but my heart starts pounding pounding pounding as the row of dominoes tumbles.

The blood last night. Hazel's panic. Big things we need to discuss tonight.

My eyes snag on the dark corner of a photo under her keys. I've never held one of these, but I know what it is.

When I pull the ultrasound photo free, I already know what I'm going to see, but it knocks the breath out of my chest anyway.

Bradford, Hazel

November 12

9w3d

And, in the very center, a round body, a head, two tiny buds for arms, two tiny buds for legs.

My own legs nearly give out and I sit heavily on the barstool, staring at the photo in my hand. I know Hazel hasn't slept with anyone but me in . . . well, a long time. And the first night we had sex—drunk sex, floor sex, *I might be falling for you* sex—was two months ago.

Emily isn't pregnant—*Hazel* is. She's been pregnant this entire time, and we had no idea.

I stand, unsteady, and put the photo back beneath her keys, tilting my face to the ceiling. It isn't panic. It isn't dread. It's shock—yes, definitely this is a surprise—but . . . I close my eyes and I can see it. I can see Hazel pregnant. Can see how it would feel to crawl into bed next to her, put my head on her belly and listen. I can see my parents losing their minds, Emily going overboard with gifts. In this moment, with these thoughts running wild through my brain, I grow nearly light-headed. And I understand completely Hazel's panic last night.

Holy shit, she was *bleeding*.

I come up behind her while she's brushing her hair and balance my shaking hands on her hips.

"Hey, you." She leans back into me and then turns in my arms, stretching to kiss me.

Shock has left a metallic tang in my mouth and numbs me, making me feel like my hands aren't mine. "I want to go with you this morning."

Her face furrows in confusion. "To school?"

"To the doctor."

She shakes her head. "You don't need to do that. I know you have a busy morning, too. It's just routine—"

"I want to be there." I think my choice of words jogs something in her, because when her eyes meet mine, she searches for confirmation there. Reaching up, she cups my face in her hands, her gaze flickering back and forth between my eyes. "Don't you think I should be there?" I ask.

She swallows, and her eyes are soft with guilt. "You know?"

"The ultrasound was on the counter."

At this, her face absolutely crumples. It hurts, the answering reaction in my chest. It's like being punched. I pull her to me, cupping her head and holding her as she breaks.

"It's okay, Haze."

She hiccups, pressing her face to my neck. "I just found out on Monday."

Two days ago. That must have been where Emily was— she was at the doctor with Hazel.

"I saw the tests at Em's house," I tell her. "Actually, I thought *she* was pregnant."

When she flattens her palms against my bare back, I can tell they're shaking. "I was going to tell you."

"I know."

Her sob rips through me. "I wanted it to be a happy moment."

"It still can be. We just need to make sure you're okay."

"They said bleeding can be normal, but . . . I'm so scared something happened." Another sob breaks her voice on the last word. "I'm already in love with this little monster, and I'm so scared, Josh."

I've barely processed what's going on, but already my panic seems to swallow the words forming in my brain. "Whatever happens, we'll deal with it, okay?" I pause, and I'm terrified of the answer to the next question. "Are you still bleeding?"

"A little."

My heart drops, and I tighten my arms around her, catching my reflection in the mirror. I look wild. Hair a mess, eyes wide and bloodshot. My mouth is a harsh frown, my pulse is a hollow echo in my throat.

....

Beside me, Hazel's knee bounces up and down. I reach over, placing a calming hand there.

"I'm going to chew my nails off," she whispers. Her eyes are fixated across the waiting room on the generic watercolor painting of a bouquet of flowers.

I reach up, coaxing her hand back down and into mine. My heart is lodged somewhere in my throat; it seems like we could both use an anchor.

To fall in love, to be loved. The reality that we are together now is enough by itself to make my breath grow tight and hot in my chest. And to be here, with an ultrasound photo clutched in my hand . . . The mind, it reels.

But this is Hazel. We're so much bigger than this moment, no matter what happens behind the wide white door leading into the exam rooms. Is it weird to think I've known for years that we would somehow end up here? Or is hindsight just the most convenient explanation for coincidence?

I squeeze her hand and she looks up at me, expression tight.

"You know," I say, giving her the most genuine smile I can muster, "no matter what happens back there, we'll be okay."

"I knew I wanted kids, but I don't think I realized how much until this happened."

"We may not have *seventeen*, but we'll get there."

She laughs. "I'm going to win you over."

"You will never win me over to seventeen children." She growls when I say this, so I add in a compromise: "But how about this: after the appointment, we'll go get milkshakes."

"Promise?"

"I promise."

"Cherry," she says. "No. Wait. Cookies and cream."

"One of each."

Finally, I get a true Hazel smile. "You know what I keep repeating over and over in my head?"

"What?"

" 'I love Josh Im more than I've loved anything in my life.' " She bites her lip. "Don't tell Winnie."

I lean forward and rest my lips on hers. Against my mouth, she's soft, shaking a little. The kiss angles, and my hand comes up to her neck, where my fingers find her pulse drilling against her skin. I could get lost in the way she leans into me, I could drown in the feel of her. But then the wide door opens, and her name is called.

EPILOGUE

JOSH

*W*hen Hazel comes bounding down the front steps, she's wearing orange tights, a black miniskirt, and a purple tank top. Her bun is hidden beneath a giant, wobbly witch's hat. In the light from the porch, she's nearly glowing.

I glance down at my own outfit—black shirt, jeans, sneakers—and then back up again. "I feel like I missed an important text today."

"Halloween stuff was out at Target."

"It's over a month away."

Shrugging, she moves to where I stand leaning against the car and slides her arms around my neck. "Just getting into the spirit."

I touch my lips to hers. "Because it would take you so long otherwise?"

"Are you by chance taking me somewhere Halloweeny?"

Every Friday night is date night, and tonight was my

turn to plan. Last week, Hazel took me to a place where we painted self-portraits with our hands and feet, and then we had a picnic on the hood of my car. My date nights tend to be a bit more standard.

"Just dinner," I say. "A new ramen place opened up near Emily and Dave's. Thought we could give it a try."

After a small rendition of the Running Man on the sidewalk, Hazel climbs into the passenger seat. Her fingers come over mine when I get behind the wheel and pull away from the curb, and with her free hand, she reaches to turn up the song playing on the radio, singing along badly, loudly, happily.

"Wait," she says, looking at me and letting out a bursting laugh. "This is Metallica."

I nod. "Takes me right back to the worst concert ever."

She lets out a mock scream. "What was I thinking? Tyler!"

"No idea."

"I wanted you to come to my apartment and say, 'I love you, Hazel Bradford, please be mine forever and ever and ever.'"

"And I did."

She nods with vigor. "You did."

At the red light, she leans over, kissing me. One short peck turns into a longer kiss, with tongue and sound and the acceleration of her breath and mine. At the green light, she lets me focus on the road but her hand on my thigh soon transitions to her fingers unbuttoning my jeans, her teeth and growl on my earlobe.

Instead of ramen, we find our way back to my old house— empty, between renters—and return to our roots: making love on the floor.

....

Our own home is dark when we pull in, avoiding the squeaky step and coming to a quiet stop in front of the door. Hazel — hair a mess, tank top slightly askew, underwear in her pocket—digs in her purse for her key, sliding it into the lock and gingerly letting us inside.

Umma meets us in the entryway, wearing her small, calm smile.

"Everything okay?" I ask.

She nods, stretching to kiss both our cheeks before padding down the hall toward the separate wing of the house she shares with Appa.

Hazel turns and grins up at me in the darkness. "Even after that greasy burger, I'm starving."

"Want me to make you something?"

She shakes her head, giving a little shimmy before disappearing down the hall.

I unload my wallet and keys near the door, slipping off my shoes. From one of the bedrooms I hear voices, and follow the sound, ducking into Miles's dimly lit room, surprised to find him still awake. Hazel sits at the edge of his bed, food apparently forgotten as she pushes a strand of hair off his forehead.

"Halmeoni made me do a bath," he whispers, full of three-year-old outrage.

"That's good," Hazel tells him. "You were stinky."

"And Jia told her that I ate the last gummy worm."

I sit down beside my wife as she asks, "Did you?"

"Yes," he says, "but she had seven and I only had two!"

Hazel bends, kissing Miles's forehead. "Big sisters are like that sometimes. Sleep, baby boy."

He doesn't fight, rolling over and immediately closing his eyes. I stare at him a little longer. Everyone says he looks just like me. Hazel stands with a smile, picking up the pile of costumes on the floor—Mulan, Tiana, and Ariel are his favorites.

We agree that inside, he is all Hazel.

....

Saturday morning, Miles bounds down the hill, feet barely staying beneath him. Today, he is Elsa—except for his red cowboy boots—with a well-loved Disney wig unraveling behind him as he runs.

Beside me, his sister, Jia, watches him, eyes narrowed as she pulls long, careful licks across her ice cream cone. "He's going to fall."

I nod. "Maybe."

"Appa." She turns her doe eyes on me. "Tell him to slow down."

"He's on the grass," I remind her. "He'll be okay."

Unconvinced, she stands, yelling down to her little brother. "*Namdongsaeng!*"

Only when she calls out to him does he tumble, tripping over a boot and rolling a few feet on the lawn. He comes up laughing. "Noona, did you see me?"

"I saw you." Suppressing a smile, Jia sits back down. Looking up at me again, she gives a dramatic shake of her head. "He's wild, Appa." She looks like her mom.

We agree that inside, she is all me.

Hazel comes up the hill, holding a tray of coffees and hot chocolates in one hand and catching Miles's hand in the other. She manages to start running with him, careening up the hill toward us without spilling anything. When she nears, I take the tray from her hand to keep her from pressing her luck.

"Mama, did you bring me hot chocolate?" Jia asks.

Bending, Hazel swoops her up from the bench, cradling her for a kiss before spinning in wild circles that make Jia giggle wildly and make my blood pressure spike.

"I did," Hazel says, "and had them put extra whipped cream on top."

"Haze," I say gently. "Careful." She's nearly seven months pregnant, and it seems like ever since the first, she has more and more energy each time.

She gives me an indulgent smile, setting Jia down, and our daughter wraps her arms around her mom's wide middle. She kisses Hazel's belly. "Mama, tell me about the time when *I* was in your tummy."

Hazel glances at me again, and plops down cross-legged on the grass. "Mama found out she was going to have a baby. She and Appa were *so happy*." She cups Jia's face, leaning forward to kiss her nose, and—not to be ignored—Miles climbs into Hazel's ever-shrinking lap.

She sweeps his hair out of his face, speaking to Jia. "But I found out that I had to be very quiet and still for a little while." She drops her voice to a whisper. "Mama was not good at being quiet and still. Was she?"

Jia shakes her head, very serious now.

"But *you* were," Hazel whispers, "weren't you?"

My daughter nods, grinning proudly.

"You taught Mama how to be quiet, and calm, and still. And so I did it, because you showed me, and that is how everything turned out okay."

"Now me!" Miles roars.

"*You*, my little wiggle monster," Hazel says, "did not know how to be calm or quiet or still. And that was okay, because Jia also taught Mama's body how to have a baby in there, and so we could be just as silly as we wanted to every single day!"

"Thank you, Noona!" Miles climbs off Hazel, tackling his sister.

The two of them wrestle on the grass, tangled up in Miles's dress, hot chocolates forgotten.

A hand comes up to my knee, tapping, and I help Hazel up from the lawn, standing to wrap my arms around her. "You sure you're ready for another one?"

"No turning back now. Almost three down," she says, "fourteen to go."

"Keep dreaming, Bradford."

Stretching, she kisses me, eyes open, lips resting on mine.

I'm an optimist; I always anticipated having a good life. But to have dreamed something like this would have felt enormously selfish.

"Sometimes I imagine going back in time," she says, reading my mind, "and telling myself that I'd end up right here. With Josh Im."

"Would you have believed it?"

She lets out a husky laugh. "*No.*"

I can't pull her as close as I want, chest to chest, thigh to thigh, so instead I dig my fingers into her bun, pulling it apart so that her hair falls around her shoulders. Her breath catches—I think at the hungry, possessive expression on my face. She looks a little wild, too: her cheeks are pink from the wind, her eyes bright and amber.

"I thought this was your plan all along," I say, kissing her again.

"In my dreams."

I look over at Jia and Miles. She's swiping grass from his

skirt, helping straighten his wig. And as soon as she's done, he tears off down the hill again under the watchful eye of his sister.

"Well," I say, "*I'm* pretty sure that if someone went back in time and told me I'd end up with Hazel Bradford, it would sound just crazy enough to be true."

ACKNOWLEDGMENTS

*S*ome characters take longer to find, and some burst onto the page, already formed and impatiently waiting for us to start typing it all down. The latter situation was the case with Josh and Hazel. Few people get to say they find joy in their job, but that's what this book was: pure, unadulterated fun. We are so very lucky.

Behind every book is a whole team of people who make it happen. Editor Adam Wilson is as instrumental to our books as we are. He helps us find what we're missing, and makes the things we get right even better. Our agent, Holly Root, is a miracle, seriously. Thank you for always being there to calm our flails and celebrate right along with us. You are our rock. Kristin Dwyer, our moon and stars and magical unicorn publicist, we would be lost without you. You did so good, girl.

Simon & Schuster/Gallery Books has been our home since we were newborn debut authors. Thank you to Carolyn Reidy, Jen Bergstrom, Diana Velasquez, Abby Zidle, Mackenzie Hickey, Laura Waters, Hannah Payne, and Theresa

Dooley (we miss you). Thank you, John Vairo and Lisa Litwack, for the cover that makes us smile whenever we see it. The amazing S&S sales team gets our books on the shelves, and into the hands of amazing readers.

Thank you, Erin Service, for forever being our biggest cheerleader and most careful set of eyes, and Marion Archer, for the thoughtful reads and all of the heart you put into your feedback.

Thank you to every reader and blogger and Instagrammer and Booktuber who has ever picked up one of our books or recommended us to someone. We laughed so much while writing this book; we hope you feel that in every page.

This book is dedicated to Jen Lum, and Katie and David Lee because they are AMAZING. We can't actually show up on their porches and thank them in person, but we would if it wasn't creepy. Thank you, Jen, Katie, and David, for sharing your lives and your stories and helping us make Josh and his family feel real. We are very grateful.

To our families! You are the reason we smile, and also the reason we occasionally drink wine by the bottle. Thank you for putting up with our deadline brains and tours and crazy schedules and our nonstop texts to each other. We love you.

To PQ, you make me so proud. Working on this felt like the best of what we do, and I love that it still makes us laugh out loud, every single time we read it. I love you!

To my Lolo, when we first started writing together it was basically to make each other laugh or swoon or blush. Nine years later and that hasn't changed. Thank you for being patient while I found my voice again and for loving me no matter what. I thank the universe every day that a sparkly vampire brought you into my life. And that you still haven't managed to escape. I love you.

The story of the heart can never be unwritten.

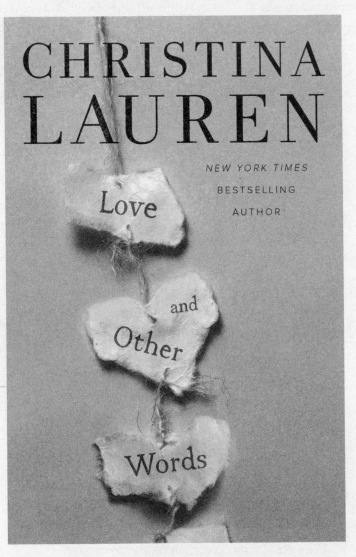

CHRISTINA
LAUREN

NEW YORK TIMES
BESTSELLING
AUTHOR

Love

and

Other

Words

Pick up or download your copy today!